THREADS
OF A
NEEDLE

DG ZITTING

DG Zitting in association with:
Elite Online Publishing
63 East 11400 South #230
Sandy, UT 84070
EliteOnlinePublishing.com

ISBN: 978-1-956642-17-9 (eBook)
ISBN: 978-1-956642-15-5 (Paperback)
ISBN: 978-1-956642-16-2 (Hardcover)

FIC028010

PSY051000

SCI057000

Quantity purchases: Schools, companies, professional groups, clubs, and other organizations may qualify for special terms when ordering bulk quantities of this title. For information, email info@eliteonlinepublishing.com.

This book is printed in the United States of America.

For more information visit

DGZitting.com

NOTE TO THE READER

Dear Reader,

This book was crafted for the inquisitive seekers of meaning, for those who have sensed that there is more to life than meets the eye, those who believe that each of us holds the power to shape reality, both at the individual and societal levels.

If you have ever questioned what exists beyond the boundaries of empirical science or the constraints of rigid religious dogma, if you've felt the presence of a bridge that unites these belief systems, or if you've dared to contemplate an infinite reality, you've arrived at the right destination.

Threads of a Needle embarks on an enlightening journey, unveiling a captivating narrative that forges a visionary connection between the domains of science and non-denominational spirituality, often regarded as the mystical.

This bridge transcends the confines of age-old debates that have revolved around various ideologies. It does not align with one ideology or another. Instead, it stands resolute upon the very foundation of reality itself, a foundation woven from the intricate fabric of consciousness in all its magnificent and universal forms.

Amidst the backdrop of political strife and societal division, it is truly remarkable to observe a convergence taking place within our most respected academic institutions. The age-old wisdom once attributed to ancient sages is now harmoniously intertwining with the latest scientific breakthroughs, leaving us to ponder: Could it be that these seemingly divergent paths are, in fact, leading us to the same destination, albeit expressed through distinct lenses?

As we advance along the path of knowledge, these seemingly disparate worlds inexorably converge. What was once regarded as mystical is now emerging as a fundamental principle. This profound synthesis invites us to contemplate the rich tapestry of possibilities that extend beyond the confines of our physical existence.

Threads of a Needle embarks on a quest to explore the extraordinary power of belief and its ability to shape our experiential reality.

Welcome to a realm where curiosity, science, and spirituality gracefully intertwine, unveiling a fresh perspective on the universe, our role within it, and the boundless potential that lies ahead.

With warm regards,
DG Zitting

P.S. Explore the Terms and Concepts section at the end of the book. Whether you dive into it before, during, or after your journey, it's a valuable resource to enhance your reading experience. Enjoy!

CHAPTER 1

Amsterdam. October 13, 2054, 6:52 p.m.

Hope's long, dark hair danced in the crisp Amsterdam breeze as she confidently strode across the historic Hogesluis, spanning the Amstel. Her tall, slender figure effortlessly cut through the chilly October air. Though the night was unusually cold for this time of year in Amsterdam, Hope had grown accustomed to facing the elements head-on.

The call resonated in her mind, its significance tugging at her intuition. Ordinarily, she would have swiftly terminated the conversation and reported it to her superiors. However, an indescribable quality in the man's voice compelled her to entertain his request. She replayed the call in her head, meticulously scrutinizing every nuance.

"I'm afraid I can't share that with you now," the man's urgent tone echoed in her memory. "Nevertheless, I must deliver the file to you in person. We need to meet in Amsterdam. Follow my instructions exactly. I'll transmit them to you in an encrypted metaverse frame. I know of the instability, but it is the only way to ensure we're undetected."

"Wait, please. How did you know to contact me?" The line went dead before she got the answer, leaving a whirlwind of questions swirling in her mind. *Why Amsterdam? Why the Amstel Hotel?*

Less than twenty-four hours later, Hope found herself on the other side of the world, burdened by unanswered questions. As she crossed the bridge, her gaze was drawn to the imposing rear façade of the iconic Amstel Hotel on the river's east bank. Despite the chaos and uncertainty that plagued the world, this architectural masterpiece stood as a beacon of preserved beauty. It held a special place in Hope's heart, evoking memories of a simpler life.

Mixed emotions coursed through her as she made her way toward the hotel's front entrance. The beloved city of her youth provided a semblance of solace, reminding her of summers spent with her grandparents and the joyous moments they shared.

Hope felt a sense of melancholy as she observed the profound changes that had taken place, both in the city and within herself. The once-familiar streets had undergone a transformative shift over the course of so many challenging years.

Her heart raced with emotions: a blend of concern, suspicion, and an insatiable curiosity. An unsettling feeling gnawed at her, setting her nerves on edge. As an operative for the League of Consciousness, revered as The LOC in intelligence circles, her role required a steady and analytical mindset, sharp thinking, and precise execution. She understood that maintaining unwavering focus was essential for survival and unraveling the threads of her work.

As she reached the end of the bridge, her attention was abruptly captured by the unexpected sound of a combustion engine. It had been over a decade since she had heard the distinctively loud, rough, and throaty ballad of a vintage T100

Triumph motorcycle, a beautiful relic from a bygone era. A sharp pang of envy settled in the back of her mind. She couldn't help but imagine the thrill of riding that exquisite machine, the raw power of combustible motive force, unlike the ghostly quietness of the nuclear-powered vehicles of her generation.

Hovercraft street lighting silently floated fifteen feet above her head, glowing steadily through the thick, polluted fog. The AI illumination drones positioned themselves strategically, creating a well-lighted path as she proceeded toward Professor Tulpplein, a street running parallel to the front entrance of the iconic Amstel Hotel. Governments worldwide sought new ways to enhance safety in their metropolitan areas, particularly at night. Yet, Hope knew it was too late for such measures. Amsterdam was no longer a haven of safety. The danger lurking in the shadows was all too real.

Just another fifty steps, Hope instructed herself, staying focused and confident.

She possessed a finely honed belief mindset, skilled in the art of self-dialogue. She understood the power of her words, the internal narratives that guided her actions, and the profound impact of how beliefs shaped her future. Her ability to choose the right thoughts and listen to her most empowering inner voice fueled her unwavering determination. As a PT-SOF agent for The LOC, she had undergone the world's most advanced special-ops training, known only to a select few.

Yet, tonight, more than ever, the words of her instructors resonated deeply within her: "Belief in the desired outcome is infinitely more powerful than any round of ammunition. You've hit the target long before you pull the trigger."

Finally reaching the hotel's grand entrance, Hope bounded up the center stairs, each step pressing against the royal blue carpet adorned with the Amstel's golden crest. Stepping through the revolving doors, she released a breath of relief, grateful to have left behind the prying lights and unknown surveillance cameras that had tracked her every move. Being inside the hotel provided a temporary respite from the nagging thought that an adversary might have intercepted her plans.

As she surveyed the opulent lobby, memories of her childhood flooded to the surface. The polished white marble floors, contrasted by the black trim at their base, brought back a sense of wonder. The grand staircase, with its intricate wooden banisters and twin archways, symbolized elegance and solidity. In her youth, it felt like a palace where she could envision herself as a reigning queen. Nostalgia enveloped her, evoking memories of long-forgotten years. *Why the Amstel? Could it be a coincidence?*

Moving deliberately across the marble floor, Hope approached the concierge desk on the right side of the lobby. Keeping a cautious eye out for any suspicious figures, she noticed a couple engaged in a lively debate, contemplating whether to venture out for an event. Another elegantly attired pair seemed poised to attend a banquet within the hotel. Nothing appeared out of the ordinary, at least not yet.

"Ency," Hope whispered through gritted teeth.

"Yes, Mum?" came the response.

Hope had deliberately assigned her Tactical AI Companion the voice of a captivating and audaciously confident character from one of her favorite classic movies. It was none other than James Bond, an alluring symbol of sophisticated charm and unwavering composure. His charismatic demeanor and ability to remain calm in the face of danger resonated with her.

"Scan the lobby for potential threats," she discreetly instructed. Although she could have communicated her thoughts directly to Ency through the NeuroConnect chip implanted in her neocortex, she found satisfaction in the old-fashioned method of communication.

"Yes, Mum," came the reply in his deep, charming voice, resonating a few seconds later. "No immediate threats detected in the lobby. However, I've observed a convergence of uncertain probable thread frequencies harmonizing. We can't afford to bumble through this one, darling. It's a long way from being a casual afternoon in the park." His accent was dry and sophisticated, dripping with sarcasm.

"Noted," Hope acknowledged as her vigilant gaze continued to sweep the area.

Making her way through the hall at the rear of the lobby, Hope entered the atrium and found herself captivated by the enduring charm of her childhood memories. The cobalt blue accents and midnight black coatings on the walls framed the scenic view of the Amstel River just beyond. The soft illumination of candelabra lighting cast an elegant glow against the dark backdrop, while delicate white shades provided a subtle contrast to the environment with its dim lighting. With a swift scan of the room, Hope located her contact—a man seated near the window, easily identifiable by the vibrant periwinkle handkerchief adorning his left lapel pocket. Gracefully maneuvering through the tables, she approached him.

"Get up. We need to move," Hope's eyes darted around the room with a mixture of vigilance and unease. Her voice revealed contempt as she chastised the man for his risky choice of seating, endangering them both. The man froze, his anxious gaze meeting hers.

"Do you know how dangerous this is?" she continued, her frustration palpable. "I spotted you from the bridge. If I wanted you dead, you'd be long gone by now." Hope scanned the surroundings for potential threats. "We need to go now," she urged, her tone insistent.

Hope extended her hand, offering it as leverage in an attempt to speed things along. However, before she could exert any pressure, the man gripped her forearm with an iron-like grasp. His hands trembled, and sweat glistened on his forehead. In his other hand, he clutched a small container revealing digital contact lenses.

"I need you to put these in immediately," the man urgently instructed, his eyes darting anxiously around the room. "You don't have much time."

Hope hesitated, studying the container in the man's hand. Her instincts nudged her toward trust, yet an unsettling feeling lingered in her gut. "What do you mean, I don't have much time?" she asked, her voice tense.

The man's eyes darted around the room. "Insert these and then look directly at the golden clock's face in the lobby at exactly 7:15 p.m.," he said urgently. "It's the only way to activate the augmented reality feature and accept the file."

Hope's heart sank as a poignant memory flooded her thoughts. *The clock.* The synchronicity was impossible to ignore. Her father, Gabriel Valencia, had once regaled her with the tale of Queen Juliana, who dialed back the time to spare a guest the embarrassment of arriving tardy for a luncheon at the hotel. The clock served as a bittersweet reminder of the man he had become: The renowned neurotechnologist, who had once been lauded for his groundbreaking work in digital thought synthesis, had subsequently and woefully played a role in the technologies now threatening their world. Despite her conflicted emotions, Hope cherished her father and clung to the image of the man she idolized in her youth. It perplexed her that his intentions and character seemed at odds.

Collecting herself with a deep breath, Hope pushed aside thoughts of her father. This was not the time for reminiscence. Was this yet another coincidence? Suspicion brewed within her, accompanied by a growing sense that the puzzle pieces were about to fit together. Trained to recognize probable synchronicities, even from a young age, Hope possessed an innate understanding of when universal alignments were at play and how to utilize her intuition to navigate the course of action.

Hope's heart rate jumped as she spotted the unmistakable red dot of a sniper's laser sight dancing brightly on the man's forehead. Instinct took over as she swiftly shoved him back onto the table. The air shattered with the sound of a silenced bullet, in unison with the crash of the window shattering to the floor. The man let out a pained cry as the bullet grazed his left eyebrow, affirming to Hope that he was not a trained operative disguising his true identity or abilities.

"Get down!" Hope shouted, dropping to the floor behind the table.

The man looked around frantically and yelled, "A broken clock . . ." but the sentence was brutally cut off.

The familiar thuds of two bullets piercing flesh were simultaneously accompanied by the chilling sound of a final breath escaping its human vessel. The man's lifeless body crumpled to the floor, a testament to the expertise of the assailant. Hope swiftly retrieved the contact lens case from the man's left hand. A fourth shot exploded on the floor just centimeters away from her head. *Too close*, she thought. In a prone position, Hope scrambled forward, seeking refuge behind a busser's cart. Luck had once again provided her life-saving protection. Though better than her previous location, it fell far short of what Hope deemed safe.

The patio door burst open, and a server darted inside, desperately seeking safety. A surge of emotions coursed through Hope's mind—a mixture of sorrow and urgency—as she recognized that another life was on the brink of being lost in seconds.

With a firm grip on her weapon, an M32-Killjoy, Hope knew she had no other option but to rely on the technology entrusted to her by her superiors. This cutting-edge weapon represented the latest advancements provided by the LOC. The instructions she received were simple, "Point and shoot," placing her faith in its capabilities to deliver.

With the gun firmly in her grasp, it seamlessly synchronized with her thought patterns, analyzing the probable trajectory of previous shots fired. This information would unveil the assailant's general location, enabling the M32-Killjoy's intelligent ammunition rounds to track and neutralize the threat. It was akin to wielding a highly sophisticated, heat-seeking missile; however, much smarter. Her task was simple—pull the trigger and survive long enough for the weapon to do its work.

Within seconds of the bullet hitting the busser's chest, Hope clenched her hand tightly, unleashing the weapon's fury upon the assailant. Feeling the recoil as the bullets silently discharged from the barrel, she trusted that the Killjoy hit its mark. Knowing she had to escape the atrium glass, Hope swiftly stood and sprinted toward the hallway leading to the main lobby. Drawing upon her LOC training, she focused on her breathing and assessed her surroundings. She needed to avoid appearing as an obvious target when she emerged from the other end of the hall. Adopting the guise of a hotel guest or staff member would attract less attention.

Slowing her pace, she grabbed a tray with a dish and raised it above her head, mimicking the actions of a busser. It was a ruse to momentarily confuse any potential shooter lurking in the expansive marble lobby. Concealing the M32-Killjoy behind her back, her finger primed on the trigger, Hope stepped into the lobby nonchalantly. She squatted down slightly, instinctively countering the possibility of a kill shot. It proved to be the right move, as the wall behind her exploded in a burst of gunfire the moment she stepped beyond the safety of the hallway. The speed of the attack made her realize that she was dealing with an AI Agent, a synthetic creature designed to resemble a muscular humanoid. Clad in a sleek black Kevlar bodysuit and a featureless face, these artificial beings instilled fear with their mere presence. A single illuminated slit, positioned horizontally in the space where eyes would be, provided them with an array of visual optics.

No disguise could have protected her from the shots that rained down. As Hope sat on the floor, bullets exploded around her, and she retaliated by squeezing the trigger of the Killjoy, letting the weapon take control. Three shots spit out of the end of the barrel, instantly halting the crossfire. Amid the chaos, screams echoed through the lobby as patrons and staff scrambled to find safety.

Taking cover behind the concierge desk, Hope wasted no time retrieving the contact lenses from the case and swiftly inserting them into her eyes. Initially, her vision was overwhelmed by a burst of digital images and colors, causing her to shut her eyes tightly. Gradually, the lenses adjusted, aligning with the permanent implants in her corneas and the NeuroConnect chip in her brain. Her vision transformed, merging all three central human realities—base, virtual, and augmented—into a complex mixed-reality experience.

This technological marvel, BR-AR-VR, was available to the public, catering to their convenience and entertainment.

Individuals could access and immerse themselves in any reality they desired with a mere thought command. It was an addictive escape that robbed people of their imaginations and programmed their minds with predefined beliefs. Hope despised its dominance, recognizing how it enslaved humanity and stripped them of critical thinking. But now, she needed to leverage the technology she loathed.

Focusing her mind and blocking out all distractions, Hope was conscious of the time ticking away. She knew the time to look at the gold clock above the grand staircase, as instructed, was approaching. Hope quickly emerged from her hiding place and sprinted up the steps with the lenses uncomfortably fixed in her eyes, hugging the handrail. Her gaze remained set on the clock as it struck 7:15. The augmented reality capabilities of the lenses activated, projecting a holographic video in front of her. The word "PASSPHRASE" hovered above an input box, accompanied by a holographic keyboard perfectly positioned for her to enter the required information.

Frustration consumed Hope as she realized that the man who had given her the task had failed to provide the passphrase. Adrenaline surged through her veins, convinced that more AI agents would storm through the doors any moment. The augmented reality feature allowed her only sixty seconds to view and capture the file, leaving little time to download it into her NeuroConnect memory frame.

In the midst of the chaos, Hope felt an unseen force whispering answers to her. The synchronicities, the memories, and the puzzle pieces aligned. Amsterdam, the Amstel, the gold clock—there was a connection.

The clues prodded at her mind, and she sensed that the answer lay just beyond the grasp of her understanding. It was then that Hope recalled the peculiar words the man blurted in the atrium just moments before his demise: "A broken clock." Those words raced through Hope's mind like a distant echo until a flash of understanding surfaced. She quickly looked back up at the face of the clock. *Impossible!* Hope thought. *Did the clock read 7:15 p.m. all those years ago?* Hope was baffled by the answer slowly coming into focus.

As a child, Hope and her family gathered at the Amstel one evening for dinner while visiting grandparents and friends. They had planned to meet at 8:15 p.m., but Hope noticed that the old gold clock was nearly an hour off upon entering the hotel. Perceiving the discrepancy, she remarked to her father, Gabriel, about the broken clock. Gabriel confirmed her observation and reassured her that it would be fixed soon. As they hurried through the lobby, Hope expressed her concern, not wanting the beautiful clock to be discarded. Gabriel eased her concerns and then playfully assured her that despite its inaccuracy, the clock still held value, or at least it did "twice a day." Understanding her father's riddle, Hope laughed and reported that one of those times would be the following day at 7:15 a.m. Gabriel praised her cleverness, and they proceeded to the restaurant. Hope leveraged this cherished memory throughout her life. She would share this riddle with others, treasuring the lessons it imparted.

Suddenly, the answer hit her. With her heart racing, Hope looked up at the clock once again. *That's it!* Hope lifted her hands to the holographic virtual keyboard and frantically typed, "A BROKEN CLOCK IS RIGHT TWICE A DAY."

WRONG ENTRY flashed in red at the top of the input box.

What? Confusion and desperation swirled in Hope's mind. How could it be anything else? Time was slipping away, and she was running out of options.

"Mum?" Ency chimed in his cool, British voice.

"What, Ency! I'm kind of busy here!" Hope snapped.

"Might I suggest you replace the word RIGHT with . . ."

"Of course!" She quickly typed the revised passphrase into the input box: "A BROKEN CLOCK IS CORRECT TWICE A DAY." As she hit enter, a video began to play.

Hope was taken aback to see her father appearing in the video, seemingly floating in front of her, invisible to the rest of the world. Why was her father in this video, and why did he always introduce himself as if she couldn't recognize him?

"Hope, this is your dad. Please listen carefully. Pause this video and leave the Amstel as quickly and safely as possible. Be ready for anything and trust no one. You will know when it's safe to play the video again. Trust me. Go now!"

Her thoughts swirled, but there was no time to process it all. Hope needed to act. Pausing the video, she commanded her AI companion, "Ency, store video, surface memory, level ten encryption." The video and virtual keyboard disappeared from her view.

Looking around the lobby, Hope noticed an eerie silence. It seemed that everyone had fled when the bullets started flying. Adrenaline surged through her veins as she bounded down the stairs, through the lobby, and toward the entrance of the hotel. Opting for the bellman's entrance, she hugged the wall and cautiously peered out the glass door. Nothing seemed suspicious, which only heightened her concerns.

Across the street, she spotted someone beside an e-bike, helmet in hand. Thankfully, the person was not an AI agent, and the bike was a Centurion X3, a fast and agile nuclear-powered vehicle. Assessing the risk, Hope decided to take action. Silently opening the bellman's door, she crouched and slipped out, her weapon concealed in her jacket pocket, finger ready on the trigger. Standing nonchalantly, she scanned the surroundings from left to right before discreetly descending the short flight of stairs leading to the sidewalk.

"Ency."

"Doing it now, Mum." Ency swiftly downloaded the latest specs and tactical driving skills program for the CX3, anticipating Hope's needs before she even asked.

"Love ya like a brotha," Hope whispered.

"Oh, stop," Ency replied dryly.

Crossing the cobblestone street, Hope noticed the rider preparing to mount the bike. With a flirtatious tone, she called out loud enough to catch his attention without arousing suspicion from others nearby. The rider looked up, surprised by her approach and striking appearance.

"Liam, is that you?" Hope said playfully. The rider hesitated, brows raised and mouth agape.

"No, sorry, you must be mistaken. My name is Arie," he replied, a hint of confusion in his voice.

Approaching him with confidence, Hope responded, "Ah, Arie, that's right." Then, taking charge, she asserted, "Arie, I need you to step away from your bike now!"

Startled, the rider attempted to saddle the bike, but Hope swiftly swept his feet from beneath him before he could react, leaving him lying on the cobblestone street. In one fluid motion, she mounted the bike, engaged its energy core, and accelerated away. Glancing at the rearview mirror, she saw the rider getting up, yelling and cursing.

"Tot ziens!" Hope called back with a smirk. However, before reaching the corner, she noticed a set of headlights in her rearview mirror. Her instincts kicked in, recognizing them as pursuing agents. In perfect synchrony, the assailants accelerated, closing in on her position.

Banking the CX3 sharply to the left, Hope leaned low, her knee nearly skimming the road's surface. As she turned, the alarm bells of a drawbridge rang out. The red and white traffic gates began to lower, temporarily halting traffic to accommodate the rising bridge and allow an approaching canal boat to pass by. With the agents mere seconds behind her, Hope didn't have time to turn back. Weaving through the descending gates, she calculated the bridge's rising motion, determining that she would undoubtedly become airborne if she continued. Skillfully, she modulated the accelerator, preparing for a flight that served two crucial purposes: clearing the rising section of the bridge and maintaining enough speed to grease the landing. *Perfect! Cheated death once again*, Hope thought as she eased off the accelerator, preparing for another sharp turn to the right.

With no time to look back and see if her pursuers had successfully crossed the bridge, Hope pushed the CX3 to its limits, racing down a narrow road along the west bank of the Amstel. She noticed security lights casting an ethereal glow over the Royal Theater Carre' on the opposite bank.

"All is not lost," Hope murmured, allowing herself a moment of nostalgia. As she reached blistering speeds, she saw two additional sets of headlamps turn, intercepting her on the other side of the Magere Brug. The translation, "skinny bridge," took on a new meaning at that moment.

"Ency," she called out.

"Confirming now, Mum," Ency replied promptly. After a brief pause, he added, "Confirmed. AI Agents."

As the bridge flashed by to her right, Hope knew they still had some distance to cover before closing in on her.

Slowing the bike, she made a sharp left turn, leaving the river behind and heading toward Rembrandtplein. She raced past the once beautiful Blauwbrug, which, in an earlier time, reminded her of Paris with its majestic pillars and ornate blue candelabra lanterns. Now, it stood defaced by graffiti and broken glass.

Just then, Ency's voice broke through the chaos. "Mum, you have an incoming call, level twelve encryption. The caller claims it was your fault that the wine spilled on the rug at last year's Christmas dinner and insisted on speaking with you."

"Poet?" Hope's voice carried a tinge of surprise as she spoke her twin brother's nickname. His given name was David, and Poet was a moniker bestowed upon him by their family, a testament to his poetic soul and eloquent way with words.

"Ency, scan for intercepts. If it's clear, open a secure line," Hope shouted over the rushing wind.

"Yes, Mum," Ency acknowledged.

Moments later, Hope heard her brother's voice resonating in the center of her skull. She never quite got used to how the NeuroConnect-comms made it feel like someone had invaded her thoughts.

"Hey, sis," Poet's voice came through, severe yet calm.

Hope raced down Reguliersbreestraat, skillfully maneuvering around a man on a bicycle. Frustrated by her brother's unexpected call, she replied tensely, "Poet, why are you calling me with level twelve encryption?"

Hope quickly looked back to see the pursuing agents had already closed half the distance and were gaining on her.

"Hope, I'm in Amsterdam. We need to meet right away," he insisted.

"Amsterdam? Poet, that's impossible. I'm in a compromised situation at the moment," Hope responded, her voice laced with a deliberate disregard that belied the intensity of the evening.

"I need you to meet me where we first watched Neo meet with the Oracle. Remember? With Dad and Mom? We were about ten years old," Poet urged. Instantly, Hope understood the reference and knew precisely where Poet was referring to.

The location he had so cryptically requested to meet up was just a stone's throw behind her. Moments ago, she had raced past the iconic Tuschinski Theater, a place that always evoked fond memories for her. The irresistible curiosity tugged at her, intensified by the unexpected involvement of her father and brother in the unfolding events of the evening. She couldn't say no to Poet and needed to find out what was truly going on.

"I'll see you there," Hope declared, then ended the call to focus on the situation.

Hope's heart raced as she reached the end of Reguliersbreestraat, with the imposing presence of the Munttoren Clock overlooking the square. Her eyes caught sight of a tram approaching from the opposite direction. Dealing with the agents before the tram arrived was crucial, as it would temporarily block her path to Singel Street, where the beautiful Bloemenmarkt Flower Market once dazzled city goers. In a flash, Hope realized she could use the tram to her advantage. Slowing the CX3, she allowed the pursuing agents to draw closer, meticulously timing her actions.

Bringing the bike to a stop, Hope reassessed her options, solidifying the plan in her mind. The key to her strategy relied on the predictable nature of AI Agents, who lacked self-preservation instincts and would persist in their pursuit regardless of the circumstances. This understanding played into her calculations.

With the agents approaching the square, Hope firmly gripped her M32-Killjoy, her feet planted on the ground as she remained saddled on the CX3. Her gaze briefly shifted to the advancing tram, calculating its progress along the tracks. She focused on steadying herself, keeping her heartbeat in check.

"Ency," she called out.

Promptly responding, Ency acknowledged her thoughts. "My calculations confirm that the tram will align quite well with your tactical strategy, Mum."

Hope adjusted her position on the CX3, extending her arm and aiming the Killjoy toward the agents' entry point. AI Agents were deadly marksmen, but Hope knew their predictable programming. The LOC had trained her to exploit those patterns, giving her precious milliseconds to react.

As the agents entered the square, their movements synchronized. One of them swiftly raised its weapon, taking aim. Hope shifted her head and pulled the trigger in a split second, firing almost simultaneously with the agent. A searing pain jolted through Hope as she realized the bullet had grazed her ear. But her shot had found its mark, obliterating the faceless head of the AI Agent. The impact sent the agent and its bike crashing through the square in a chaotic swirl of destruction.

Gripping the accelerator tightly, Hope propelled herself forward, knowing the next move required even greater precision. With the remaining agent closing in, only meters behind her, she navigated the narrow gap between her bike and the tram. Hope calculated that the agent might hesitate to fire, aware she possessed the lethal M32-Killjoy. She seized the moment, making her daring move.

Hope's heart pounded as she raced ahead of the tram, her plan unfolding before her eyes. She aggressively banked the CX3 to the right with calculated precision, crossing the tram's path. The agent, caught off guard, attempted to mimic her maneuver but misjudged the distance. Its rear wheel collided with the tram's cowling, sending the agent crashing into an abandoned fast-food restaurant window.

Breathing a sigh of relief, Hope buried the accelerator, her determination fueled by the success of her plan. The few dilapidated shops floated in desolation. Hope had a plan to ditch the CX3. Ahead, she spotted a partially opened security gate of one of the old floating shops.

With the wind whipping against her, Hope estimated the narrow gap between the front and back of the shop to be just three or four meters. Beyond that lay the dark, unforgiving waters of the canal. She clenched the brakes, sharply turning the bike into the abandoned shop while maintaining momentum, then launching herself off the bike in one swift motion, landing on a cart that cushioned the impact. The CX3 accelerated through the back of the shop, soaring through the air before crashing into the canal's dark waters.

Painfully, Hope rose to her feet, her movements hindered by the fall. She limped out of the shop, her determination unwavering. With a quick scan of her surroundings, Hope sprinted southward, seeking refuge in the shadows. Making her way eastward, she navigated the dark alleyways, heading toward the theater's rear entrance.

"Ency," she called out.

"You're clear, Mum. Potential threats averted, for now," Ency reassured her.

Keeping to the shadows, Hope pressed on until eventually, her destination came into sight. She moved swiftly, blending into the darkness of the night as she made her way toward Reguliersdwarsstraat. Each step brought her closer to the theater, where she would reunite with her brother and hopefully find some answers.

Hope's heart raced as she neared the theater, her anticipation growing each minute. She and her brother had sneaked into the theater as teenagers, so she knew exactly where the employee entrance was located. There was a risk of surveillance cameras capturing her presence, but it was still her best option for entry.

She kept her head down and moved swiftly to evade facial recognition algorithms, constantly checking her surroundings for any signs of a tail.

Finally, she arrived at the entrance, taking one last glance around to ensure she was not being followed. Her friends from her teenage years had shared the audio-lock password, a long shot that might still work after all these years. She whispered, "Quattro-Quattro-Quattro," entering the audio code into the lock. *Still works!*

The grand hall of the Tuschinski was shrouded in darkness. Yet, even in the dimness, Hope could make out the ornate red velvet theater chairs and the intricate gold and red decorations adorning the mezzanine levels. The theater had become a historical landmark, preserving its original charm and still showcasing films from the bygone eras of the 2020s, '30s, and '40s.

Her gaze fell upon the crimson central curtains, elegantly draping over the screen. To her surprise, they parted, revealing a ghostly grey screen as a movie started to project. The sudden illumination allowed her to survey the entire auditorium. It was an old-fashioned sci-fi film that held a special place in her and her brother's hearts.

Silence enveloped the theater, but Hope recognized the scene playing out on the screen. The protagonist, Neo, stood in the Oracle's waiting room, observing two children displaying extraordinary abilities. One levitated three toy blocks, while the other effortlessly bent spoons with his mind. Something about this scene tugged at Hope's emotions, stirring a deep sense of wonder.

Illuminated by the light of the ancient projector, Hope noticed a figure sitting in the third row from the front, on the far left edge of the theater. It was a strategic position, close to the exit, offering temporary protection in case AI Agents were to enter the grand hall. The utilization of tactical situational awareness by her brother, an AI engineer, was confusing.

Hope's heart raced as she knelt beside her brother, her confusion growing with each passing moment. Poet seemed engrossed in a hologram visible only to him through his mixed-reality lenses. Frustrated, Hope addressed him in a whispered voice, demanding an explanation. Instead of responding, Poet remained fixated on the hologram and issued a command to his Tactical AI Companion, instructing it to transfer the video to Hope. Instantly, the hologram materialized before her, revealing an aerial map with blue and red dots. The blue dots marked their location, while the red dots indicated immediate threats, some dangerously close.

Realizing the urgency of their situation, Poet expressed his concern in a nervous but oddly confident tone. Hope couldn't help but feel a pang of worry for her brother.

"We need to get you out of here," Hope insisted, aware that her pursuers would soon pinpoint her location. The thought of Poet caught in the crossfire troubled her deeply.

Poet reassured her, explaining that he had deployed countermeasure drones to scramble their location for a limited time. He pointed to the map, showing her their positions as the drones scattered and the red dots veered off course.

Rising to his feet, Poet pulled Hope into a firm embrace, offering a comforting gesture to distract from the chaos. But Hope couldn't shake her concern.

"Poet, please tell me what's going on," Hope pleaded. "You're scaring me, and that doesn't happen easily."

Apologizing for the unsettling turn of events, Poet inquired about Porter, the man who was supposed to meet Hope at the Amstel.

"Do you mean the sacrificial lamb that was assassinated right in front of me? He had no business being in that position, Poet! Whose idea was *that*?" Hope's voice shook as she pressed her brother for answers. "What's happening? I need to know what this is all about."

Poet revealed that Porter had willingly taken on the dangerous assignment despite the slim chances of survival, driven by a deep sense of duty to the mission objectives and their father. Hope struggled to reconcile this new information. "Why haven't I ever heard of this person before?"

Poet explained the necessity of their decisions and actions, emphasizing the secrecy surrounding the data. He spoke with respect for Porter's sacrifice and the crucial role he played in their mission.

Frustrated and impatient, Hope demanded answers. "Why are you and Dad involved in this? What's the purpose?"

With an urgent tone, Poet responded, "Play the rest of the video. There's a lot more you need to see."

Hope quickly activated the last saved video file. Floating a meter in front of them, they saw their father fill the holographic projection.

"Hello again, Hope. If everything has gone as planned, you and your brother are at the Tuschinski Theater. I love you both very much and need you to trust me. We don't have much time."

Hope and the Poet heard the sincerity of his love for them.

Gabriel continued, "I've been working on a plan to correct my mistakes. When I started working for Encephalon. . ."

A proximity alarm sounded, automatically shutting off the video and replacing it with the holographic map for them both to see. Somehow, the AI Agents had slipped past Poet's countermeasures and surveillance.

Realizing the imminent threat, Poet activated the compromised extraction plan, but it was already too late. The theater doors burst open, and three AI Agents immediately opened fire. In the chaos, a bullet slammed Hope to the ground in a flash. Now face-down on the floor, she gasped for breath as she fought to stay conscious, knowing Poet was next in line for an attack.

Despite her injuries, she watched in disbelief as Poet skillfully wielded an M32-Killjoy, his shots finding their marks, obliterating two of the agents. However, the third agent remained unharmed, and the Killjoy lacked a zeroed target. The AI Agent swiftly leaped to the second-floor balcony, gaining the advantage over Poet. Helpless on the floor, Hope witnessed the exchange of gunfire. In a fraction of a second, the auditorium fell silent and Poet arose from behind the seats he had used to take cover.

With the immediate threat neutralized, Poet hurried to attend to Hope's wound. Although her protective jacket slowed the armor-piercing round, she was still gravely injured, blood steadily seeping through her clothing. Poet's shock was evident as he realized the severity of Hope's condition. Frantically searching for assistance, he reassured her that an extraction team would arrive soon.

In what seemed like an instant to Hope, she found herself lying on a hover gurney, her body weak and her mind clouded. The extraction team swiftly maneuvered her through the theater's rear entrance, following the captain's commands. They carefully placed her in the ePAV-VTOL, a medical airlift vehicle spacious enough to accommodate the entire team and provide a comfortable space for her to lie flat. Hope drifted in and out of consciousness, her condition rapidly deteriorating.

Poet knelt beside her, his voice trembling with urgency. "Hang on, Hope. You can't leave me now. I need you to fight, just a little longer." He held back tears as his unyielding grip tightened around her arm.

Amid the clamor of the moment, Poet's plea stood as a beacon of unwavering support. He raised his voice, a desperate cry for help, "We need to go! Now!" The tension in his voice was palpable, and the team rallied, moving with precision.

Hope's eyelids fluttered, her gaze locking onto Poet's, a profound connection that transcended words. In that moment, they shared a universe of unspoken sentiments, a love that defied the chaos surrounding them. As her strength waned, Hope struggled to utter her deepest truth, a lone tear carving a path down her cheek. With all her might, she whispered, "I love you . . ." Her voice then trailed into a breathless silence as consciousness slipped away.

The operating room buzzed with frenetic activity. Medical professionals swiftly prepared the room, bathed in the bright halo of overhead lights. Hope's body lay on the operating table, her arms immobilized at her sides, and a cervical collar supporting her neck.

From an otherworldly vantage point, Hope observed her body on the table. She felt no pain as she peered over the shoulders of the doctors, watching their every move. One surgeon's hand was stained crimson as they skillfully tended her chest wound. Urgent commands were accompanied by beeping machines, clanging instruments, and nervous chatter among the medical staff. Observing the whirl of activity, Hope felt as if she existed in a hazy state where her senses were alert, yet her understanding of the unfolding scene remained foggy. *How am I witnessing all of this? What is happening? How is this possible?*

A soft voice, seemingly emanating from an invisible presence nearby, addressed her. Hope turned toward the sound, but saw no one. Nevertheless, she sensed the reassuring presence of a man.

"Hello, Hope," the voice said gently, reassuringly. "I want you to know that you are in a coma."

Hope's gaze remained fixed on the scene below as questions flooded her mind. "Why? How did I get here? What's happening to me?"

Free from pain and devoid of recent memories, she felt a deep bewilderment, unsure of what to do next.

"Everything will be alright, Hope," the voice assured her, as the figure of a man slowly materialized. "My name is Gentry. Please, come with me. We have much to share with you."

CHAPTER 2

Present day, October 10, 2024, the here-and-now converges with a rapidly unfolding future. Fueled by an unwavering determination, a visionary embarks on a journey driven by profound insight, serendipitously stumbling upon a groundbreaking discovery.

Gabriel Valencia's heart quickened as electric tension filled the auditorium. At the podium, he readied himself to unveil his groundbreaking research to an expectant audience at the Harvard Science Center. A scan of the crowd, a final check of his equipment, and he was set. The moment weighed on him like the tension of gladiators before a Colosseum battle, heightening his nervous anticipation.

The lecture hall was teeming with eager attendees, leaving the tardy stragglers with no choice but to squeeze into the back rows. It was a testament to the unforeseen level of attention Gabe's work had garnered. Whispers of conversation swirled around him, weaving an unsettling symphony of skepticism surrounding the "fringe science" he had ventured to explore. Gabe's thoughts ricocheted between the meticulously prepared notes, his frayed nerves, and the formidable array of equipment that stood before him. Public speaking was hardly his forte, and the spotlight had always felt like an unwelcome intrusion on his comfort zone.

A gentle tap on his left shoulder jolted him from his thoughts. He turned to find a young woman in smart attire sporting a bright smile. "We're ready when you are, Dr. Valencia," she said. "Just let me know when you're prepared to start. I'll introduce you to the audience and guide the Q&A session. You'll have control over the slides with the clicker on the podium."

"Thank you. I'm ready to get started," Gabe replied, confident and focused. Comfortable or not, he was determined to deliver the presentation of a lifetime.

The audience applauded as Gabe took the podium. Glancing up and to his left, he caught sight of Ella, seated at the end of the aisle halfway up the auditorium. Their eyes met, and a private joke played out silently between them. She mouthed the words, "Olive juice." In that simple moment, he understood her true sentiment: *I love you*. Ella was his rock, the unwavering support he couldn't imagine life without. She never questioned his ambitions, always passionately championing his career objectives despite the doubts circulating around MIT and the scientific community at large.

Gabe had recruited Ella onto his research team years ago, captivated by her brilliance and unique ability to discern truth in the abstract. As they spent more time together, their connection grew more substantial, and they fell deeply in love. At that moment, as he caught sight of her beautiful face among the crowd, a surge of confidence coursed through him.

With a deliberate pace, he scanned the room from left to right, anchoring himself in one spot. His hands clasped confidently atop the podium, he made eye contact with random individuals in the audience, each connection fueling his energy. With unwavering enthusiasm, he launched into his presentation.

"Welcome, esteemed colleagues. I am Gabriel Valencia, head of MIT's Neurotechnological Research Studies Team." All eyes were fixed upon him. "What began as a mere research project has evolved into one of the most profound discoveries in neurotechnology. We have crafted an artificially intelligent algorithm that harnesses the intricate web of neural activity within the human brain. We can extract the electric signals coursing between synapses in the human neural pathways for the first time in history. Put simply, we can now digitally read people's minds. Initially, our objective was modest, to explore neurological technologies that could aid in addressing and curing various health ailments. However, what we uncovered surpassed the scope and objectives of our scientific inquiry, as our research combined cutting-edge neuroscience, artificial intelligence, and mixed-reality technologies."

Gabe knew he had captured the audience's attention, and with each passing moment, he seized the opportunity to illuminate their minds with the possibilities his work presented. His voice reverberated through the lecture hall, his words weaving a complex tapestry, intertwining the profound intricacies of the human brain with the enigmatic nature of reality itself.

"Through millions of years of evolution, the human brain has amassed the utilization of hundreds of billions of neurons," Gabe proclaimed, his voice infused with a sense of wonder and passion for his discoveries. "Examining just one of these remarkable cells, we uncover a set of simple rules not dissimilar to those followed by technology hardware in response to binary commands from software. A command of one triggers a specific action, while zero initiates another. Yet, when billions of these neurons coexist within the confines of our skulls, the result is nothing short of sentient, conscious life on Earth."

Gabe wondered how long he could continue speaking without taking a much-needed breath. He reminded himself of Ella's advice: "Remember to breathe, honey. Everything will go better than you ever imagined." He valued her unwavering support, even as he navigated the divergent opinions of his colleagues, some of whom had cautioned him against venturing down this unconventional path. His best friend, Jake, had expressed his doubts during a candid conversation in a pub years ago.

"Gabe, really? You're an MIT graduate fixated on bridging the gap between the physical and metaphysical realities?" Jake had exclaimed, skepticism lacing his words. "We're still grappling with understanding what we can observe with our own eyes, let alone entertaining these outlandish new-age ideas. You're wasting your time, my friend."

While Gabe held a deep respect for the opinions of his colleagues, he clung steadfastly to his pursuit, his conviction unshaken that a groundbreaking discovery lay just beyond the horizon. Yet, to propel his research to the next level, a substantial influx of funding was imperative, and securing it posed a daunting challenge for him and his dedicated team. No longer limited by the confines of MIT's research budgets, Gabe found himself thrust into the unfamiliar role of a fundraiser.

Undeterred, he continued his presentation, capturing the audience's attention with each carefully chosen word. "This remarkable family of neurons operates instinctively, working in harmonious orchestration to achieve the ultimate goal: sentient intelligent faculty. Trillions of electrical pulses, in harmony with the brain's biological foundations, allow for synaptic processes that transcend the boundaries of our physical minds, leading us into an infinite universe of imaginative human consciousness. This duality allows us to recognize our multifaceted reality—the physical brain and the metaphysical mind. We explore the interplay between our external sight, which perceives the physical world around us, and our internal sight, fueled by our creative imaginations. The question that lingers is: Which one precedes the other?"

Pausing momentarily to quench his thirst with a sip of water, a surge of confidence propelled him forward as he resumed.

"The age-old question of what came first, matter or consciousness, has ignited fierce debates in the halls of prestigious scientific institutions worldwide," Gabe explained, his voice carrying a tinge of intrigue. "It is widely accepted within the scientific community that reality itself harmonically resonates from the foundations of mathematics. Some even postulate that we might be living within an intelligent mathematical simulation. While I won't delve into the latter, I can unequivocally state that the images before you offer nearly irrefutable evidence of the programmatic nature of our known reality."

Gabe gestured toward the screen behind him, drawing the audience's gaze. "These visual AI renderings depict the mathematical summation of various string theory calculations. In our relentless quest to unravel nature's fundamental structures, we have stumbled upon mathematical clues and equations intricately woven into the fabric of the universe. These images reveal a fascinating revelation: The same programmatic equations employed by basic search engines and web browsers are identical to these captivating visuals of string theory mathematics."

The audience buzzed with renewed energy, whispers intertwining with the rustling of anticipation. Gabe pressed on, fully immersing them in the realm of his research.

"By mere chance, we have stumbled upon an intriguing echo—a reverberation we believe—caused by the existence of quantum consciousness. To be more precise, a theoretical particle known as the Conscious Agent," Gabe's voice brimmed with excitement. "This remarkable revelation has afforded us glimpses into the realm of probable realities, woven within the intricate tapestry of human thought patterns, visually unfurling the very fabric of the universe. To be more precise, we find ourselves exploring the depths of the multiverse. We have coined the term 'Trans-Dimensional Probability Threads' to encapsulate these visual findings. They have set us on a daring scientific trajectory, aiming to unveil a profound truth: The world we perceive around us is an intricately interwoven manifestation of consciousness itself, forever shaped by our beliefs and thoughts."

The sound of murmurs filled the room as the audience grappled with the profound implications of Gabe's claims. Gabe cleared his throat, his voice rising above the commotion as he pressed forward, fueled by his eagerness to share the results of their groundbreaking experiments.

"The remarkable strides made in NeuroConnect brain installations have profoundly propelled our research," Gabe declared. "The capability to seamlessly stream neurological data directly from the human brain into specialized data servers marks an achievement of unparalleled significance."

Gabe's presentation sought to illuminate the mysteries surrounding these pioneering neocortex-chip installations while deftly establishing the links between human consciousness and the realm of physics. It was paramount to meticulously assemble his findings, much like placing tiles individually, to construct the complex mosaic of his groundbreaking work.

"Imagine this," Gabe began, his voice captivating the room. "We surgically embed the NeuroConnect chip into a subject's brain, forging a complete neurological connection to every known receptor. The chip becomes a conduit, supplying raw data and information from the subject's electrochemical neuronal signals—motor movements, hearing, visual cues, desires, feelings, dreams, hunger, anticipation—everything experienced during the experiment."

He continued, shedding light on the early versions of the NeuroConnect transmitter. Early prototypes could decipher data reflecting the subject's intentions. In these experiments, chimpanzee test subjects astoundingly controlled a cursor on a computer monitor using only their thoughts harnessed from the primary motor cortex (M1). While neurotechnology had previously focused on utilizing digitized thoughts to manipulate electronic devices or explore theoretical health applications, the NeuroConnect technology laid the foundation for something far more profound.

Gabe explained how he and his team embarked on a transformative mission, capturing human thoughts in digital form. These thoughts were then guided through a cutting-edge Quantum Thought Dynamics AI protocol named QTD-AI. With meticulous precision, they directed the flow of these captured thoughts, aiming to unleash the untapped potential hidden within human consciousness and explore its mysteries through digital experiments.

As these "digital thought packets" passed through the QTD-AI, they underwent a revolutionary transformation. The result? An extraordinary inventory of digital thought probabilities, each offering a glimpse into the artifacts of human cognition. This breakthrough allowed them to delve into uncharted territories, mapping the intricate connections between thought and the enigmatic quantum field—the very fabric of consciousness.

"With our system in place, we were ready to take the next steps," Gabe enthusiastically shared. "But what really fueled our curiosity was the chance to test Dr. Adrian Bannister's visionary theories surrounding quantum consciousness. Imagine if the universe was comprised of tiny building blocks called Conscious

Agents, gradually coalescing to form atoms and matter. Could thoughts themselves be constructed from these very same energetic quanta? Could we deconstruct thoughts into these fundamental building blocks? Our research strongly indicates the potential."

Gabe's excitement was contagious, and the audience seemed captivated by the possibilities. The mysteries of human consciousness and the enigmatic quantum realm were on the brink of convergence, ushering in an era where human cognition would no longer be an undiscovered frontier.

"After exploring various paths in the realm of Quantum Thought Dynamics-AI, we finally discovered a series of commands that would reveal the incredible findings of our work," Gabe declared, his voice filled with determination. "With precision, we routed the subject's thoughts, freshly collected from the NeuroConnect chips, through the QTD-AI protocol. The outcome was a precisely structured data compilation, enabling us to synthesize organized cognition. Using state-of-the-art mixed-reality visual systems, we then made an astonishing discovery."

Gabe directed his attention to the floating screen behind him and activated a video. Instantly, his colleagues were transported into his MIT laboratory. In the video, a young lady reclined in a lounge chair, adjusting the mixed-reality headset. As the test subject settled into the augmented experience, the audience, seeing everything from her perspective, watched as the room shifted in accordance with her gaze.

Through the chaotic visual display, fleeting glimpses of Gabe appeared on the left side of the frame. Clad in his customary white lab coat, he commanded a mobile computer cart adorned with a tangled web of wires stretching in all directions. His fingers danced across the keyboard while his gaze remained fixed on the monitors suspended above the cart. On the left screen, digital code scrolled rapidly, punctuated by Gabe's periodic checks. The right monitor displayed a captivating animation of a colossal server bank pulsating with raw computational power.

Gabe's voice, filled with excitement and confidence, resonated through the speakers. "Everything looks great on my end," he declared. "The server array is smiling and ready to roll!"

A pleasant female voice interjected, tinged with a hint of anxiety. The woman's words conveyed their limited time within the leased bracket. "They'll shift the server bank capacity over to us in two minutes and thirty-five seconds," she warned. "We only have ten minutes for the QTD-AI run today. Let's be ready the second we go live." The urgency in her tone was palpable, underscoring the immense computational power required for Gabe's groundbreaking technology. The limitations of the MIT mainframe necessitated leasing server capacity from technology giants, a calculated risk he had embraced to push the boundaries of his theory.

Gabe's face loomed large on the video screen. With kindness in his voice, he asked the test subject if she was ready to get started. Nervously, she nodded affirmatively.

A loud voice resonated through the auditorium, announcing the countdown. "Ninety seconds," the female voice declared, firmly capturing the audience's focus.

Another member of Gabe's team provided reassurance from deep within the lab. "The servers are online. We're set for full compression today. Everything is tracking perfectly. No power surges or interruptions in the past hour. We've got this."

The tension grew as the countdown continued, amplified by the female voice. "In ten!" The woman exclaimed, her voice ringing out louder than before. The test subject's gaze locked forward, her movements settling into a moment of stillness. The audience could hear the sound of her heavy breathing.

Then, Gabe's voice reverberated through the lab, cutting through the anticipation. "On Ella's mark, we'll synchronize the activation," he shouted across the room in an urgent tone.

As if choreographed, Ella's voice filled the space, each cardinal second enunciated clearly. "Five . . . four . . . three . . . two . . ." Her voice hung in the air, building anticipation. And then, with a resounding finality, she called out, "One!"

In perfect unison, the team pressed the keys on their keyboards, a synchronized motion that sparked the transformation. The audience instantly witnessed the extraordinary spectacle that Gabe and his team had seen in the lab. The video playing on the screen unveiled a breathtaking distortion, a mesmerizing display that captured the imagination.

The video frame came alive with fine vertical lines elegantly strung from top to bottom. Like an intricate tapestry, they weaved together with translucent grace, creating a pattern reminiscent of a loom's artistry. Clustered tightly on the sides, they gradually spread apart, leaving a central gap. As the test subject explored the laboratory with her gaze, the vertical lines whimsically responded to her every movement. They danced and flowed elegantly throughout the laboratory, perfectly aligning with her shifting perspective. It was as though the very fabric of reality had seamlessly adjusted to her vision.

The audience was captivated, their eyes fixed on the screen, immersed in the ethereal beauty unfolding before them. The unique patterns provided a tangible glimpse into the test subject's mixed-reality experience.

The mixed-reality headset seamlessly projected a holographic representation of the test subject's stream of thoughts, augmenting them into the physical laboratory space.

Powered by the Quantum Thought Dynamics-AI protocol, the system processed the young woman's digital thoughts and displayed them visually, yielding truly astonishing results.

Amid this technological marvel, the test subject couldn't contain her awe. Her voice, filled with wonder, broke the silence. "It's so . . . beautiful," she whispered, struggling to find the right words. "I see these . . . beautiful shimmering threads. It's indescribable. They are simply breathtaking!" As her gaze wandered across the room, the translucent vertical threads gracefully danced and shimmered, painting vivid strokes of color across the frame.

Gabe swiftly pressed the pause button, bringing the captivating display to a momentary halt. The audience's heightened sounds of anticipation and restless movement filled the air.

Gabe attempted to regain their attention. "What we believe we are witnessing in this video is a remarkable visual representation of the Fecund Universes, or simply the Multiverse. Although we have yet to grasp its underlying mechanisms, it's clear that we've discovered something profound. We generated dual visual streams by reprojecting the subject's mental images simultaneously within the mixed-reality framework and the physical laboratory. Think of it as overlaying a digitally rendered representation of probable reality onto the physical world, deliberately kept slightly out of sync.

"Initially, we thought the time-lapse would blur the image, and these vertical threads were a calibration glitch. However, we now believe the experiment visually represents the subject's probable future timelines." Gabe paused allowing his revelation to set in. "We're referring to them as Trans-Dimensional Probability Threads."

Murmurs filled the audience as Gabe noticed many engaged in conversation. He then attempted to clarify the possibilities. The combination of science, advanced mixed-reality technology, NeuroConnect brain installations, and the dynamic Multiverse had led to an extraordinary revelation. It was a scientific journey beyond imagination. Nevertheless, Gabe and his team remained resolute in believing that what was once deemed science fiction would ultimately become a scientific reality.

Gabe now confronted the formidable task of demonstrating that human neurological functions could influence this framework. Could thoughts, he pondered, have the power to transport one's consciousness into an alternate reality? They embarked on a journey of rigorous experimentation to uncover the answer. Their mission was clear: to ascertain whether humans possessed the capacity to select their probable realities, or if the Trans-Dimensional Probability Threads adhered to steadfast, unchangeable universal laws.

Gabe continued, "Hollywood often portrays parallel universes as accessible only through exotic portals or dimensional gateways. This makes for great entertainment, but it's an unreliable prediction of the future. Our experiments suggest something different. Each of us gathered here today may function as a doorway to an expansive range of parallel universes, which we refer to as 'probable life dimensions.' Remember the saying, 'Do you think the world revolves around you?' Well, there might be some truth to it. Numerous probable worlds may orbit around each of us, and we have the ability to select the one we wish to experience. We believe this selection process occurs countless times daily, molding our reality in ways we are only just starting to comprehend."

A silence descended upon the room as Gabe's words hung in the air. It was as if the atmosphere bore the weight of his claims. Gabe could see that the audience was challenged by the notion that the once solid boundaries dividing imagination from reality had unveiled a remarkable fluidity.

"What does this mean for us as individuals and as a society?" Gabe's voice broke the silence. "Could it mean that we hold the power to transcend our current realities and choose new ones within us? We're setting out to prove that our beliefs, emotions, and thoughts are not mere passive components of our experience; they are the very catalysts that can propel us onto new threads of probable reality."

As Gabe made his last claim, the audience grew restless. Still, he pressed on. "Through our experiments, we've unearthed a key concept at the heart of our research: the Dimensional Algebraic Reality Equation, or D.A.R.E., represented as $B \in E+T=R$. This symbolic equation illuminates a core process that operates subconsciously as humans select their preferred thread of reality. Our beliefs, emotions, and thoughts collaborate to shape the very essence of reality itself. It offers insight into how our inner world profoundly influences the external reality we experience.

"Our research led us to suspect that human neurological functions, particularly thoughts, somehow align with Trans-Dimensional Probability Threads at the quantum level. To gain a deeper understanding, we incorporated a sub-function research team of psychologists tasked with identifying potential connections between human consciousness and the threads we've uncovered. The results have offered the opportunity for real-time testing and experimentation."

As Gabe surveyed the room, he explained the equation $B \in E+T=R$, breaking it into elemental components. "B represents beliefs, E represents emotions, T represents thoughts, and R represents reality," he explained. "We aim to unravel the interactions between these variables as they determine an individual's probable life dimension. By intentionally manipulating any of these variables, we believe we can guide a person onto a different thread of reality."

Gabe then noticed several confused looks etched on the faces of his audience. He pressed on, determined to make his point resonate. "Our beliefs (B) act as triggers for our emotions (E), and we've discovered that these variables are intrinsically linked—they exist in set membership ($B \in E$). Consequently, this connection influences our thoughts (+T) and fuels our creative imagination."

Gabe hesitated briefly, considering whether or not to reveal the next aspect of their research. It hinted at a possible connection between thoughts and reality, although they were still in the process of providing concrete proof. Ultimately, he chose to share it. Gabe firmly believed in introducing the bridge that would become the central focus of their upcoming research phase.

"We've yet to prove this conclusively, but we're convinced that a quantum connection exists between conscious thought and the physical reality surrounding us. Thoughts appear to be more than mere neurological functions; they are energetically charged echoes of our beliefs. Like a tuning fork, these beliefs harmonize with universal frequencies, initiating a quantum resonance we've termed 'Quantum Thought Dynamics.' This resonance acts as the catalyst, propelling individuals into uncharted probable realities. In this dynamic interplay between beliefs and thoughts, we witness the very fabric of reality taking shape, unveiling the extraordinary power we hold to choose from an infinite set of probable realities ($=R$)."

Gabe paused to allow his words to set in. "We recognize a missing piece in our puzzle—an essential component within the realm of theoretical quantum particles known as a 'Conscious

Agent.' This subatomic particle precedes all other quantum functions. A particle endowed with a conscious process would serve as the bedrock from which all other quanta spring into existence and bridge the gap between thought and our perceived reality. To deepen our understanding, we are collaborating with other projects at MIT, pooling our efforts to unveil this intricate connection."

Gabe summarized their innovative therapeutic approach, Neuro-Symbolic Programming (NSP), developed with psychologists. NSP used personalized visualizations and belief programming called Future Memory Recalls (FMRs). He likened NSP-FMR to watching a personalized movie of one's future. With the guidance of psychologists, Gabe and his team assisted subjects in replacing their limiting beliefs with empowering ones. The goal was to unlock their ability to transition onto new Trans-Dimensional Probability Threads and theoretically access alternate realities.

"In essence," Gabe explained, "this process rewrites beliefs, allowing conscious selection of a more desirable reality. It unlocks the power in subconscious thoughts shaped by beliefs. By updating the test subjects' beliefs, we aim to assist them in selecting a more desirable reality."

The audience was captivated by the implications of Gabe's claims. The notion that human beings are not passive observers of reality but active co-creators suggested a sense of empowerment that many thought previously impossible. It was a paradigm shift that challenged the prevailing narrative of limitation and opened up a world of infinite potential.

Gabe concluded his lecture, his voice resonating with conviction, "Envision a world where the true potential of every individual is realized, where the power to shape reality resides within each of us. Envision a society where collective beliefs foster harmonious coexistence. Armed with the potential of Quantum Thought Dynamics-AI protocol and the $B \in E + T = R$ equation, we can dare to bridge the seemingly insurmountable gap between the physical and metaphysical realms."

The room erupted in applause as Gabe's final words settled in the air. The audience was now captivated by the vision of a future where the boundaries of reality were no longer fixed but malleable, inviting their conscious participation. It was an audacious and untested proposition that, if validated, would irrevocably reshape the world's perception of reality.

As the applause faded, a captivating figure caught Gabe's attention as she gracefully made her way down the center aisle. Among a sea of threadbare tweed sports jackets and conservative dresses, she exuded an aura of elegance and sophistication, as though she had just descended from a high-fashion runway in Milan, Italy. His curiosity piqued, Gabe wondered who she was. Something about her striking presence tugged at his intuition.

As the woman made her way up the aisle, her strides purposeful and determined, she retrieved a phone from her crocodile bag, symbolizing her enigmatic persona. The instructions she had received were crystal clear: Provide an immediate assessment of Gabriel Valencia's latest achievements.

A voice broke the silence. "This is Hayes."

The woman wasted no time. Her words were concise and laden with urgency. "Hello, Ronan. Gabriel Valencia just shared his discoveries with the entire academic community. He's further along than we thought."

The line went dead. The woman stood frozen, her hand gripping the phone tightly, a mix of anticipation and apprehension coursing through her. She considered the consequences of the report she had just delivered. One thing was sure—Gabriel Valencia had become the focal point of her world.

The auditorium emptied, leaving Gabe to navigate the lingering conversations. Ella stood among a group of colleagues and engaged in their intense conversation. They had recognized her in the video of the experiment and bombarded her with their hypotheses. Gabe approached, greeted by their recognition.

"There's our man with the plan!" one of them exclaimed, acknowledging Gabe's achievements. These post-presentation encounters were always a mixed bag, filled with curiosity and skepticism, leading to occasionally awkward introductions.

As always, Ella stepped forward with unwavering confidence. "Gabe, meet Dr. Jennings and Dr. Serrano. They're interested in learning more about your work."

After conversing with the doctors, Gabe and Ella shared their contact information with them and promised future connections. Eagerly inclined to speak with anyone in the auditorium about his work, Gabe was equally predisposed to invest his time with those specifically willing to support his work, either with financial grants, state-of-the-art lab space, or other resources. These doctors seemed merely interested in uncovering more than what Gabe was willing to share about his research. So he and Ella bid them farewell and walked up the aisle together hand in hand.

"I hope we made progress today." He expressed his aspirations, knowing deep down that he had done well.

Ella halted their steps, her hands resting on Gabe's shoulders. She peered deeply into his eyes, her voice filled with unwavering support. "You crushed it today, honey. All the hope you need resides right here." She gently guided Gabe's hand to her belly.

A smile stretched across Gabe's face as he locked eyes with Ella. "And I believe the name Hope is perfect for our daughter," she declared.

"It's a girl?" Gabe's astonishment was evident. "I mean . . . she's really a girl?"

Ella chuckled, her joy radiating. "Yes, darling, she's real, and she has a brother keeping her company!"

Confusion momentarily clouded Gabe's expression. "But, how . . .?" Then, in an instant, understanding dawned upon him. "Twins?"

"Yes!" Ella affirmed, her excitement palpable. "We're having twins! A girl and a boy!"

Gabe's face rapidly transformed, a whirlwind of emotions playing across his features in seconds. Joy, surprise, and a touch of trepidation danced in his eyes as he absorbed the news. Their shared journey had taken an unforeseen twist, steering them onto a new path brimming with the promise of double the joy, love, and adventures.

CHAPTER 3

Hope's consciousness finds itself adrift, detached from her physical form. Yet, she remains anchored to her earthly reality. It is 9:37 p.m., October 13, 2054 in Amsterdam. Following her encounter with the AI agents at Tuschinski Theater, Hope is drawn into the ethereal embrace of The Inverse.

Hope's thoughts spun in a whirlwind of confusion and curiosity, emotions intermingling like a storm within her. The gentle voice she had previously heard in the hospital room now materialized as a man named Gentry. His presence exuded an enigmatic fusion of mystery, wisdom, and compassion.

"Why am I here? What's going on with me?" Her voice quivered with concern, seeking answers in this moment of uncertainty.

"You have been seriously injured, Hope. Try to recall the last thing you remember," Gentry's words carried a comforting weight, like a guiding hand in the darkness.

Her thoughts turned inward, retracing the path that had led her here. The searing agony of ammunition tearing through her body and crushing her chest clawed its way into her consciousness.

"My brother, Poet," Hope's words trembled with fear, "is he safe? Is he okay?"

Gentry's voice offered a calming reassurance. "Poet is just fine, Hope. He is just outside in the waiting room. Please, try not to worry."

As Hope hovered beside her physical form, a haunting unease settled over her. "Am I dead?"

Gentry's presence remained an anchor of calm in the turbulence of her thoughts. "No, Hope, you are not dead. Everything is going to be okay. You are experiencing a unique state of consciousness that has unveiled the ability to perceive a reality beyond the physical realm."

Hope grappled with her thoughts, fixating on the intricate medical procedure below. The urgency and tension in the voices of the medical staff hinted at trouble.

"Am I going to be okay?" Standing beside Gentry, she found solace in his aura as though he were an old friend, here to offer comfort.

"Yes, everything is going to be okay, Hope," Gentry reassured her.

Hope continued to unravel the enigma before her. "Why is this happening to me, and who are you?"

"I am here as your guide, Hope. We have work to do. We will leave when you are ready."

Hope inquired further, her words latching onto her thirst for understanding. "Leave? Where are we going? You said I'm not dead. I'm not prepared to leave! I need to return to . . ." Words eluded her, lost in the labyrinth of her concerns.

"Please, try not to worry, Hope," Gentry consoled her. "It will be clear once you meet with your advisors. You can return here anytime. But I strongly suggest considering the journey with me. There is much to be explained."

Desperate for answers, Hope found herself inexplicably drawn to Gentry. "So, I can return at anytime?"

"Yes, Hope. You can return instantly if you wish."

Hope watched the medical team's frantic efforts to save her. Despite the ethereal disconnect, she felt tethered to her physical self, like a fragile thread linking her to life. Simultaneously, she sensed the pull of a forgotten responsibility, an unspoken duty she couldn't ignore. Gentry's words resonated with undeniable comfort. Her instincts led her to trust him, and she knew that following him was the right course of action. Gathering her resolve, she pushed her fears aside and uttered, "I'll go."

"Excellent, Hope. I am very proud of you," Gentry's voice brimmed with pride. "I will be right by your side."

Gentry extended his hand, and Hope hesitated momentarily, glancing back at her earthly vessel. Curiosity led her to grasp his hand despite her reservations, and in a heartbeat, they departed the hospital room.

The surroundings blurred into a vortex of motion, and Hope found herself immersed in a celestial realm bathed in delicate shades of baby blue. Its elegance seized her senses, but the most captivating sensation was an overwhelming and pure contentment that permeated every inch of this seemingly infinite space. Within its embrace, she felt secure, cherished, and liberated from the shackles of time. It was unlike any experience she had ever encountered on Earth.

As they traversed this ethereal expanse, Hope marveled at the seamless motion that carried them forward, yet its source remained elusive. No familiar landmarks or rushing winds gave clues to their velocity, leaving Hope astounded and inquisitive.

"Where are we going?" Hope's curiosity remained unquenched by the mesmerizing surroundings.

"Like I said, Hope, you are going to meet your advisors."

Still lacking answers, Hope's confusion deepened, prompting another question. "Is this the afterlife?"

Gentry's reply attempted to clarify the nature of this enigmatic realm. "Think of this place more as a state of consciousness, Hope."

Hope's search for comprehension persisted. "Am I dreaming? Is all of this a dream?"

"No, Hope. This is not a dream, not in the way you are accustomed to. You are now within a reality as tangible as the one you have known on Earth, but here, you have transcended your current dimensional boundaries."

"Dimensional boundaries? What do you mean by that?"

"In your current state, you have been set free from the space-time continuum you, and the rest of your species, perceive as reality. Beings that are native to this realm are not restricted by time or space. Anything and everything we can imagine is reality."

As they continued to travel, Hope felt as if she were moving at speeds she never thought possible, but she had no sense of direction or any sort of destination that might lie ahead.

"What do you call this place?"

"We do not necessarily have a name for it. Humans find it necessary to label everything under their sun, so for your benefit, we call this place The Inverse."

"The Inverse? Why The Inverse? What does that even mean?"

Gentry offered a contemplative look before answering. "The Inverse is where you are from, Hope. You have returned home, so to speak, temporarily."

Gentry's words only fueled Hope's curiosity, but he continued. "You asked if this was the 'afterlife.' That label suggests there is a start and an end to life, whereas life is infinite in this greater reality. So, there is no before or after. We are not bound by dimensional restrictions here."

Hope looked confused and countered, "But I still don't understand why you call it The Inverse?"

Gentry carefully constructed a more complete answer. "On Earth, humans understand their reality through certain dimensional constraints. For instance, you perceive time as linear, always moving forward and never backward. This linear perspective of time governs your understanding of cause and effect, past and future. It is a unique way of experiencing reality, but it greatly limits the boundaries of your understanding. The Inverse is a profound juxtaposition to the constraints of physical reality. Here, beings of pure consciousness dwell in a space that embodies the unlimited expression of the universe or, more precisely, the multiverse. Unlike the three dimensions of space, defined by height, width, and length that bind your physical existence, The Inverse unfolds within a singular, infinite space dimension.

"Moreover, time here is not the linear, unidirectional flow experienced on Earth. In The Inverse, time manifests as past, present, and future simultaneously, coexisting harmoniously as one dimension. So, for your understanding, The Inverse can be thought of as a metaphysical space where the very fabric of existence is turned inside out, in human terms."

Hope took a moment to absorb the profound concepts Gentry had presented. It was indeed a lot to digest, but her sharp intellect allowed her to grasp the dimensional realities in which she found herself. She whispered to herself, "I see. The Inverse."

"Yes, Hope. You are starting to perceive a reality that directly opposes what you have known," Gentry affirmed.

In the distance, faint outlines of buildings emerged, exuding an air of sophistication and modernity. However, the gap between them and the structures was not closing, as if they were suspended in a perpetual distance.

With a cautious tone, Hope asked, "Are those buildings where we're headed?"

"Yes, that is where you will meet your advisors," Gentry replied.

Hope's curiosity grew, prompting her to inquire further, "How much longer until we reach them?"

Gentry's response carried a hint of mystery, "That, my dear Hope, depends entirely on you."

Frustration tinged Hope's voice as she pressed for a straightforward answer. "No more riddles, Gentry. Please, just tell me when we will be there."

Gentry's tone conveyed understanding, "Hope, trust me when I say I have never seen those buildings before. They exist solely within your imagination, a creation of *your* thoughts alone. I am simply here to accompany you on this journey. When I mentioned the need to move forward, you interpreted it as embarking on a physical voyage. As a result, everything around us, including the sense of progression toward a destination, instantly manifested according to your conscious commands. Within The Inverse, nothing comes into existence without first being consciously contemplated. All potential realities coexist simultaneously in this realm, already complete and realized. The only thing that separates you from any of these infinite possibilities is your choice, or more precisely, your beliefs, thoughts, and imagination.

"Remember," Gentry continued, his voice filled with profound wisdom, "that in this reality, a singularly infinite dimension of space exists intertwined with multiple dimensions of time. Here in The Inverse, there is no delay between desire and experience. Thought and manifestation are seamlessly intertwined. The notion of anticipation, so familiar to those who have undergone multiple life experiences on Earth, is foreign to most beings residing within The Inverse. We will arrive at our destination the moment you decide we are there. Over there is here, and here is over there. You are both everywhere and nowhere simultaneously."

Hope closed her eyes, allowing Gentry's words to permeate her consciousness. When she opened them once again, she found herself standing in front of a magnificent, modern building. An air of familiarity surrounded it, almost as if it held a significant place in her memories. The structure stood tall, its glass walls reflecting the gleaming steel beams that adorned its frame. It radiated a brilliant light that seemed to engulf its surroundings. Peering inside, Hope caught sight of individuals traversing its expansive corridors.

She turned to Gentry, her eyes seeking understanding. "This place . . . it feels familiar," she uttered, her voice filled with a mix of intrigue and confusion.

Gentry finished her thought, his voice laced with vagueness. "Yes, it is indeed familiar. But its true meaning eludes you, for now," he replied.

Hope's gaze remained fixed on the building as she contemplated its significance.

Gentry extended his arm with a gesture, inviting Hope to step forward. Curiosity guiding her, she took a determined step toward the towering glass doors. The doors parted with hardly a sound, granting her passage, then gently closed behind her as they entered, enveloping them into a space that exuded grandeur and elegance. The sheer magnificence of the interior left Hope in a state of awe. Above her stretched a breathtaking glass ceiling, supported by colossal steel beams, creating a majestic canopy beneath the flawless expanse of a blue sky.

Modern lighting hovered at varying levels, defying gravity with its ethereal glow. The floors, walls, and ceilings emanated a luminescence that surpassed anything she had ever seen.

The vast space was framed by two parallel mezzanines positioned high above, their railings crafted from mesmerizing baby-blue crystal material. Further ahead and to her left, a floating staircase appeared to materialize before her eyes, each step falling into place effortlessly, accommodating the footsteps of those ascending and descending. At the back of the expansive lobby, a solid glass bank of elevators stood, while suspended words, high above, proclaimed a profound message for all to see: *Multis filis unum sumus.* Hope whispered the meaning of the Latin phrase, "Of many threads, we are one." She stood transfixed, absorbing the splendor that enveloped her.

Gentry broke the silence, his voice resolute. "Just ahead and to the right, we will find the main conference room. Your advisor is waiting for you there. She will share details of the mission. Shall we proceed?"

Hope's brow furrowed in confusion as she asked, "Mission details? What exactly do you mean by that?"

Gentry's demeanor remained unfazed, a faint smile touching his lips as he replied, "You will find the answers you seek from someone more suited for the task, Hope. Let us make our way to the conference room."

As they continued, a magnificent structure was suspended in midair. Its enchanting form appeared both functional and artistic. The floor resembled the cool blue hue of an iceberg, while the walls flowed in a circular embrace. Ascending the levitating stairs that led to the entrance of the conference room, Hope entered the space to be greeted by a woman who emanated a presence of wisdom and grace.

Aiko's dark eyes held a depth of ancient understanding, like windows into the mysteries of the universe itself. Her regal poise was complemented by the warmth of her smile, which carried a wealth of compassion and insight.

"Hello, Hope. I am Aiko. It is a pleasure to make your acquaintance."

CHAPTER 4

Massachusetts Institute of Technology, MIT - Present day, April 27, 2025. Before the births of Hope and Poet, during an era when Gabriel's passions were woven into academia, society stands on the precipice of choosing its destined thread of reality. Embedded within his creation lies the potential for individuals to navigate a digital labyrinth of probable reality. However, Gabe, grappling with a life burdened by overwhelming challenges and seemingly insurmountable odds, finds the allure of the corporate world too tempting to resist.

Ella and Gabe toiled away in the dim light of the laboratory hours after most of their team had gone. Gabe cherished every moment he spent in Ella's company, regardless of the surroundings. His fingers fumbled nervously as he adjusted the instrument panel, his thoughts focused more on Ella than the work at hand.

"Where is your mind, sweetheart?" Ella asked, noticing Gabe's distracted demeanor.

Gabe, lifted his head and locked eyes with Ella. In that moment he felt an overwhelming rush of affection and knew it was time. With a soft, tender smile, he said, "El, every day I spend with you is an experiment in happiness, and I've discovered that there is no hypothesis needed when it comes to my love for you."

Kneeling before her, he said, "Will you marry me?" Gabe's voice resonated with love, his smile reflecting the depth of his affection for Ella.

Her soft laughter filled the room, a beautiful harmony of surprise and joy. "Gabriel Valencia, proposing in the lab, of all places? You certainly know how to sweep a girl off her feet," she playfully teased, her eyes shimmering with genuine emotion.

Gabe looked deeply into her eyes, his own brimming with love and a touch of nervousness. "Ella, I couldn't wait any longer. Every moment with you feels like a dream, and I never want it to end." He placed his hand on her round belly where their unborn children grew. "I can't wait to meet them, to watch them grow, and to share every moment with you, El."

In a soft voice filled with emotion, Ella responded, tears glistening in her eyes as she reached for his hand on her belly. "Yes, Gabriel. Yes, a thousand times yes." It was a beautiful confirmation of their love and the promise of a shared future that brought tears of joy to both their eyes.

As Gabe's words hung in the air, his nerves got the best of him, causing him to lose balance. He stumbled backward, arms flailing, landing on a table. The sudden jolt sent a few manuals and a piece of equipment tumbling on the floor, creating a brief commotion in the lab. Ella's laughter filled the space, a delightful mix of surprise and amusement. Gabe gently placed the simple gold band on Ella's finger, a meaningful symbol of infinite beauty that captivated them both. In that fleeting instant, the weight of their commitment and the promise of a lifetime of love filled the air.

They were ensconced in a technological fortress, a world humming with the whir of servers, blinking with the glow of monitors, and teeming with the energy of scientific pursuit. This labyrinth of equipment formed the backbone of their life's work, standing as a testament to the intellectual leaps they had made together.

Gabe found himself running to catch up at times, managing the rapid shift in the dynamics of their lives. The euphoria of impending parenthood was tempered by the financial strain gnawing at the edges of their accomplishments. He and Ella had chased their groundbreaking research fervently, squeezing incredible results out of the barest resources. But as time slipped through their fingers, so did the funding they desperately needed to propel their work, and life, forward.

Their work had been successful, yet the mounting challenges were impossible to ignore. In a landscape crowded with scientific discoveries and projects competing for a finite pool of funding, their Quantum Thought Dynamics-AI Protocol was labeled as "fringy," a term that hindered its acceptance by mainstream grant providers and research expenditure allocations. The academic sector, once a potential wellspring of support, had all but closed its coffers to them, leaving Gabe with no choice but to seek private funding. It was a necessary compromise that neither he nor Ella had envisioned, but was now indispensable.

When the situation seemed dire, Ronan Hayes, Encephalon Media Group's founder and CEO, appeared on their horizon. Celebrated for his technological ingenuity, and commanding a global empire, Hayes was a beacon of salvation. His expressed interest in their work did more than just present a lifeline—it provided an affirmation that invigorated Gabe's resolve.

Gabe understood the gravity of this opportunity and the sweeping changes it could bring to their lives. But at what cost?

Unbeknownst to anyone on the research team, Ronan Hayes had been tracking Gabe's academic career meticulously from the moment Gabe began winning science competitions in the field of neurology. He followed Gabe's journey through the years at MIT, scrutinizing every published paper and tracking his groundbreaking research. During a private symposium, rumors of Gabe's revolutionary Quantum Thought Dynamics-AI Protocol had started to circulate, and Hayes's curiosity was piqued. Quietly, he conducted an extensive investigation into their work, leaving no stone unturned. His clandestine fascination with Gabe's achievements and groundbreaking research led Hayes to conclude that a collaboration might be the catalyst for the next technological leap in human consciousness. So he invited Gabe to a private meeting at his office in New York.

The bright prospect of Ronan Hayes providing much-needed funding served as a glimmer of hope amidst a cloud of uncertainty. Yet, the excitement was tinged with dismay. Gabe and Ella were acutely aware of what Ronan and Encephalon Media Group represented. They had watched as unregulated social media giants shaped public perception through their powerful algorithms, delivering an endless stream of tailored content, videos, and images that kept users glued to their platforms. Gabe and Ella had even coined a term for it: "Dopamatic Programming," playing on the dopamine-fueled addictive nature of the technology.

However, Ronan Hayes was not just another tech titan. His well-publicized philanthropy, especially his contributions to mental health causes, painted a more promising picture. He advocated using the powerful potential of social platforms for good. This aspect of Ronan's persona gave them a glimmer of hope. But the question remained: Was he genuinely different, or was it just a sophisticated PR game?

Their reservations notwithstanding, the meeting with Ronan was too good an opportunity to ignore. They needed the funds, the support, and the lifeline that Encephalon represented. With their twins on the way and their groundbreaking work hanging in the balance, the prospect of this partnership was not just an opportunity, it was a necessity.

As Gabe's face revealed his thoughts, Ella gently squeezed his arm, offering a comforting reassurance. "We've faced challenges before, and we've always come out stronger," she said confidently. "I have complete faith in you, honey. We all do. When you walk into that meeting tomorrow, you'll blow them away. Trust me. Everything is going to be okay."

A smile tugged at Gabe's lips. "Thank you, sweetheart. It's just that leaving now, with the due date so close, isn't what I had planned."

Ella nodded, her smile offering reassurance. "I get it, Gabe. But we still have a few weeks, honey. The babies aren't going to make their grand entrance tomorrow," she said with a playful tone. "But I can tell something else is on your mind. What's bothering you?"

Gabe's smile faded as he searched for the right words. "It's hard to explain. I'm not worried about securing funding from Encephalon. I'm confident I can handle that. It's more about what they represent. I just wonder if our intentions are aligned."

Ella squeezed Gabe's hand as an act of solidarity for the weight of his concerns. Ever since the invitation from Encephalon arrived, she, too, had expressed her concerns about the integration of their research into the powerful conglomerate's social media empire. She and Gabe acknowledged the immense potential for positive change. Still, they needed to be conscious that Encephalon Media Group was a for-profit global conglomerate, prioritizing profits and shareholder returns over the well-being of the public at large.

"You have good instincts, Gabe," Ella reassured him, her voice filled with trust. "You're a man of integrity, and I, for one, trust you. If Encephalon isn't the right fit, you'll know it."

It's just a meeting. I haven't signed anything yet, Gabe thought.

"You're right, El. I'm sure I'm overthinking it. I can't expect a perfect scenario. I'm grateful for the opportunity to meet with Hayes and hear them out," Gabe admitted, feeling his shoulders relax. "Let's see what they have to offer. But for now, let's head home so I can pack, and then I'll make you one of my famous fried egg and bacon sandwiches you love."

"That's a deal," Ella replied, and they walked hand-in-hand toward the Static Free, shutting off the lights behind them.

Gabe's heart raced as the plane touched down, jolting him awake from a restless sleep. He glanced at the amused passenger next to him, wondering if he had unwittingly provided some entertainment. His embarrassment grew as he discovered a trail of drool on his chin, hastily wiping it away with his sleeve.

The flight attendant's announcement blared over the speakers, welcoming them to John F. Kennedy Airport. Gabe tried to drown out the noise, his focus shifting to his phone as he deactivated airplane mode in anticipation of any urgent messages. The anxiety of potentially missing important news about Ella's labor weighed heavily on him. Being so far away from her at such a crucial time was unsettling.

Relieved to find no urgent messages, Gabe exited the plane and headed through the terminal, following the signs to ground transportation. A man holding an iPad with the name VALENCIA caught his attention. Approaching him, Gabe confirmed his identity.

"Hello, I'm Gabriel Valencia."

The man in the dark suit introduced himself as Maurice, or Mo for short, his driver for the next twenty-four hours. Gabe was grateful for the convenience of not having to depend on Uber to get him around the city.

"I only have my backpack," Gabe informed the driver.

Mo gestured for Gabe to follow him, advising of a short walk ahead. Gabe settled into the luxurious leather seats of the Maybach. It was a fitting introduction to the vibrant energy of New York City, even as the Manhattan skyline appeared hazy in the distance.

Gabe's mind buzzed with a mix of hope and apprehension as they made their way to Encephalon's corporate headquarters. The failures of previous funding rounds lingered in his thoughts, fueling his nervousness. Yet, he was confident and determined in his work and knew he had developed something that would change the world forever.

Entering the underground parking, Gabe marveled at the collection of luxury cars parked there. Stepping out of the Maybach, they walked through a sleek glass vestibule, awaiting the elevator that would transport them to the highest floor. As the elevator ascended, Gabe felt a sense of altitude, his ears popping with the change in pressure. The doors opened, revealing a breathtaking view of Manhattan and Central Park through seamless floor-to-ceiling windows, a stunning backdrop to the forthcoming meeting. Although a bit intimidated by the grandeur of the space, Gabe couldn't help but be impressed by the elegance surrounding him.

A strikingly beautiful woman captured Gabe's attention at a half-moon reception desk ahead. Her jet-black hair cascaded around her piercing blue eyes. He felt a flicker of familiarity but couldn't place where he had seen her before.

Finishing a call, the woman greeted them with a warm smile as she arose from her seat. "Good morning, gentlemen. And you must be Dr. Valencia," she said, extending her hand. Her sophisticated demeanor added to her allure as she walked around the desk. "I'm Sophia Mendez, Mr. Hayes's business affairs coordinator. Welcome to Mr. Hayes's office."

Gabe swallowed hard and his eyes widened. "This entire eightieth floor is his office?" He realized he sounded like a kid in an extraordinarily large candy shop, but he couldn't help but be impressed at the sheer scale of it all.

Sophia giggled lightly, then informed Gabe that Ronan was running a few minutes late but would be landing shortly.

Landing? Gabe thought.

Suddenly, a helicopter echoed through the air, drawing his attention. The Sikorsky S-92 VVIP business ship made a graceful approach toward the building's rooftop, its presence commanding.

"Almost perfect timing," Sophia exclaimed with a broad smile as they continued toward a massive conference room. The solid glass doors stood tall, reaching thirty feet in height. Before them sat a contemporary table crafted from steel beams, cable, glass, and remnants of what looked like a historic aircraft to Gabe. It was a breathtaking piece of art, blending functionality and history seamlessly. The windows overlooking Central Park framed the view with precision, inviting a sense of wonder. Gabe wished Ella could see this, knowing that words alone couldn't capture the experience.

"Please make yourself comfortable. Refreshments are available at the far end," Sophia pointed toward the designated area. "Enjoy the view while I fetch Mr. Hayes." With a smile, she exited the conference room, leaving Gabe to immerse himself in the extraordinary surroundings.

Gabe poured himself a cup of hot coffee and returned to the center of the room. Overlooking Central Park, he found himself caught in the spectacle of the unfolding Manhattan day. The sprawling green oasis lay beneath him, a vibrant tableau dotted with countless individuals. Each one a small story in the grand narrative of the city. Thousands of lives in motion, yet so distant. It was humbling and exhilarating from this vantage point.

The clear blue skies stretched endlessly, mirroring the uncharted horizon of possibilities before him. His heartbeat quickened in his chest, a rhythmic testament to the adrenaline coursing through his veins. Despite the twinge of intimidation that clung to him, he felt a surge of confidence. He was eager for what the day had in store. As he waited for the meeting to start, the world seemed full of promise. The future was uncertain, but it invited possibilities.

"I never take that view for granted." The voice broke the silence, causing Gabe to spin around, nearly spilling his coffee on the plush wool carpet. Startled, he found Ronan Hayes standing in the doorway, commanding attention. Gabe swiftly regained his composure.

"Hello, Mr. Hayes," Gabe greeted, his voice betraying a hint of flustered excitement. "I was just lost in thought. It's truly a pleasure to finally meet you." Gabe extended his hand as Ronan entered the conference room.

"The pleasure is mine, Gabe. And yes, this place can be quite distracting," Ronan replied, leading Gabe toward a luxurious leather chair at the table. "But with a little focus, we know how to make a big difference around here. With that said, how about we get down to business. I've been eagerly anticipating our meeting."

Ronan's no-nonsense approach took Gabe aback. Evidently, he was not one to waste time on small talk. Ronan gestured for Gabe to focus on the table's end, then commanded, "Raise monitor. Play Valencia overview." Turning back to Gabe, he added, "Gabe, as you'll see, I'm a huge fan of your work."

Suddenly, the center of the conference table sprang into action. Silent doors slid open, revealing a massive solid glass monitor underneath the table's surface. Within seconds, the windows darkened, casting a dim light in the room, and the monitor came to life. Gabe recognized the familiar translucent vertical threads displayed before them, his Trans-Dimensional Probability Threads. However, he had never seen them outside the secure confines of MIT's lab.

Gabe's concern grew, and he immediately responded defensively, "How did you get this video feed?"

Ronan reassured him, "I assure you it was acquired legally and is well-protected. Trust me, Gabe. I want to keep this as secure as you do."

Anxious, Gabe's heart raced, and tension filled the room. "What do you mean it was acquired legally?" he demanded.

Ronan took a moment to collect his thoughts. "I should have approached this differently," he admitted, his tone indifferent. "I tend to dive headfirst into things. I apologize, Gabe. Do you remember when you were negotiating server-bank capacity for your Quantum-Thought Dynamics-AI protocol? You were struggling to secure the allocation you needed within your budget. But then, a last-minute discounted leasing opportunity presented itself. Does that ring a bell?"

Gabe recalled the transaction. "Yes, but how do you know about that? And what does it have to do with having our proprietary content in your possession?"

Ronan leaned forward, his eyes focused. "Gabe, it's my business to stay informed about potential advancements in my field. While the world sees me as a social media mogul, my true interest lies in human consciousness. Yes, I've built and acquired billion-dollar social media platforms, but they are just pieces of a larger puzzle, not the whole picture."

A video on the monitor showcased significant moments from Gabe's life. It started with him accepting an academic award in his late teens and highlighting his achievements since then, including a segment from his lecture at Harvard. As the scenes unfolded, Ronan began to speak.

"I've been tracking your work, Gabe, along with many other brilliant minds like you," Ronan revealed. "You showed the most promise. I must admit, I was puzzled and intrigued by your need for such a massive amount of processing server capacity. The company that leased your computing capacity is a subsidiary of Encephalon Media Group. Did your attorneys not inform you about the backdoor language in the agreement that gives us legal access to your digital domain?"

Confusion etched across Gabe's face as he responded, his voice tinged with frustration and defensiveness. "Backdoor language? What do you mean?" Gabe felt a rush of embarrassment and vulnerability, his cheeks growing warm and his stomach churning.

Ronan offered feigned reassurance. "I understand, Gabe. Limited budgets rarely allow for thorough legal review. The lease agreement included provisions granting access to any system connected to the server bank, even through their APIs. I assume you were unaware of this lease feature?"

Gabe's confusion deepened. Initially, he believed that Ronan Hayes wanted to invest in his work, but now he realized that Encephalon Media Group had been monitoring him. He had unwittingly walked into what suddenly felt like enemy territory, feeling threatened and exposed. A sheen of anxiety-induced sweat started to form on his forehead. Anger surged within him, prompting Gabe to stand up with the intent to leave abruptly.

Ronan quickly rose from his seat. "Please, Mr. Valencia, don't leave. Jumping to conclusions based on limited due diligence and my desire for transparency in our relationship won't lead to anything positive. Take a moment to think it over before you do anything rash."

After an uncomfortable silence, Ronan motioned for Gabe to sit back down, prompting him to return to the table. Ronan then offered, with uncharacteristic sincerity, "I had hoped you would appreciate my interest in your work. The deal we struck with you on the server bank cost me millions. My board of directors was quite displeased," Ronan explained. "The power distribution units went off the charts! I even received a call from the Transaction Processing Performance Council after they reviewed our utilization reports. They thought there was a problem with our hardware. I had to separate your experimental capacity from the server bank in the name of research and development. It wasn't easy and it cost me a fortune."

Capitulating, Gabe asked, his voice laced with suspicion, "Then why did you grant us the computing capacity in the first place?"

Ronan chuckled before confessing, "I had no idea what you were up to or hoped to achieve with your experiments. Curiosity got the better of me. Fortunately, it led us to this meeting and your groundbreaking discoveries."

Gabe felt a momentary ease as Ronan's transparency and complimentary tone sank in. He became more curious about the direction of the conversation, realizing that he could at least learn more about how much Ronan knew about his work.

"Thank you for being transparent, Mr. Hayes. I wasn't aware of your ownership of the servers and the access through our

APIs. However, I need reassurance that my work is secure and that you stop spying on me and my team," Gabe asserted.

Ronan responded, "First and foremost, please call me Ronan. I want to establish a trusting friendship, Gabe. I'm quite impressed with your work, and I would love to be a part of it. I truly believe it can change the world . . . for the better. I can help you, Gabe. I can give you access to a bank account with no bottom, but that's just the beginning. I can bring much more to the table. First, however, to address your concern, I will instruct my team to draft a new lease agreement for the server bank, closing the access to your APIs immediately. How does that sound?"

Silence hung in the air as Gabe absorbed the unanticipated confusion of the past few minutes. He then spoke, genuinely relaxedly, "Thank you, Ronan. That's a good start."

"Excellent, Gabe. I'm confident your time invested with us today will not disappoint. Now, let me show you what else a partnership with us has to offer."

Ronan's command activated another video on the monitor, displaying a world map with clumps of various colors representing different geographic areas and major cities. With a voice command, Ronan zoomed in on Manhattan, bringing the city to life on the screen. Thousands of colored dots spread throughout the city, fluidly shifting and changing shades.

"This is a live data-visualization feed of the city, Gabe," Ronan explained, pointing at the screen. "We overlay real-time user data organized into color-coded visual layers. The bottom right-hand corner of the screen shows a legend for the color coding. We track and analyze user visitations and navigation across our social platform assets, providing live surveillance."

Gabe watched as the dots on the screen changed color and moved. "So, this tracks real-time social media activity?" he asked.

"Yes, exactly," Ronan replied. "But it's not just tracking activity; it also analyzes it. Our system identifies patterns and trends in the data, providing insights into the behavior and preferences of the social collective."

"That's incredible," Gabe remarked. "But why? What's the application motive?"

"Just imagine the possibilities," Ronan enthused. "With this technology, we can anticipate and address the community's needs and desires before they even realize them. We can use this data to tackle social issues proactively, ensuring the well-being of society."

Gabe nodded, acknowledging Ronan's response but maintaining a skeptical stance. "I appreciate the social benefits, but how do you address privacy concerns?"

"Privacy is always a concern, and we take it seriously," Ronan assured. "Our system employs advanced encryption and anonymization techniques to protect user identities and ensure data security."

Gabe squinted as he observed Ronan navigating through the colorful dots on the screen. "How does it work?" he inquired.

Leaning over the table, Ronan tapped on a red dot, causing a pop-up with user information and activity to appear. "Like you, we leverage sophisticated AI. Each dot represents a user," he explained. "The color reflects their mood or emotional state based on social media activity, thanks to our advanced MoodSense AI sentiment analysis algorithms. For instance, red dots indicate high excitement or energy, while blue dots signify calm or relaxation. Each dot reveals even more visualized data layers within."

Gabe was captivated as he watched as the dots on the screen shifted, representing the complex layers of user behavior and preferences. The possibilities that emerged from this immense data collection fascinated him, igniting a fire of curiosity for the potential applications this kind of access could have for his research.

"We've recently stumbled onto an extraordinary anomaly," Ronan confided, his words laced with intrigue.

Gabe couldn't help but lean in closer, "What kind of anomaly?" he pressed.

"One of our data analysts came across a news report about a dead humpback whale washed ashore on Staten Island. The image caught her attention, as it closely resembled an illustration shared by a local artist on one of our social feeds she'd been auditing just a few days prior. It was a fluke that she saw it in the first place. The feed discussion focussed on the issues associated with polluted harbor waters and the devastating impact on marine life. The artist posted the rendering of what a dead whale washed up on a beach might look like. It was almost exactly the same image as the news report."

Gabe listened intently, his mind racing to grasp the significance of the connection. "So, what did she find?"

Ronan's eyes gleamed with a mix of astonishment and excitement. "She applied probability theory to calculate the likelihood of such a coincidence. It came back at approximately one in thirty-seven trillion."

Gabe's eyes widened, revealing his disbelief. "That's an astronomically improbable coincidence," he said, his tone tinged with skepticism.

Ronan nodded in agreement, acknowledging the incredulity of the discovery. "Indeed, it is. We adhere to a strict R&D protocol that compels us to investigate any anomalies, regardless of their significance. We were motivated to uncover similar coincidental anomalies within previous social feeds. By cross-referencing historical platform data with newsworthy events in specific geographic areas, we were astounded by the sheer number of positive findings. Some were conspicuous, while others required a more abstract perspective. Nevertheless, the results are irrefutable."

As Gabe absorbed Ronan's revelations, a whirlwind of questions began to churn in his mind. He was caught between fascination and skepticism, enticed by the underlying mathematical models, yet wary of the staggering implications. Ronan's explanations ignited his curiosity, but a nagging doubt remained.

"So, what you're implying is that your social platform possesses a form of precognition?" Gabe sought to clarify with a skeptical tone.

Ronan's enthusiasm was visible, "No, Gabe. It's not precognition. I'm surprised that you, of all people, aren't seeing it yet. It's more equivalent to collective consciousness. Think of it as an extension of your breakthrough but on a grander scale. Instead of belief-based reality manifesting at the *individual* level, we're exploring the possibility your Trans-Dimensional Probability Threads are chosen *collectively* as well. One person may harbor a belief in their specific thread of reality, but that belief must resonate within the tapestry of reality's greater whole. Regardless of an infinite set of dimensions, it appears that collectively, we may be choosing, or at least influencing, a common thread of reality."

Gabe's skepticism began to wane as the pieces fell into place. The conversation had opened the door to the undiscovered territories of thought, and he could feel the pull of the unknown beckoning him forward. His eyes remained fixed on the screen. The words echoed in his mind, resonating with their significance.

Ronan's voice cut through the silence. "You see, Gabe, your invention has allowed us to form a hypothesis about what is happening," Ronan explained, his voice filled with admiration and excitement. "We could spend years trying to replicate your Quantum Thought Dynamics-AI protocol, but it wouldn't be the same without your expertise driving it forward."

Gabe was still reeling from the profound implications of what Ronan had shared with him. The idea of collective consciousness influencing Trans-Dimensional Probability Threads struck a deep chord within him. It was a groundbreaking perspective that filled gaps in his research, answering questions he hadn't even known to ask. His mind was abuzz with the excitement of new possibilities.

But as Ronan continued, a new proposal unfolded that Gabe had not anticipated. "Gabe, the trails you've blazed in neurotechnology have led to profound breakthroughs," Ronan said, his eyes alight with respect. "Your explorations of Trans-Dimensional Probability Threads have been instrumental in forming the hypothesis we now pursue. We recognize the genius in your work and the potential it holds. We want you on our team to lead this effort. Together, we can uncover the deeper connections within our shared reality and push the boundaries of what's possible . . . and what's really happening all around us."

Gabe's heart seemed to skip a beat. The outcome of this meeting was a far cry from his initial intention of merely securing funding for his research. The future Ronan presented, filled with the opportunity to collaborate with him and tap into his global resources, was overwhelmingly enticing. Building upon their shared discoveries, the chance to revolutionize an entire field sent a thrill of excitement coursing through Gabe.

It was a chance to escape the struggles at MIT, where he had often felt stifled and unsupported. With twins on the way and financial pressures mounting, the offer held even more allure. Yet, this was a massive shift, a leap into an unknown world far removed from his comfort zone as a scientist. His emotions were a mix of excitement, trepidation, and disbelief. Could he really leave behind academia, his colleagues, and his students? Could he take this bold step into a corporate environment where the stakes were higher, the challenges different, but the rewards potentially monumental?

He looked into Ronan's eyes and recognized a genuine passion and conviction. A spark of determination had been ignited within Gabe, giving rise to a thought he hadn't entertained before. It may be time to think bigger, to step beyond the confines of his expectations. The path ahead was far from clear, laden with risk and opportunity, but Gabe knew he had to carefully consider Ronan's enticing proposal. The potential to revolutionize the world and steer humanity toward a better future beckoned him. Yet, a sense of caution and concern lingered, reminding him of the risks and responsibilities associated with such power.

Lost in his thought, Gabe approached the glass wall. It automatically became translucent in an instant. As he gazed out at the bustling city beyond, the panorama of possibilities stretched before him, but so did the uncertainties. He struggled with the fear of his technology being utilized for something other than improving the world.

Ronan's voice interrupted his contemplation as he commanded the monitor once again. Gabe's image flickered on the screen, a reminder of the impact he had already made. His words echoed in the room, reminding him of the profound realization he had shared with the Harvard audience.

"Hollywood often portrays parallel universes as accessible only through exotic portals or dimensional gateways. This makes for great entertainment, but it's an unreliable prediction of the future. Our experiments suggest something different. Each of us gathered here today may function as a doorway to an expansive range of parallel universes, which we refer to as 'probable life dimensions.' Remember the saying, 'Do you think the world revolves around you?' Well, there might be some truth to it. Numerous probable worlds may orbit around each of us, and we have the ability to select the one we wish to experience. We believe this selection process occurs countless times daily, molding our reality in ways we are only just starting to comprehend."

As Gabe settled back into his seat, a wave of conflicting emotions erupted within him. Pride surged through him, a testament to the years of dedication and perseverance he had poured into his work. In just a few hours, one of the world's most influential media companies acknowledged his invention as a potential cornerstone of human history. An intoxicating feeling washed over him, and he basked in the glow of recognition.

But beneath the surface, a different voice tugged at Gabe's thoughts. The realization that human consciousness played a role in shaping the physical world corroborated all of his work. Ronan's conclusion that society's collective imagination acted like a projector manifesting the world around us stirred both fear and a whirlwind of excitement within Gabe's mind. Questions crowded his thoughts, seeking answers that seemed just beyond reach.

Ronan offered a comforting perspective. "We are all searching for answers, Gabe. For too long, we have placed blame on external forces, failing to recognize the true power of our own free will, the ability to create and destroy the world around us . . . individually and collectively."

At that moment, Gabe's mind wandered to the various belief systems he had explored in his research, unearthing glimpses of truth in every tradition. The notion of the multiverse found echoes in ancient wisdom, and he realized that the power of belief and imagination served as the doorway to different dimensions, guiding the selection of a chosen reality.

Gathering his thoughts, Gabe fixed his gaze on Ronan, his expression earnest. The weight of the offer hung in the air as he asked, "What exactly are you proposing? What would be my role in all of this?"

Ronan's eyes sparkled with excitement as he leaned in, his response immediate and filled with conviction. "I'm offering you an entire division within Encephalon Media Group. You'll work directly under me, with an unlimited research budget and stock options in the business. As we achieve our goals together, you'll win right alongside me. But more than that, you'll be able to change the world. Imagine the possibilities, the endless discoveries awaiting us. This is the new frontier, where belief and imagination hold the key. Together, we can unlock the mysteries of consciousness with humanitarian achievements as our compass. It's your destiny, Gabe, and together we can shape humanity's future."

Gabe's heart raced, torn between the excitement of embarking on this groundbreaking partnership and the gravity of its responsibility. The choices before him held the power to alter the course of his life and, potentially, the trajectory of human history. Gabe tried to process the information that had unfolded before him. The conversation had taken an unexpected turn from the profound implications of their research to the philanthropic philosophies of Ronan Hayes. It was a lot to take in, and Gabe couldn't deny the fear and uncertainty that tugged at his thoughts.

"I think I understand your fear, Gabe," Ronan reassured, leaning forward earnestly. "I share the same worries, and I want you to know I'm committed to ensuring this technology doesn't fall into the wrong hands. But tell me, do you know the true meaning of philanthropy?"

Gabe's eyebrows raised, a hint of mockery in his voice as he responded, "Beyond the notion of the ultra-rich making themselves feel virtuous by giving away a tiny fraction of their wealth?"

Ronan's smile thinned, a touch of offense in his eyes, but he retained his composure. "The word philanthropy comes from the Greek words philein, meaning to love, and anthropos, meaning humankind. It signifies the love of humanity," he explained, his tone softening. "Writing checks and boasting about being an altruist is one thing, but true philanthropy is much more profound. It's about empowering people by giving them the tools and knowledge they need to shape a better future for themselves and others. Honestly, what could be a more powerful gift than giving someone the ability to choose their destiny?"

Gabe felt a sense of relief as Ronan's definition resonated with him. The tension in his neck eased as he began to see the alignment in their visions. Still, Gabe knew he needed more time to fully trust Ronan's intentions and ensure that his technology would indeed be used for the betterment of humanity.

Ronan's demeanor shifted, indicating that their conversation was ending. "Think it over for the next seventy-two hours, Gabe," he suggested firmly. "Process everything we've discussed, but understand this: If I don't hear back from you within that timeframe, I'll have no choice but to explore other avenues. There are many researchers out there who are eager to work with Encephalon, and I won't hesitate to take your findings to market on my behalf if necessary. Time is of the essence."

Caught off guard by Ronan's sudden change in tone, Gabe felt a mix of confusion and gratitude. Just moments ago, he had been uncertain about his place in this partnership, and now it felt as if Ronan had just handed him his hat.

"Thank you, Ronan," Gabe replied, his voice steadying. "I appreciate your offer. I'll certainly take the time to think it through. I've been more than impressed with everything I've seen here."

Ronan's grin widened, "I'm glad to hear that, Gabe. I believe we can achieve great things together."

Sophia's almost magical entrance interrupted the conversation. "All done here, gentlemen?"

"Yes, our meeting has concluded, thank you, Sophia," Ronan replied with a polite nod.

Sophia's attention turned toward Gabe, her tone filled with warmth. "Wonderful. Mr. Valencia, can I assist you with anything for your stay in the city this evening?"

Gabe considered her offer for a moment. "Thank you, Sophia, but I have a flight to catch later. I'll be heading straight to the airport after our meeting."

Ronan's expression turned thoughtful. "Ah, I see. In that case, let us take care of your logistics. Sophia, is Sam still available?"

A knowing smile played on Sophia's lips. "Yes, Mr. Hayes, Sam is standing by."

Ronan nodded in approval. "Excellent. I'd like Sam to give Gabe a lift to the airport."

"Of course, Mr. Hayes. Sam will be happy to assist you, Mr. Valencia. Please stop by my desk on your way out."

Gabe felt a mix of gratitude and hesitation. "That's very kind of you, but it's not necessary. I can take an Uber to the airport. I wouldn't want to trouble anyone."

Ronan waved off his concerns. "Nonsense, Gabriel. It's our pleasure to make your trip a bit more convenient. After all, you came a long way to meet with us. Allow us to take care of the details."

"Thank you, Ronan. I appreciate your hospitality, and the opportunity to work together. Your passion is contagious."

Ronan's eyes sparkled with enthusiasm. "I'm glad to hear that, Gabe. Our media platforms have so much untapped potential, and I believe we can positively impact the world."

As they prepared to leave the conference room, Gabe reflected on the unexpected turn of events. He had come to Encephalon Media Group with skepticism, but now he found himself open to the possibility of collaborating with Ronan Hayes. There were still many unanswered questions, but today's meeting had planted the seed of excitement within him.

"I look forward to our next meeting," Gabe said with a nod, his mind filled with anticipation.

Ronan motioned toward the door, and they walked toward the front of the office. The bustling energy of the workspace gradually faded as they approached the main entrance. Ronan paused, turning to face Gabe, his hand extended for a final handshake.

"Until next time, Gabe," Ronan said, his voice filled with conviction. "I'll have Sophia set up another meeting to explore our partnership further."

Gabe firmly shook Ronan's hand, feeling connected and having a shared purpose. "Thank you, Ronan. I appreciate your time as well."

With their farewell exchanged, Gabe made his way to Sophia's desk. She stood and gestured toward the elevator.

"Right this way, Mr. Valencia," Sophia said soothingly. "I've arranged a delightful trip to the airport."

Gabe thought it was peculiar that Sophia had pressed the elevator button pointing up. As the door opened, Sophia swiftly hit the "ROOF" button. A sudden realization struck Gabe: *Sam must be the pilot.*

Exiting the elevator, they found themselves in a glass vestibule serving as the rooftop helipad's lobby, where Gabe saw the most exquisite helicopter he had ever laid eyes on. A tall, slender man dressed in a meticulously pressed airman's uniform approached them.

"G'day, Mr. Valencia. I'm Sam, and I'll be takin' you to the airport. Have you eva' flown in a beauty like this before?' Sam's warm Australian accent perfectly matched his amiable nature.

"It's nice to meet you, Sam, and no, I haven't. I'm looking forward to it," Gabe replied, genuine excitement coursing through him.

"We'll have a grand time, mate," Sam replied enthusiastically.

As they approached the Sikorsky S-92 VVIP, Sophia chimed in, "I took the liberty of putting a bottle of Chateau Cos d'Estournel and a nice charcuterie onboard for you. We couldn't subject you to the likes of airport dining. I hope you're a fan of Bordeaux. Ronan acquired this Chateau three years ago and is thrilled with this latest vintage. I've also asked Sam to give you a VIP tour of our beautiful city. There's nothing quite like seeing it from the air; no one does it better than Sam."

"Thank you, Sophia. I really appreciate it," Gabe replied, amazed by the helicopter's luxurious interior as he stepped inside. The scent of leather permeated the cabin. He settled into the seat nearest the table, which showcased the delectable food and wine Sophia had arranged. The plush leather seats, mahogany wood accents, and subdued lighting gave the space a residential feel.

Before bidding farewell, Sophia addressed him again, her bright smile shining. "Have a pleasant flight, Gabe, and safe travels home. I'll reach out early next week to schedule another meeting for you and Ronan. Until then!"

With a graceful motion, Sophia closed the door. Soft classical music filled the cabin as Gabe felt the Sikorsky's engines rumbling to life under Sam's skillful command from the cockpit. Gabe heard Sam's voice through a hidden speaker just above his head.

"I've got quite the nice little flight planned for you, mate. Sit back and enjoy. We've got plenty of time to get you to JFK."

As they ascended from the rooftop helipad, the tower of Encephalon Media Group faded into the distance. They flew perilously close to the Empire State Building, creating the illusion that Gabe could step out onto its spire. Cruising north along the East River, they circled back over the Bronx, where Gabe spotted the Yankees players in the outfield. Sam shared expert commentary on each landmark they passed, recounting the historical events that had shaped them. Gabe felt pride as they approached the Freedom Tower, heading directly toward the Statue of Liberty.

Sam quipped in a playful and sarcastic tone, "I might get a call from the FAA, considering how close we'll likely get to that Sheila with the torch in her hand, mate."

Gabe chuckled, feeling as if Lady Liberty were right next to them, her intricate design visible in all its glory. He had never imagined this was how he would wrap up his visit with Ronan Hayes. He wished that Ella could have experienced it with him. Gabe quickly dialed Ella's number, hoping for a good connection. The phone rang, and Ella's beaming face appeared on the screen.

"Hello, darling! I've been so excited to hear from you. How did it go?"

"It was fantastic, El. I'm still a bit in awe, to be honest. And you won't believe where I am right now. Take a look." Gabe held up his phone to the window, giving Ella a glimpse of the view from the window of the Sikorsky.

CHAPTER 5

Present day, August 5, 2025. On the Franco-Swiss border near Geneva, at the European Council for Nuclear Research, known as CERN, unfolds. The birth of twins Hope and David infuses Gabriel and Ella's budding family with joy. As Gabriel shifts from academia to the bustling corporate world of Encephalon Media Group, their lives hum with optimism, blissfully ignorant of the subtle undercurrents of change taking place.

A serene alpine view greeted Gabriel and Ella as their private shuttle eased to a halt, having journeyed from the vibrant pulse of Geneva to the peaceful outskirts of CERN. It was a journey through many kilometers of winding alpine road and across a chasm of contrast as the urban tempo yielded to the tranquil rhythm of the Swiss Alps.

Ella's mind wandered briefly to the twins, now in the safe care of their nanny at the elegant Le Richemond Hotel. The separation from their infants, though necessary, tugged incessantly at her heartstrings. Just months old, their cherubic laughter and the innocent marvel in their eyes filled her and Gabe with joy incomparable to any scientific achievement. The twins pulled at their every thought. The invisible thread of love entwined their hearts, connecting them to little Hope and David in a way they never imagined. Despite the allure of unraveling the enigmas of the universe, their babies had become their most wondrous mystery, their own personal universe.

As the shuttle entered the CERN complex, Ella's grip on Gabe's hand tightened, an unspoken recognition of the journey ahead. The setting was a symphony of human ambition nestled amid nature's grandeur—verdant meadows dotted with vibrant wildflowers, tall pines whispering tales from ages past, and the formidable CERN structures bearing testament to the groundbreaking research within.

A man of distinction approached. His salt-and-pepper hair and thoughtful creases on his face identified him as none other than Dr. Adrian Bannister. Known as a trailblazer in the realm of consciousness and physics, he was a figure of admiration for Gabe. Despite his illustrious reputation, Bannister radiated an aura of unexpected warmth.

"Welcome to CERN," his greeting came in a soft British accent, his eyes alight with anticipation.

"We're honored, Dr. Bannister," Gabe responded, his voice heavy with heartfelt respect.

Ella, joining the exchange, chimed in, "The fusion of nature and human innovation here is truly awe-inspiring."

Bannister's reply was light-hearted. "It certainly keeps us grounded in our quest to decipher the mysteries of the universe amid such a beautiful canvas."

The conversation shifted to their work as Dr. Bannister gestured for them to follow, leading them deeper into the scientific sanctuary.

Turning to Gabe, his face showing genuine curiosity, he asked, "In your address at Harvard, you referenced my work in the field of Conscious Agents. I'm curious as to the connection you've found between our studies and your Trans-Dimensional Probability Threads."

Gabe nodded, grateful for the chance to articulate the connection. "Your work, Dr. Bannister, has been a major influence on me," he began. "The notion of quantum conscious observers holding the power to open doorways into parallel probable dimensions led me to my hypothesis. It struck me that perhaps there is a quantum mechanism activated by thoughts, more specifically, by our beliefs. Your work offers the closest explanation we have."

As they ventured further into the heart of CERN, they were struck by the enormity and precision of the operation. Nestled deep within the earth's embrace, the Large Hadron Collider, a marvel of mechanical engineering, sprawled beneath them. The circular tunnel, stretching almost twenty-seven kilometers in circumference and buried up to 175 meters deep, appeared to throb with potential energy. Before them, the massive detector structures, bristling with tubes, wires, and instruments, bathed in a golden hue. The intricate, almost labyrinthine configurations were a testament to the unbounded human endeavor to decipher the universe's elusive codes. The collider was a vision of breathtaking complexity. Scientists in white lab coats dotted the multi-leveled scaffoldings, like bees attending their hive. Clipboard in hand, each of them diligently monitored the behemoth that hummed and pulsed.

Ella and Gabe, gazing at the impressive scene, felt a wave of awe wash over them. It was a poignant reminder of how far human ingenuity had come in pursuing knowledge and how much further it dared to go.

Bannister gestured for them to enter a small office adjacent to one of the many subterranean corridors that made up CERN. They stepped inside and each took a seat around a small table in the center of the room. The bland utilitarian space included a small desk nestled against the wall opposite the doorway.

Papers sprawled haphazardly across the desktop indicated that it must be Bannister's office.

Ella then asked, "So, could these Conscious Agents also be the conscious observer interfacing with the Trans-Dimensional Probability Threads?"

Bannister shook his head slightly. "In a way, I suppose that is possible, but it's not exactly what we believe is happening. In this scenario, the conscious observer is represented by entities with a more complex consciousness, essentially, us humans. We interact with these Conscious Agents through our perceptions, decisions, thoughts, and actions."

Intrigued, Gabe ventured, "So, to be clear, if our thoughts and beliefs can mold reality, it suggests that these Conscious Agents are triggered or directed by our mental processes."

Bannister nodded approvingly. "Exactly, Dr. Valencia. That's one of the primary reasons I brought you both here today. Your pioneering exploration of human cognition and belief systems, along with their profound influence on reality, presents a unique opportunity to bridge the gap in my work."

In a reflective silence, Bannister's words lingered in the room, their significance apparent to Gabe and Ella. They shared a knowing look, understanding the gravity of the situation. It appeared that thoughts possessed a tangible presence, capable of initiating the actions of Conscious Agents when projected into the quantum realm. While the precise mechanism or underlying functions behind this phenomenon remained a mystery, it represented a vital component of the intricate puzzle they aimed to decipher. Their partnership with Dr. Bannister held the promise of unraveling the answers they had long sought.

"Ella, forgive my curiosity," Bannister began, adjusting his spectacles with a thoughtful look. "But it intrigues me how someone with a background in theology is so deeply involved in such scientific research and doing so impressively, if I might add."

Ella smiled. She was used to this question. "I've always found the idea of hidden truths intriguing, Dr. Bannister. It's what drew me to theology and science in the first place. The search for meaning and the interconnectedness of everything. But a single verse in the Bible initially sparked my interest in all of this."

"And that verse is?" Bannister leaned back in his chair, genuinely interested.

"Ecclesiastes 1:9," Ella offered. 'What has been will be again, what has been done will be done again; there is nothing new under the sun.'"

Bannister considered her words, his brows furrowing slightly. "Quite philosophical. But how does it connect to our work here?"

Ella leaned forward, excitement in her eyes. "This passage reflects an infinitely dynamic reality based more on science than spiritual conjecture. It suggests the power of human thought, pointing toward an infinite array of dimensional realities already complete in nature. All that is required is choice. Isn't this what we've come to understand as the multiverse?"

The physicist's eyes widened in realization. Ella continued, "Deuteronomy 11:24 is another such verse: 'Every place where you set the sole of your foot shall be yours.' Some theologians argue that the 'sole of the foot' symbolizes conscious awareness. The verse implies that wherever one directs their imagination, visualizing a desired outcome, that outcome already exists somewhere in the realms of probability."

Ella paused, her gaze on Bannister's eyes ablaze with passion. "These are just a couple of examples. The point is that perhaps our ancient sages understood something profound about the nature of reality and consciousness, something we are just beginning to explore scientifically. It's as if they were hinting at hidden truths about the nature of existence, consistent with what we now discover in neurotechnology and quantum physics."

In the silence that followed, Gabe reached out, gently squeezing Ella's hand, a sign of his quiet admiration for her brilliance. Bannister, on his part, leaned back in his chair, his mind grappling with the novel perspective Ella had presented.

"You've given me quite a bit to think about, Ella," he admitted, a wistful smile on his lips. "I can see why your insights would be valuable in this field. You've approached the intersection of faith and science from a unique angle."

Ella nodded, a gentle blush coloring her cheeks at the compliment. "When I understood the depth of what Gabe had discovered, I knew I wanted to be a part of this. Little did I know that I'd also find a life partner and become a mother to two wonderful children along the way." Her smile radiated across her face.

Bannister chuckled, a warm, rich sound. "Indeed, life has a way of surprising us all. I look forward to seeing how your unique perspective continues illuminating our research."

Dr. Bannister then put his hands in his lap, seeming to delve into a realm of thought. "You know," he began, his voice filled with curiosity and wonder, "as we delve deeper into this research, it's intriguing to consider what it could mean for our understanding of consciousness and . . . our very existence." He paused, eyes focusing on some far-off point, then shifted his gaze back to Gabe and Ella. "One idea that's been building in my mind is that the concept of a 'soul' or a 'spirit' could very well be an intelligent collective of Conscious Agents."

Both Ella and Gabe perked up at this. It was an idea that resonated with them both, and it sparked a flurry of thoughts.

"It's a bit of a leap," Dr. Bannister continued, "but hear me out. Consider this: What if what makes *us* up, as individuals, is not merely our flesh and blood, our brains and physical bodies, but this incredible, vibrant assembly of trillions upon trillions of Conscious Agents? They form a kind of 'sentient village,' where each Agent has its unique part to play. And when they come together, they give rise to this collective consciousness that we experience as . . . *us*."

Gabe interjected, "Then, would this collective of Conscious Agents persist beyond physical death?"

Dr. Bannister nodded, "I really don't see why not. Imagine that these collectives represent the very essence of who we are. And that essence, once formed, could endure, could carry on. And why not infinitely?"

Ella blinked, a slow smile spreading across her face as Dr. Bannister's words echoed her thoughts, theories, and beliefs. She felt a warm glow of affirmation. This was what she'd been trying to articulate all along, the foundation of her enthusiasm for their work.

"You know," she began, her voice steady but with an unmistakable note of reverence, "what you're saying, Dr. Bannister, echoes my understanding of existence, of what it means to be human." She glanced at Gabe, sharing a moment of silent connection before she continued. "This concept, this idea of an enduring consciousness, it's why I find such profound significance in our research."

She paused momentarily, her gaze shifting, becoming distant as she recollected her personal experiences. "When we had our twins, I knew. I just *knew* that they came from somewhere beyond this place. They weren't just blank slates. Their little smiles, their laughter, it wasn't new. It felt ancient. Like an old soul was looking out through their eyes. And that could be the essence of those Conscious Agents you're referring to." Ella took a deep breath, her gaze returning to Dr. Bannister. "I believe we're onto something truly profound here. It transcends the boundaries of science and religion. We're tapping into the essence of existence itself."

Dr. Bannister smiled, his eyes indicating a deep respect for Ella's insights. He nodded, adding, "It's a magnificent journey we're embarking on, isn't it?"

The room vibrated with the energy of their combined enthusiasm and the enormity of their discoveries. There was so much more to explore, and they were at the forefront of it all.

Dr. Bannister removed his spectacles, holding them up as though inspecting them for imperfections. As he returned his gaze to Gabe, the questioning look on his face was unmistakable. "I must admit, Gabe," he began, his tone thoughtful, "your move to Encephalon Media Group raised more than a few eyebrows in the scientific community. Some even felt . . . let's say, betrayed by what appeared as your swift leap from pure science to the world of capitalism."

Gabe nodded, meeting Dr. Bannister's gaze evenly. "I know, and I understand the skepticism," he replied. "I faced a choice. Our research was perceived as fringe science at best. The funding was drying up. We were at risk of losing everything we've been working toward."

Bannister's eyes flicked to Ella, then back to Gabe. "And this . . . Ronan Hayes, the media mogul, he convinced you otherwise?"

Gabe's features relaxed, meeting Dr. Bannister's scrutinizing gaze with earnest assurance. "Indeed, Dr. Bannister, Ronan Hayes is more than just a business tycoon. He sees the potential of our research. His media empire and the diverse social platforms he has amassed are not just tools for revenue generation. Hayes envisions them as conduits for spreading awareness and bringing about a positive shift in the collective consciousness of humanity. The power of these platforms could help democratize the benefits of our discoveries."

Ella interjected, her voice gentle yet firm. "We didn't make this decision lightly, Dr. Bannister. We were aware of the risks, but we also saw a rare opportunity to bring our work to a global stage, to help people understand the true nature of reality, the immense power of their consciousness."

A pause hung in the air, punctuated by the soft hum of the air conditioning in the office. Gabe added, "We trust Hayes. He's shown us that his intentions align with our vision. We're willing to take this risk for the greater good."

Dr. Bannister's expression softened, and he nodded slightly, the thoughtful look on his face belying his still lingering doubts. Carefully selecting his next words before speaking, he said, "Well, perhaps this is the paradigm shift our work needs," finally admitting a reluctant concession to Gabe and Ella's unconventional course. "And, I suppose there are worse places your work could have ended up."

Just as he was about to continue, a loud, sharp alarm rang. Dr. Bannister's face broke into a smile. "Ah! Speaking of our work, it seems we're about to conduct another test in the collider," he said, leaping out of his chair with surprising agility for a man his age.

Gabe and Ella exchanged a look, intrigued and slightly startled by his sudden enthusiasm.

"Come, come!" Dr. Bannister beckoned them, nearly bounding toward the door. "We're about to smash a few billion atoms into each other. It's not something you want to miss."

They followed him into a large room filled with buzzing monitors and researchers poised at various stations, their faces a mix of focused intensity and palpable excitement. The atmosphere was electric, filled with the potent thrill that always preceded a significant experiment.

Standing at the front of the room, Dr. Bannister raised his hands. The chatter fell silent. "Ladies and gentlemen, our esteemed colleagues Dr. Gabriel Valencia and Ella Valencia are joining us for today's experiment. Let's show them why we're at the cutting edge of this scientific revolution."

Applause filled the room, and Gabe and Ella were swept up in the electrifying anticipation of the imminent collider run.

Dr. Bannister's eyes sparkled with unmasked excitement as he turned to them and said, "What we're searching for isn't merely the 'God particle.' If our theories are right, we're on the brink of uncovering Conscious Agents, the real divine entities at work in our universe. If there is a God, we're all part of it at the quantum level and about to get a closer look."

Their whirlwind tour through CERN left Gabe and Ella with minds buzzing and hearts pounding. Meeting the intellectual giants of particle physics, exploring the enormous tunnel where the collider path ran, and witnessing live particle accelerated collisions was nothing short of overwhelming. Yet, amid the flurry of activity and ideas, there was a sense of unity, a feeling of convergence. The theories and ambitions of Dr. Bannister and themselves were no longer isolated fragments but parts of an emerging, groundbreaking picture. They were beginning to see how the puzzle pieces could fit together.

The drive back to Geneva was silent, and both Ella and Gabe were lost in thought. Dr. Bannister had become an unexpected ally, and the possibility of achieving their goals seemed closer than ever. But that evening, as they settled in their hotel room with the twins, the grandeur of scientific discovery was momentarily dwarfed by the simple yet profound pleasure of being a family.

The city's hustle and bustle provided a lulling backdrop to the peaceful slumber of little Hope and David, nestled between them on the bed.

Gabe and Ella's eyes shifted between their precious babies and each other. No words were spoken, yet there was an understanding, a shared awareness of the life they were creating together. Not just the revolutionary path they were paving in the realm of science, but also the warmth and love they were weaving as parents and partners. This juxtaposition of their ambitious professional pursuits and the tender moments of parenthood were an enigma they cherished. They were walking on a path unknown, creating a new world where science, love, and parenting intertwined seamlessly.

In the night's stillness, under the glow of Geneva's city lights, they held each other close, silently reveling in the grandeur of the journey ahead, their hearts echoing the exact unspoken words: They were ready to change the world. Their world. For the better.

CHAPTER 6

On Earth, the time is just shy of midnight on October 13, 2054. Hope's consciousness remains deeply immersed within The Inverse, and the urgency of her situation becomes increasingly apparent.

Hope was momentarily speechless as she and Gentry followed Aiko into the Command Center. The glass doors silently parted, revealing a vast chamber resembling Earth's NASA Space Center.

The room buzzed with the energy of intense activity. A cascade of thirty levels spread out before Hope, with a hoard of individuals filling each floor, their gazes locked on the screens of their workstations. Walls plastered with rows of video monitors flashed with cryptic images. Yet it was the central display that demanded attention. Towering over the command center, it loomed thirty feet high and fifty feet wide, radiating a hypnotic glow. A timer pulsed at the heart of the screen, relentlessly counting down.

As Hope took in the overwhelming scene, Gentry turned to Aiko and asked, "Is there anything else you need from me?" His voice was respectful and attentive.

Aiko met his gaze, her expression appreciative and firm. "Gentry, I cannot thank you enough for your help," she said.

"You have been instrumental in getting Hope here safely. From this point on, we have it under control. Your services are no longer needed. Thank you."

Gentry nodded with understanding. "It has been an honor," he replied with a nod to Hope, then turned and quietly exited the Command Center.

The timer seemed to have a sense of urgency that resonated with Hope. It captured her full attention, making it nearly impossible for her to divert her gaze from the relentless countdown.

12:44:11 . . .

Looking up, Hope asked: "What will happen in twelve hours and forty-four minutes?"

Aiko turned toward Hope, her expression a balance of solemnity and resolve. "A precious rose petal will be pulled from the stream of time, dear." Her words echoed a sense of imminent significance.

Aiko's cryptic response stirred a mix of curiosity and apprehension within Hope. The tone of her words caused Hope to instinctively form a connection between her current situation and surroundings, and her existence on Earth.

"Will I be okay?" she asked, her voice filled with uncertainty.

Aiko's eyes held a depth of knowledge as she met Hope's gaze. "Indeed, I can assure you of that," she began gently. "Imagine this dimension as an interface, a nexus between the finite, physical world you know on Earth and the infinite realm of The Inverse. Here, different layers of reality interlace, all shaped by the collective beliefs of countless entities." She paused for a moment, letting the weight of her words settle. "On Earth, you are rooted in a reality defined by its unique logic, sensory experiences, and perception of time. But now, your consciousness has been freed, temporarily. The essence of what many on Earth term 'soul' is, in fact, a manifestation of your expansive consciousness, your infinite self. This version of you is temporarily detached from your physical form, and there is still an intangible link, a tether that keeps you connected to your Earthly timeline."

Aiko gently took Hope's hand. The warmth of her touch created a deep connection between them. As the ambient noise of the command center receded, Aiko's voice was laden with a weight that emphasized the gravity of the situation.

"Hope, you and your family—Poet, Gabriel, and Ella—were selected for an important mission, orchestrated and designated by The Council." Aiko's tone became softer, imbued with a warmth that felt almost maternal. "All of you serve as reflections, extensions of your Lubhyati counterparts here in The Inverse. Your ability to be here underscores your exceptional role and destiny in this vast continuum."

A commanding figure entered the room with an air of quiet authority. The man walked with purpose, his long coat adding a touch of elegance to his presence. His eyes, a striking shade of steel blue, held a depth that seemed to encompass boundless wisdom. His hair, an almost white-grey, framed features that were both captivating and enigmatic.

Aiko's face lit up. "Epoch," she greeted, a blend of reverence and fondness in her tone. "I'm glad you are here."

Epoch turned to Aiko, an acknowledgment passing between them. "Aiko," he responded simply, tilting his head slightly in her direction.

"Hope Valencia, allow me to introduce you to Epoch, a Lubhyati of considerable influence within The Inverse. Epoch, this is Eada's Pneuma, Hope."

An unspoken connection seemed to unfurl as their eyes locked, bridging the divide between them. Hope glimpsed a reflection of her reality in Epoch's gaze, a sense of shared purpose.

Aiko continued, "I have not shared the details surrounding our mission and was just about to inform Hope of our connection to each other."

Hope turned to Aiko, her expression revealing her perplexity. "What do you mean by 'our connection?' And what is a Lubhyati? You mentioned I'm a Pneuma . . . of Eada? But who is Eada?" The questions tumbled out in rapid succession.

Aiko paused momentarily, her gaze distant as she searched for the right words. "In The Inverse, Lubhyati parallels what on Earth humans call Oversouls. They encompass a broader spectrum of consciousness, the pinnacle of an entity's conscious existence. Visualize the Lubhyati as a vast expanse of consciousness, much like the universe itself; limitless and teeming with potential. To comprehend and delve deeper into the mysteries of the cosmos, the Lubhyati emit countless fragments of themselves, which you on Earth might recognize as souls. Here, we refer to them as Pneuma. Although the Lubhyati and Pneuma share a symbiotic relationship, they are simultaneously distinct and unified in the vast tapestry of the quantum realm. The very core of a Lubhyati's being is crafted from a distinct quantum makeup, anchored in a particle that Earth's brightest minds are on the brink of unveiling," Aiko concluded, smiling with a blend of pride and anticipation.

Suddenly, memories of her parents and their collaboration with Dr. Adrian Bannister flashed in Hope's mind. With a hint of realization, she whispered, "Conscious Agents?"

Aiko's eyes brightened with approval. "Exactly, Hope. Dr. Bannister, a pioneer in particle physics who frequently worked with the Hadron Collider at CERN, was on the cusp of unveiling their existence. Conscious Agents form the essence of all that is. You and me. Everything, my dear. They form every human, Lubhyati, Pneuma, and every known object in existence, infinitely. And in your world, they bridge the gap between consciousness and the tangible physical world around you."

The weight of this revelation caused Hope to lose her composure momentarily. The pieces of the puzzle were starting to fit together. She recalled those evening discussions at her family home, where her parents passionately debated these theories with Dr. Bannister.

Hope's gaze intensified, "So, my parents and Dr. Bannister were indirectly interacting with The Inverse?"

Aiko nodded, "In a sense, yes. Their pioneering research illuminated the path, drawing them nearer to The Inverse and the intricate dance of human consciousness with the universe. They were on the cusp of demonstrating that consciousness was the precursor to matter rather than its byproduct. Moreover, your father was convinced that within every human resided the potential to select from an endless expanse of possibilities, the only requirement being belief, and an understanding of what belief *truly* meant. He was right, Hope."

Absorbing each word, Hope sensed that she had an essential role in all of this. A hint of curiosity colored her voice as she inquired, "If Eada is my Lubhyati, then who serves as my parents' Lubhyati? And my brother's?"

Aiko's eyes gleamed with a blend of affection and amusement. "I am your mother's Lubhyati, Hope."

Epoch chimed in, his smile radiant. "And I am your father's." His joy was evident in the play of his expression. Aiko and Epoch exchanged a brief, almost celebratory glance, an unspoken acknowledgment of the profound significance of this moment, a reunion that transcended the boundaries of existence.

Aiko continued, "Regarding your brother, his Lubhyati is named Pax. This mission is unlike any other, Hope. It is the first time our celestial family has sent Pneuma to Earth. While we have dispatched Pneuma to explore diverse realities across the universe, there is an exceptional allure to humanity. It is important to know that our family stands together in unity, Hope, and this mission carries profound significance."

Hope shook her head, grappling with the profound implications of Aiko and Epoch's revelation. A surge of realization dawned upon her, an understanding that resonated with her lifelong intuition of being a part of something greater, a celestial force of love and wisdom silently guiding her path. It walked beside her and even visited her in her dreams.

Interrupting Hope's introspection, Epoch gently interjected, "Hope, let us proceed with your briefing. Shall we continue in my office?" He gestured toward an impressive chamber adorned with a grand table and sleek, modern seating.

Epoch settled into his chair, his fingers intertwining as he spoke with deep contemplation. "The Council, Hope, they are the seers of infinite possibility. As Pneuma assigned by The Council, your family . . . ," Epoch paused. "Well, our family is entrusted with a critical mission to shape the course of human history. Guiding its destiny, threading it through the eye of the proverbial needle, is a task of profound magnitude. Every choice, every fleeting moment, held the power to either further our objectives or disrupt them."

With a momentary pause, the weight of his words lingered, their significance sinking in. "When your parents met, it was no mere coincidence. Their union was a meticulously planned convergence of heart and mind. Every one of us, Eada and Pax included, carried the weight of this essential mission. Others, carefully chosen and recruited, contributed their Pneuma to play pivotal roles. For instance, your father's friendship with Dr. Bannister was not a random occurrence but a meticulously woven set of probabilities within the mission's framework. Their paths converged by design, intended to guide humanity toward a future of enlightenment and growth."

Aiko's gaze remained fixed on Hope, her tone a mixture of solemnity and care. "When your father descended to Earth, his mission became a part of him, even from childhood. It was encoded within his very being, a calling that blossomed into a consuming passion that evolved through orchestrated relationships. His dedication and destiny intertwined with him falling in love with your mother. Their love was, in fact, destiny. And your birth, as well as Poet's, were meticulously planned pieces in a cosmic puzzle. Each of you bore a distinct role, an indispensable contribution, crucial to fulfilling our shared mission."

Hope's curiosity ignited. "The Council? Who is the Council?"

Aiko's gaze held a mixture of empathy and caution, her dark eyes conveying understanding and restraint. "We do not have clearance to share details surrounding The Council with you at this juncture, dear. That knowledge must remain beyond your current reach. For now, what is paramount is that we stay committed to the task at hand."

Hope's inquisitive nature stirred a longing to know more, tugging at her thoughts. Yet, an unspoken wisdom cautioned her against prying further.

Epoch's countenance grew solemn as he delivered the unsettling truth they were confronting. His voice carried the gravity of their circumstances. "Somewhere along the way, Hope, things diverged from the intended path. Instead of remaining in an academic career, your father was drawn into the corporate sector and joined Encephalon Media Group. Initially, this choice was not an immediate concern. We had contingencies for diverging threads, accounting for deviations from the expected realities. Our objective was to guide your father, and by extension humanity, back onto the proper track, realigning their trajectory. Just one pivotal message from you to your father, conveyed at a critical juncture in your life, had the potential to correct the course of humanity. This task fell to you, Hope. But the specifics of that message and its timing elude us. What we do know is that it did not occur."

He continued, "Your father's creations, his inventions, were designed to be a guiding beacon for humanity's ascension. But instead of freeing human minds, it entrapped them, resulting in humanity's descent into the dystopian technocracy that now grips your world."

Hope's mind raced with worry and confusion. "Hold on," she interrupted, her tone defensive. "You're saying I was supposed to deliver a critical message to my father? I don't understand. How is that possible?" Her voice trembled as the gravity of the situation hit her.

A weighty silence pervaded the room, matched only by the uncertainty in the air. Just as Hope was about to ask another question, a radiant orb, roughly a meter in diameter, materialized abruptly. It hovered above the table, illuminating the space around it. Within the orb's core, an equation gleamed: $B \in E+T=R$. Hope instantly recognized the symbolic equation. It was her father's work, a representation of the intricate interplay between Beliefs, Emotions, Thought, and the sum of human Reality. It symbolized humanity's power to shape entire worlds within worlds, as individuals, and through collective consciousness.

Epoch tilted his head slightly, drawing Hope's gaze. "Hope, this equation stands for the very core of our universe's existence. Before any reality unfolds, it is a belief that sparks its existence. A belief creates every experience and moment. But it is more than just a thought in one's mind; belief is the cornerstone of creation and perception. Now, this concept takes a distinctive form on Earth within your singular dimension of time. Through belief, individuals traverse a vast expanse of possibilities, charting their paths along chosen trajectories, solidifying their experiences into what *seem* like unchangeable timelines."

Hope's voice trembled with a mixture of reverence and recognition. "This is what my father tried to convey to the world," she whispered, her words trailing off, a shadow of unspoken emotions casting a weight in the room.

Epoch nodded, "And now, you must understand the reason for our intervention, Hope. You being here is not a mere coincidence; it is a fortunate chance to rectify the events that, from your perspective, deviated at some point along your timeline."

Aiko added, with compassion and conviction: "Eada, your Lubhyati, received extensive training at The Academy here within The Inverse. Her education was meticulously designed to encompass the unique human experience, specifically focusing on the equation and your family's mission. Each lesson delved into the fundamental components of human reality: Belief, Emotion, Thought, and the resulting sum of Reality, all interwoven within a single dimension of time. Hope, these lessons were intended to be passed on to you, as you are Eada's Pneuma. However, something seems to have gone amiss. It appears that the crucial message meant to be conveyed to your father did not fully connect with your awareness and purpose."

Aiko paused, allowing the weight of their situation to settle before continuing. "The Council believes that a lesson was misunderstood during Eada's training. And now, with you here, we can find whatever did not get passed down to you. We want you to revisit Eada's training at The Academy. Your unique perspective might be just what we need to find the message."

Hope blinked, processing the information. "You're asking me to re-experience my Lubhyati's training? How is that even possible?"

Aiko nodded. "Yes, dear, by revisiting Eada's training, we hope you will be able to uncover the missing message. And then we want to send it back with you. You're the only one that can find it, Hope."

Hope's eyes, already wide from the revelation about her Lubhyati's training, grew restless as she processed Aiko and Epoch's request. "What happens if I find the message?"

Aiko's gaze shifted to the orb floating above them, where a single rose petal drifted gently in a delicate stream. "This," she began, pointing at the petal, "represents your time on Earth, Hope. You have been removed from the flow of your timeline. Once you have found the message, we can place you back into your timeline, but only at the point where life begins. You must understand that we cannot return you to your previous moment on Earth. I regret to say," Aiko paused, her voice filled with empathy, "your physical life, on its current thread of existence, is nearing an end." Aiko subtly directed her gaze to the timer on the central monitor, silently acknowledging the relentless seconds ticking down.

Seeing the weight of realization dawn on Hope's face, Epoch added, "Your only viable option is to retrace Eada's steps, identify the message, and then return to the day you and Poet were born. You would live your life over, Hope, but this time with the intended message for your father."

Hope's internal mind plunged into chaos. As Epoch's words became a distant echo, she was transfixed by the central monitor, and its brutally persistent countdown as a stark reminder of her transient existence. Every challenge she had overcome, every mountain she had climbed, and every change she had undertaken felt like it might vanish, rendering all her life's efforts moot.

With her voice trembling, barely holding back tears, Hope said frantically, "You're asking me to relive my *entire* life?"

Aiko's eyes, a pool of empathy, responded, "We understand the enormity of our request, Hope. But consider the magnitude of what is at stake. Your life's work will not be lost. No, the foundations built can now be reinforced. You are the key to getting humanity back on track, Hope. Back on the right probable thread of reality."

Hope's emotions—rage, fear, sorrow, and an enduring flicker of hope—threatened to drown her. Memories of her struggles played out in rapid succession. "After everything I've accomplished . . . how can I just start over?" Her voice tapered off, the weight of the impending decision seeming insurmountable.

Epoch approached her, gently placing a comforting hand on her shoulder. "We understand, Hope. We truly do. But imagine the profound mark you could leave on your world if we can find what went wrong and correct it."

Meeting Aiko's compassionate gaze and then Epoch's determined eyes, Hope understood the unspoken message, a sincere appeal for understanding, faith, and the unwavering conviction in her capacity to steer Earth and humanity back onto its proper timeline. The weight of the decision bore down on Hope. Taking a deep breath, she finally spoke, "Show me. Show me how I can find the message."

Aiko nodded, gesturing toward the shimmering orb that floated above them. It pulsed softly, and its glow intensified. "As you are aware, in The Inverse," Aiko began, "linear time does not exist. Instead of merely watching recordings, you will immerse yourself in Eada's training. Think of it as your consciousness visiting Eada's dimensional reality."

Hope's gaze fixed on a scene playing out within the orb, she squinted to focus on the details of what was taking place within. Suddenly, the orb's boundaries expanded, and Hope stood beside a figure of such extraordinary beauty that it captivated her and rendered her nearly speechless. It was the most stunning being she had ever encountered. An immediate recognition surged within her. This was her Lubhyati. The woman standing before her was Eada.

Every moment in Hope's life where she had felt guidance, every whispered word of wisdom during her trials, every comforting embrace in her loneliest hours, and even the messages in her dreams suddenly made sense. It was Eada. She was her guardian angel, her protective force throughout her life on Earth. It was as if they shared a sacred bond that transcended time and space.

Remembering the countless times she'd felt a presence by her side, Hope realized those weren't mere coincidences or flights of fancy. When people on Earth spoke of guardian angels, Hope had always known hers was real. Her protector was no abstract concept; Eada was by her side, and their love and connection were undeniable. Hope could feel their bond rekindling in the gentle cadence of Eada's steps and the purposeful way she moved, reminding her of a love that had always been there.

"That's . . . my Lubhyati?" Her thoughts running to catch up.

"Yes," Aiko affirmed softly. "And she is about to start her lessons at The Academy."

The mere thought that she was about to enter Eada's reality was overwhelming. The vividness of the orb's portrayal was unlike anything Hope had ever experienced.

She turned to Epoch, a hint of uncertainty in her voice. "The experience feels so real. Will Eada sense my presence?"

Epoch shook his head, "No, not exactly, Hope. While the experience is immersive, it is merely a window for you to observe. You will be a silent participant, free to examine without influencing. Your observation and keen awareness of unfolding events is crucial during this assignment. This is the only way, and you are the only hope for finding the lost message in Eada's training."

Hope was in awe, her trepidation momentarily forgotten. The experience was surreal and mesmerizing. "It's . . . beautiful," she whispered.

Aiko smiled gently. "It is a unique opportunity, Hope. A paradoxical experience that no Pneuma has experienced. To witness your Lubhyati's training sessions is truly a gift."

Hope felt an overwhelming rush of emotions, each one battling for prominence. Her heart ached as memories of her life on Earth flooded her thoughts. She remembered the gentle warmth of her mother's embrace, the loving banter with her brother, and her father's guiding wisdom. The laughter of friends, the serene moments of solitude, and even the everyday challenges she faced seemed tangible yet impossibly distant.

At that moment, the orb's expansive scene began to contract like a lens narrowing its view. The grandeur of The Academy, the ethereal light, and Eada herself slowly dissolved, fading into the confines of the shrinking orb. The majestic scene transformed into the previous scene of Epoch's office.

The abrupt transition left Hope momentarily disoriented, her senses readjusting to the shift in reality. The room around her seemed to snap back into place, and the tangible space of the Command Center replaced the all-encompassing presence of Eada's reality. Now diminished in size, the orb hovered above the table, its glow illuminating the area.

As the scene settled, the Command Center's familiarity struck Hope again, only now it tinged with a sense of déjà vu that was even more profound. There was an underlying connection to this place that defied explanation, a significance that remained just out of reach. Hope turned her gaze to the digital timer on the wall, its countdown continuing with relentless precision. Each passing second carried weight beyond mere time, symbolizing fading memories, lost opportunities, and the escalating stakes of her crucial mission.

The faces of her loved ones appeared in her thoughts. Their shared moments, lingering conversations, quiet understanding, and the simple, unspoken bonds resonated with her soul. She loved these people, and she would fight for them at all costs.

Drying her tears, she murmured, primarily to herself, "For them. For every one of them. I'll do it."

Pausing to collect herself, Hope looked out into the vastness of the Command Center. "On Earth, everything felt so defined. The paths I took, the battles I fought, the enemies I knew. Here, everything feels . . . intangible. I'm trying to understand, to grasp a reality that keeps shifting." Her voice quivered, but determination burned in her eyes. "But if it offers a glimmer of hope for my family, for everyone back home, I'm committed to this mission."

Sensing the internal battle within Hope, Aiko approached and gently placed a comforting hand on her arm. "This mission, dear, transcends anything we have ever embarked upon. But remember, you are not stepping into the unknown alone. We are with you at every turn, guiding, supporting, and *believing* in you."

As Hope processed Aiko's words, her resolve became evident. Planted firmly in the heart of the Command Center, the weight of entire worlds bore down on her. Each conscious thought and every introspective moment solidified her commitment. This mission transcended her personal needs or desires; it represented the hopes and dreams of an entire civilization. As the Command Center's lights cast their gentle glow, a single thought crystallized in her mind: *I hope this works.*

CHAPTER 7

In Manhattan, the date is July 20, 2041. Amid the upper echelons of Manhattan's social circles, the Valencia family strives to balance family and career, even as the world faces troubling times. While they navigate the consequences of Gabriel's career choices, a daunting question looms: Is it too late to choose another path?

Hope awoke with a start, the intensity of her vivid dream still lingering in her mind. The golden sunlight streamed in as her eyes fluttered open, casting a soft, warm glow across the spacious bedroom. The antique clock on her bedside table displayed 6:52 a.m.

Unlike her previous dreams, this one carried a distinct weight, she mused, gently tucking a strand of hair behind her ear. It left her wondering if she shared a connection with the enigmatic figure that often graced her dreams. Each encounter felt like a fleeting glimpse into another realm, a window to a reality beyond her own. Yet, this recent dream held an exceptional gravity. Its message implored her to listen to her heart and trust that her beliefs have the power to shape the world around her. Her voice held the key to unlocking change.

While similar dreams had previously left her feeling restless, today's held a pressing sense of duty. The reason eluded her, but she couldn't shake the feeling that there was something more significant about this day than just the date itself.

Thud!

Her thoughts were interrupted by the abrupt noise. Before she could identify its source, a series of impatient knocks followed, obnoxiously reverberating through the still morning air.

"Who's there?" Hope shouted, her voice slightly muffled by the plush comforter she pulled over her head.

"It's me, Poet! Open up! You know what today is!"

Hope heaved her bedding aside and rolled her eyes as her feet touched the cool floor. It was baffling how Poet could act as if he were the sole custodian of the knowledge of their shared birthday. The rhythmic knocking reverberated, highlighting the vastness of her bedroom. Above her, ornate coffered ceilings hinted at the room's grandeur, while the intricately designed walls whispered tales of opulence. Enormous windows framed by carved stone offered a panoramic view of the bustling city of Manhattan below.

Hope had barely unlocked her door when Poet pushed past her, dashed to her bed, and began energetically bouncing on it.

"Poet! Seriously? Off the bed. Now!" she ordered.

He stopped, shooting her a grin. "This is the day, sis! Sweet sixteen! We can finally drive!"

Still rubbing the sleep from her eyes, Hope replied, "It's early, Poet. Everyone's still asleep, even the staff. Can't it wait?"

His eyes sparkled mischievously. "I bet they got us cars! Let's sneak to the garage and find out."

Hope sighed, then climbed back into bed, pulling the covers over her head. In a muffled voice, she said, "Cars? Why? We live in Manhattan. The only people who drive here are chauffeurs, AI coaches, and cab drivers. Ever heard of Sol and Jacob?"

Poet rolled his eyes. "Sol and Jacob smell like old books. And I'm tired of the backseat view. You seriously don't want to drive?"

Hope lifted a brow and said, "Oh, I'd love to drive, alright. Or rather, ride!"

He frowned. "What do you mean?"

She smirked. "If they're getting us vehicles, I'd prefer a vintage 2002 V7 Moto Guzzi III Racer. Now, that would be something to cruise around Manhattan."

"You're so weird," Poet murmured as he walked toward the door.

"Hold up," Hope called, shaking off her remaining drowsiness. The thrill of their birthday was starting to catch up with her.

She hopped out of bed and breezed toward her luxurious bathroom and into her expansive wardrobe chamber. She quickly selected a robe from her favorite designer and met Poet in the grand second-floor gallery. The towering mezzanine ceilings, framed by elegant stone arches, stretched another thirty feet overhead. To their right, ornate stone balustrades guarded an emblem inlaid into the timeless stone flooring below. Skylights bathed the abundant space in the morning sunlight.

Hope had always thought their life wasn't normal. She likened their luxury to the homes of her favorite animated princesses, specifically the foyer of Valencia Castle. Yet something felt off. Every evening, as the day's panorama wound down, she felt like an actor in someone else's life. While grateful for the luxury, a sense of larger purpose eluded her. She half-expected a messenger at the palace door, holding a telegraph pointing her to her true path.

"No, no, no! Hold it right there!" Their mother's voice, filled with mock sternness, echoed from the bottom of the grand staircase. Hope and Poet halted, exchanging looks.

Pivoting to the corridor leading to the dining hall, Ella called out, "Gabriel! The twins are up! I've got them cornered . . . for now." Her face softened into a radiant smile, winking up at the duo.

"Ready or not, I think it's time!" came Gabriel's distant reply.

Giggling, Hope whispered to Poet, "Race you to the dining hall!"

The siblings sped downstairs, almost tripping over each other. "Careful! No broken bones on your birthday!" Ella chided as they dashed past.

Entering the dining hall, the twins halted, mesmerized by the vision above; a sea of vibrant balloons suspended as if defying gravity.

"Sixteen hundred balloons, to be precise. I thought the house might float away!" Gabriel joked.

Now recording the moment with her mixed-reality eyewear, Ella herded the family toward the breakfast table. As they took their seats, staff members brought two mini cakes, candles atop and shining brightly. After a hearty rendition of "Happy Birthday," Poet blew out his candles with a cheeky grin, whispering to Hope, "Choose your wish wisely."

His words echoed in Hope's mind, feeling eerily familiar. Pushing the strange sensation aside, she took a deep breath and blew out her candles.

"What got you two early birds up?" Gabriel asked, his eyes crinkling with amusement.

"That goof barged into my room before sunrise," Hope said, tilting her head toward Poet.

"Well, you only turn sixteen once," her brother retorted.

Laughing, Ella interjected, "This might be the first day during summer vacation that you two didn't sleep in. It means we get to spend the whole day with you, kiddos."

Poet arched an eyebrow. "The *whole* day?"

"We've got plans with friends," Hope added. "After all, we're sixteen now!"

Gabriel and Ella exchanged amused glances. "Did you draft their bedroom lease agreements?" Gabriel teased.

"Absolutely," Ella played along. "Rent's due on the first. Any late payments, and you're out on your ear!"

Gabriel grinned. "And the kitchen's off limits. Better find new dining arrangements."

Exchanging an exasperated look with his sister, Poet mumbled, "Always with the jokes."

"We get it, guys. We're just saying we've got our own lives, too," Hope clarified gently.

"We know, sweethearts," Ella replied, her voice soft. "We just want to make every moment count."

Poet sighed, "We get it. It's chill."

The aroma of a hearty breakfast wafted in as the kitchen staff presented a lavish spread, marking a rare instance of the Valencias sharing a meal.

"Mr. Valencia?" The deep voice of the head butler broke the air. He approached, holding a pair of mixed-reality glasses. "My apologies for the interruption, but Mr. Ronan Hayes is on the line. He insisted on confirming if you'll accompany him and Mr. Ash Bertram for dinner tomorrow night. Shall I connect the call?"

Ella gave Gabe a pointed look. "Remember, honey, we also have dinner plans with Dr. Bannister tomorrow night."

Gabe nodded in acknowledgment, his expression thoughtful. He then put on the mixed-reality glasses, signaling for the call to be connected. It was odd for Ronan to call personally instead of going through his business affairs coordinator, Sophia Mendez.

"Hello, Ronan," Gabe greeted, his voice even.

The room shifted as Gabe engaged in the conversation. His features became more severe as he listened intently to Ronan's words.

"I see," Gabe responded at one point, his tone neutral yet attentive. "Yes, I understand."

Gabe's attempt to decline the dinner invitation became apparent as the conversation progressed. "Actually, I had plans with a colleague from Switzerland who's in town," he explained, a note of polite regret in his voice.

However, Gabe's attempt to back out seemed ineffective. Ella, Hope, and Poet exchanged concerned glances as Gabe's expression remained composed, "Well, of course. I understand."

After a pause, Gabe's voice took on a hint of resignation. "Yes, I'll be there. Gramercy Tavern sounds fine. Okay, I'll see you then." Ending the call, he removed the mixed-reality glasses.

Ella's brow furrowed. "What was that about, Gabe?"

Gabe sighed, "Seems like I'm attending dinner with Ronan Hayes and Ash Bertram tomorrow night."

Hope raised an eyebrow. "But you declined, right?"

Gabe shook his head. "I tried. Ronan can be quite persuasive."

Ella exchanged a knowing glance with her children. Her concern evident in her eyes. "Is there any way you could change the dinner plans, Gabriel? Adrian's only here once a year for the International Physics Conference. We've all been looking forward to spending time with him."

Gabe sighed, his expression a mixture of frustration and resignation. "Ella, I wish it were that simple, but it's impossible," he admitted, his voice tinged with regret. "Would you mind going without me? Hey, we both know you're Adrian's favorite." Gabe attempted to infuse a touch of charm into his words, hoping to ease the palpable tension in the room.

Ella's disappointment was evident, but more so, she was surprised by what she had just heard her husband say. She knew that spending time with Adrian was one of his most treasured experiences, both socially and intellectually. Her shoulders tightened as she sighed and nodded understandingly, acknowledging that sometimes circumstances were beyond their control.

Hope struggled to contain her mounting frustration. Her fists clenched, knuckles whitening as she battled to stay in her seat. The rising tide of anger within her was overwhelming, and she suddenly sprung up, her voice cracking with pent-up fury. "This is absurd! Utterly absurd!" she exclaimed, her voice oozing exasperation. "How could you, Dad?" Her tone verged on a shout. "He's a tyrant who exploits women, harms children, and enslaves anyone ensnared in his web using the C.A.I.N. Hive! You're prioritizing that slimeball Ash Bertram over your friend who traveled all the way from Switzerland? It's beyond messed up!"

Gabe's face tightened, his jaw set as he absorbed Hope's outburst. He tried to respond, but the words caught in his throat as Hope's words stung with a truth he couldn't deny.

Ella exchanged a glance with Hope, her expression a mix of sympathy and frustration. The tension in the room grew thicker, the atmosphere heavy with unspoken emotions.

With a final glare at her father, Hope stormed out of the dining room, the scrape of her chair against the floor marking her departure. The milieu of the room grew uncomfortably still. Gabe's gaze lingered on the empty chair where Hope had sat just moments before, a mixture of regret and concern etched his features.

As the seconds ticked by, Gabe felt a pang of sadness deep within him, like a weight settling in his chest. He knew his decision had repercussions beyond just disappointing his family. He had sensed a shift, a disturbance in the very fabric of their reality. It was as if his choices were causing a ripple that extended beyond their immediate circumstances. Shaking his head, Gabe chided himself for overthinking it. Hope would be alright, he reassured himself, and he would find a way to make it up to her.

Although the start of the twins' birthday did not unfold as planned, the day drew to a close. The Valencias had a genuinely enjoyable time as a family, the earlier tensions seemingly dissipating. Gabe was relieved that the day had taken a positive turn, his deepest wish being the happiness of his loved ones. He had always strived to provide them with everything they needed and more.

As Gabe walked out of his closet, holding a robe, Ella entered their master suite bathroom. He was on his way to the rooftop swimming pool, a place of solace for him during times of stress, and tonight was certainly one of those times. The weight of the day's tensions was evident in Ella's expression.

"Ella, please. Can we move past this?" Gabe began, his voice thick with earnestness and exhaustion.

"Of all the nights, Gabe, and of all the people," she responded, her voice barely audible but her accusation resounding clearly.

"I'm sorry, El. I really need to go to this thing. I need to find out what Ronan is up to," Gabe's tone tinged with frustration. "I have meetings scheduled in France next month. I'll extend my trip and meet with Adrian afterward. I'll also give him a call tomorrow. He'll understand, I promise."

Ella's eyes reflected a blend of empathy and concern. "When you partnered with Ronan Hayes, it held so much promise for us. But this . . . Ash Bertram? He's far from the vision we had in mind. What's happening, Gabe?"

Gabe's gaze lowered, his expression clouded. "It's like everything's spinning out of control, El. I didn't anticipate any of this. Honestly, I didn't."

She approached him, her hands gently resting on his shoulders. "We'll find a way through this. But this isn't helping."

Gabe embraced her, pressing a reassuring kiss to her lips. "I promise, El, I'll figure this out," he said, trying to lighten the mood.

Ella half-smiled, "You need to make amends with Hope. And contributing to her foundation isn't going to cut it."

He paused, eyebrows furrowed. "Any advice?"

Ella chose her following words carefully, "Have you ever considered stepping back from Encephalon and transitioning back into the public sector?"

Gabe let out a wistful chuckle as he stepped into his slippers, the weight of her words evident in his expression. "Ella, that's impossible. Encephalon is like a runaway train now. It feels like a technological virus has taken over my life. My responsibility is to keep it in check and direct it toward something good. Leaving now would be letting go of the wheel during a storm. No, I'm afraid that's impossible."

Ella's expression twisted into confusion and concern, her voice blending frustration and genuine curiosity. "Since when did 'impossible' become a part of Gabriel Valencia's vocabulary? That's not who you are, Gabe. Remember that quote you often share with the kids? You know, the one by Walt Disney?"

Gabe walked over to the window, gazing at the sprawling city lights that stretched before him. It was as though his gaze pierced through the darkness, reaching far into the distance. "It's kind of fun to do the impossible," he murmured, the words barely audible.

Ella strained to hear him and asked, "What was that, honey?"

Gabe's distant expression returned to the present as he replied, "Oh, nothing, love. Just talking to myself." In his heart, Gabe grappled with the overwhelming sense of things spiraling out of control. The situation seemed far beyond the realm of possibility, and nothing was remotely enjoyable about it. He had intentionally shielded Ella from particular worries, not wanting to burden her with additional stress. Yet, the truth weighed heavily on Gabe. He wasn't just exhausted; he was deeply troubled.

The technology he had developed was intended to empower individuals, unveiling the boundless potential within themselves to shape their futures. However, it had now become focused on maximizing profits through controlled influence, and it was spiraling out of control. The dreams he had once nurtured were fading if they hadn't already vanished entirely. A sense of helplessness gnawed at Gabe's core.

Just then, Gabe's mixed-reality device chimed, signaling an incoming call from his friend and colleague Adrian Bannister. In his exhaustion, Gabe lacked the energy to take the call, which would involve disappointing his friend by explaining that he couldn't meet for dinner the next night. He decided to let it go to voicemail, planning to call him in the morning.

The voicemail piqued Gabe's curiosity. Adrian's voice was laced with excitement. "Hey, Gabe, it's Adrian. I can't wait to connect tomorrow night. I've got something that's going to blow your mind. You know how it is, always something new with Conscious Agents."

Gabe chuckled to himself, thinking of how Adrian's enthusiasm for groundbreaking discoveries was a constant in their friendship. With a knowing smile, he figured there was no rush and that he would return his call in the morning. Gabe couldn't yet imagine the profound significance this report would hold.

As Gabe headed to the rooftop pool, he couldn't shake the memory of his earlier argument with Hope. Her fiery outburst replayed in his mind, leaving him worried. Gabe had always held great respect for the timeless wisdom within her spirit. If someone as intuitive as Hope believed he was on the wrong path, he couldn't ignore it. The urgency to regain control of Encephalon weighed on him as time slipped by.

CHAPTER 8

In The Inverse, Hope encounters the Wisdom Complex. As her journey unfolds, her unconscious body on Earth faces a ticking clock, with only 10 hours and 23 minutes remaining. Drawing from Eada's training, Hope begins her mission to uncover the crucial message destined for her father.

The Command Center's grandeur highlighted the importance of the task ahead. As Hope's gaze swept across the expansive surroundings, a faint echo of familiarity resonated within her, a distant memory that slipped through her fingers, a hint of having traversed this space in a different time and context.

She inhaled deeply. Anticipation surged through her thoughts. The orb hovered above the grand table at the center of Epoch's office. Its gentle radiance, enticing her forward, suffused the space with an ethereal glow. It was a threshold, an entrance not only into Eada's reality but a rare wrinkle in time allowing her to right a past wrong and correct the trajectory of humanity's future. As the orb expanded, it seemed to envelop Hope's very essence, cocooning her within its luminous embrace until she stood immersed in its radiant field. Every fiber of her being resonated with the currents of dimensions, knowledge, and memory that swirled around her.

Her fingertips brushed the orb's inner surface. Then, a subtle vibration invited her to plunge deeper into her experience. Aiko's guidance resonated within Hope's mind, a calming presence amid infinite possibilities.

"Hope, allow yourself to be enveloped by the orb. Let the current of existence flow through you."

Hope yielded to its pull, a sensation that was both exhilarating and grounding. She felt like a leaf carried by some kind of trans-dimensional river, her consciousness woven into the fabric of Eada's experiences.

Images and sensations streamed around her, a whirlwind of colors, emotions, and memories. Then, within, a figure emerged. It was Eada, radiant and captivating. Tears welled in Hope's eyes as the familiarity and connection enveloped her. It wasn't just Eada's lessons that Hope was revisiting; it was the essence of Eada herself. Hope sensed Eada's thoughts, intentions, and emotions echoing within her mind, an intricate dance of consciousness transcending time and space.

Hope cast a last glance toward Epoch and Aiko, giving them a confident nod to indicate that she was ready. Then, in a flash, she was transported into another reality, a sprawling lecture hall where Eada sat beside a figure that Hope didn't recognize but with whom she felt an intense familiarity. *Pax?* Hope thought. Aiko's previous words echoed in her thoughts, revealing that Pax was her brother Poet's Lubhyati, and they had attended Academy together. They were now engaged in an orientation, marking the initial steps of their education on human reality.

Hope's heart swelled with a blend of emotions as she observed the interaction between Eada and Pax. She understood that each moment held significance. Any word or experience could be the message that she sought.

At that moment, Epoch's voice resonated in her mind. "Open your heart, Hope. Listen closely, especially to messages you may not believe."

As the audience's applause subsided, Eada and Pax took their seats in the grand lecture hall. The dean of The Academy approached the podium, his warm smile accompanying his words.

"Good infinity," he began. "It is an honor to share this occasion with all of you—students, faculty, and citizens of The Inverse. I am honored to be here as we weave new threads of reality into the fabric of your Pneuma's experiences."

As the dean continued, Eada leaned toward Pax and whispered, "Have you met your instructors yet?"

Pax shook his head subtly, his gaze still fixed on the dean. "Not yet," he replied in a hushed tone, surveying the vibrant assembly. "But I have heard good things. I believe they were all notable Pneuma Speakers on Earth."

Eada's eyes brightened with curiosity.

Gentle "Shss's" from nearby attendees occasionally interrupted their quiet exchange.

The dean's words resonated, carrying an air of anticipation. His call to open their minds to new dimensions sparked contemplation in Eada and Pax, inviting them to consider the richness of the impending experiences of their Pneumas.

As the dean's speech continued, Eada's thoughts drifted to Earth's concept of time—a singular dimension that moved in only one direction. The idea intrigued her, an intricate facet of the human experience.

Turning to Pax, she spoke in barely audible tones. "Do you understand anticipation?" she inquired, her curiosity evident.

Pax furrowed his brows thoughtfully. "It's a mystery," he confessed. "I've gathered fragments, like waiting, patience, and something called faith. It's a puzzle, for sure."

They shared smiles, a silent acknowledgment of their training partnership and mission. The Academy was their portal to comprehend these unfamiliar concepts and prepare their Pneuma for life on Earth. However, as they knew, the importance of their lessons extended beyond mere scope of experience. Eada and Pax occupied crucial positions within an exclusive team of Lubhyati tasked with a significant mission—to send Pneuma Speakers to Earth. Earth inhabitants teetered at a crossroads, delicately poised between contrasting threads of reality.

The Council's call echoed throughout The Inverse, a resonating summons answered by Epoch—a seasoned Lubhyati revered for successfully leading an array of pivotal missions. Epoch established bonds with kindred Lubhyati, enlisting Aiko as his second-in-command in the company of Eada and Pax, voyagers across countless realms of existence.

Epoch's own Pneuma, Gabriel, had already made his fall to Earth. Aiko's Pneuma, Ella, met Gabriel there. They fell in love, married, and were preparing to have twins—Hope and Poet—the Pneuma that Eada and Pax were now preparing for. With the dean's speech concluding, an air of excitement lingered, carrying the promise of fresh beginnings. Applause resonated throughout the assembly hall, a collective approval for the inspiring words that opened pathways to unexplored dimensions. Eada and Pax exchanged a knowing smile and silently acknowledged the lessons that awaited them.

Conversations filled the auditorium as attendees dispersed, each venturing toward their next education phase. Eada and Pax skillfully navigated through the crowd. Outside, Eada turned to Pax and casually remarked, "I'm headed to meet with my Orientation Counselor."

Pax nodded, "Likewise. Always an interesting session," he replied warmly.

Approaching The Hall of Counselors, their paths diverged. Eada looked back at Pax and called out, "Catch you later."

Pax replied, "Read your brief!"

Eada's gentle knock on Mr. Parson's door was greeted with an enthusiastic invitation, "Come in!" She entered, then settled into the chair directly in front of his desk. He welcomed her with a warm smile.

"Hello, Eada," he said, perusing a file that likely held records of her prior experiences and training at The Academy. His eyes had kindness, complementing his balding head and intellectual mustache.

"Epoch and Aiko's Pneuma have already begun their journey," Parsons remarked, breaking the ice.

Eada nodded, sharing the details. "Yes, that is correct. Their Pneuma are now living on Earth, already twenty-seven human years into their experience. Pax and I will follow up with our Pneuma once we graduate. They will arrive as twin human children, with Epoch and Aiko's Pneuma taking the roles of their parents."

"That should make your connection easier on Earth," Parsons noted.

Flipping through the brief, he continued, "I'm familiar with your instructors. Extraordinary Pneuma personalities who all became famous on Earth as Council Speakers."

Pausing thoughtfully, he added, "You have an exciting mission ahead of you, Eada. Your Pneuma will find Earth captivating. Humans are a fascinating species. They navigate a unique blend of social systems. The singular dimension of time and their individualized egos shape intricate relationships. It is a reality system unlike any other, and humans struggle to realize their interconnectedness, despite evidence at every turn." Passion resonated in Parson's voice as if he had invested intensely in understanding this facet of humanity.

"You are in for a treat with your other instructors. I've attended their talks and a couple of panels. Let me tell you, I am a big fan of their work. Most Lubhyati would jump at the chance to learn from just one of them, let alone all three. There's something big happening down there," the OC remarked with a spark in his eyes.

Eada wasn't quite sure what to make of Parson's curiosity or the assignment of instructors. Just then, she glanced out the door into the hallway, catching a glimpse of Pax strolling past the office with his instructor. He peeked in and shot her a goofy face. Eada rolled her eyes and couldn't help but chuckle.

Interrupting her amusement, Parsons cleared his throat, regaining her focus. "Your training," he began, each word emphasized, "will revolve around the symbolic equation of human reality: $B \in E + T = R$. Your first instructor, Walt, is a true magician regarding human beliefs. He spun fantastical tales and crafted entire fantasy realms on Earth to help humans embrace the possibility of any world they can dream of. He is a trailblazer in human belief, and having him as your Academy Instructor is an immense privilege."

Parsons paused, flipping to the next page of the mission brief. "And the excitement doesn't stop there. Your instructor for human Emotion, John, is quite the musician. His poetic contributions to humanity were extraordinary, and I was a devoted fan. I can only imagine how captivating his lessons will be for you.

Parsons added, "Lastly, you will have the honor of learning from my dear friend, Stephen. I must emphasize, Eada, that the significance of these instructors is profound. They have made remarkable contributions to humanity, opening doors to the deepest secrets of the universe. There must be a vital reason for them guiding your training on Earth. Stephen, in particular, is a brilliant mind whose work has transcended boundaries, providing humanity with the knowledge to explore the vast mysteries of the universe."

Eada found it intriguing that her OC was so impressed by her instructors. While she understood the importance of her mission, she also recognized the significance of other instructors. She couldn't quite grasp why her instructors were deemed exceptional. Nevertheless, she listened attentively to Mr. Parsons's guidance.

He continued, "Be sure to review the mission briefing. It contains crucial details to support your training."

"I'll make that a priority," Eada affirmed.

"Good. Any questions?" Parsons asked.

After a brief pause, Eada responded, "Not that I can think of."

"Great. Your training will take care of the rest. I see a note here from Walt, your instructor. He would like to meet you at the Temple of Healing. Have you seen the new crystal frequencies?"

Eada shook her head. "No, it's been many lifetimes since I've had a light cleansing."

"Walt highly recommends it. He believes in starting fresh before a new training cycle, releasing lingering negative energies from your Pneuma experiences. You'll feel rejuvenated," Parsons said with a warm smile.

As he stood, he added, "It was a pleasure meeting you, Eada. I wish you and your Pneuma a remarkable journey on Earth."

The temple guardian guided Eada to the center of the grand chamber. As Eada gazed upward, she marveled at the countless crystals that adorned the massive dome. Like prisms, they captured and amplified the light from above, casting a breathtaking display of radiant energy. *How is it possible?* Eada thought, almost speechless. The light seemed to seep into every particle of her consciousness, enveloping her in a healing embrace that seemed to originate from within.

Amid her meditation, a gentle voice broke the silence. Eada turned to find a friendly man standing beside her. He was of medium height, with a physique that balanced slender and slightly stocky features. His presence exuded a sense of purpose and vitality. His hair, tinged with silver, framed his forehead in a receding pattern, while a neatly groomed mustache added a touch of character to his face. Bright blue eyes sparkled with creativity and curiosity, reflecting enthusiasm and contemplation.

With a warm smile, she greeted, "Oh, hello there."

"Hello, Eada. It's a pleasure to meet you. I'm Walt," he introduced himself, extending his hand in a gesture familiar to humans.

Eada's eyes widened. She glanced at her mission brief and excitedly replied, "Oh, yes, Mr. Disney, it's wonderful to meet you too." She shook his hand, unable to contain her smile.

Walt chuckled warmly. "No need for formalities, dear. Please, call me Walt."

"Walt, it is," Eada agreed.

"You were pondering the same thing," Walt remarked.

"I'm sorry?"

Walt continued, "You were wondering how they managed to improve on perfection, referring to the light from the crystals."

Eada nodded, impressed by his insight. She recalled that instructors could grasp and analyze students' thoughts, emotions, and conclusions, a skill integral to accelerating the learning process at The Academy.

"Perfection is a matter of belief," Walt explained. "In the vast expanse of the multiverse, perfection only exists when a conscious being *believes* in its magnificence. What one perceives as perfection might be seen as flawed by another." He raised a finger, gesturing toward the crystal-adorned dome. "This suggests that perfection is a subjective concept molded by individual preference. Isn't that intriguing?"

Eada glanced at the dome of crystals, awestruck. She couldn't fathom anyone perceiving the kaleidoscope of colors and light as anything other than perfect.

Walt chuckled once more. "Touché, dear. How about we get started, shall we?"

Eada's smile widened. "Let's." She already felt a connection with her instructor in Human Belief.

As they strolled toward the Temple's exit, Eada observed Walt's relaxed demeanor, clad in a three-piece grey-striped suit that draped comfortably over his frame. Leaving the temple, Eada recognized several impressive buildings flanking their path. Familiar with the campus layout, she realized they were heading toward the Experiential Training Facility, the ETF. It lay just beyond the gardens connecting the sprawling Wisdom Complex.

"Follow me, if you will," Walt beckoned confidently, guiding the way. "Here in The Inverse, we hold belief as the very foundation of reality. On Earth, humans tend to see belief as a bundle of ideas and principles helping them make sense of the world and distinguish right from wrong. Yet, what often eludes them is that they are carting around thousands of unrecognized beliefs in their everyday lives.

"Humans have a special relationship with beliefs. They build their life experiences around them. But there's this funny thing; humans have a knack for treating a belief as a hard fact without a second thought, unlike any other critter out there. They dodge important questions that could lead to deeper insight into their beliefs, like 'Why am I holding onto this belief?', 'When did I adopt this belief in the first place?', or 'What was the influence behind it?'"

Walking through the central gardens of the Wisdom Complex was always a delight for Eada. Every part of it was a product of the student body's collective imagination, guaranteeing a fresh experience for everyone to enjoy. Tall, impressive trees stood like sentinels, watching over vibrant bushes, sparkling water features, and illuminated paths that wound playfully through the gardens.

Walt continued, "Humans have cooked up a whole buffet of belief systems to include over 4,200 religions, 18,000 gods, and ten key philosophies; and those have branched off into more than 2,000 philosophical disciplines. And if that wasn't enough, there are fifteen flavors of science, each with its crowd of followers and schools of thought. And guess what? These societal beliefs are like the opening act for a never-ending circus of even wilder ideas, leading to a number of personal beliefs."

As they stepped into the foyer of the Experiential Training Facility, Eada found herself, once again, swept away by its grandeur. Despite having frequented the place countless times, the sheer beauty, intricate design, and vibrant energy never ceased to amaze her. Walt gestured to the left, and Eada's gaze followed, revealing one of the three primary corridors leading to the chambers dedicated to instruction. Embarking on their journey through the expansive lobby, they continued along the corridor until Walt's voice broke the silence. "Ah, here we are." His outstretched arm directed her attention ahead and to the right.

Eada's gaze was irresistibly drawn to the magnificent threads that gracefully hung within the archway of the Oculus. They pulsed with vibrant life, emitting a gentle hum that resonated with anticipation, like a whispered promise of endless possibilities.

The expanse beyond was devoid of any flicker of light or movement. Above the archway, in elegant Latin script, Eada read the words "Oculus Relatorum – Quattuor," translated as "Eye of Threads - Four." The graceful words melded seamlessly into the exotic fusion of metal, stone, and crystal that comprised the exquisite portal. Eada's eyes then caught the familiar emblem adorning the archway's side, displaying the details of their class reservation:

INSTRUCTOR: Pneuma Speaker—Walt Disney
LUBHYATI: Eada
TRAINING SESSION ONE: Human Belief
MEETING PLACE: Experiential Training Facility—Oculus Quattuor
3D-Coordinates: Earth - 33.81° N/117.92°W, 157'

As they stepped into the Oculus, Eada felt the familiar embrace of the light blue luminescence, a realm that welcomed boundless exploration.

"Welcome back to the Oculus, Eada," Walt's voice brimmed with anticipation. "I am thrilled to show you the extraordinary power of human belief and how it molds their reality. It is a lesson I've held dear throughout my life."

Once they ventured further into the realm of the Oculus, Walt gracefully waved his hand, and the serene blue space around them instantly transformed. They now stood at the entrance of a magnificent and enchanting castle. Walt gestured dramatically, his voice filled with awe, "Behold, Eada, the Magic Kingdom!"

Eada's eyes widened in wonder as she looked out over a vibrant world where families laughed, children beamed with joy, and iconic characters strolled through bustling streets. The air seemed to crackle with topical wonder and boundless belief, infecting everyone with a contagious sense of magic and delight.

Walt led Eada across a bridge that spanned the castle's moat through a beautiful square where people lingered and then casually strolled down the bustling Main Street, USA. Shops of all sorts lined the street, their façades evoking a sense of charm and nostalgia. Old-fashioned street lamps framed the scene while the sweet scent of cotton candy and popcorn filled the air. Eada's senses were ablaze with the sights and sounds of this enchanting world, and she felt the magic of the place.

Just then, a dinging noise resonated through the air, and Walt swiftly grabbed Eada's hand, pulling her to the side of the street as a horse-drawn trolley adorned with colorful decorations passed by. Walt walked beside her with a radiant smile, emitting a sense of pride that his creation had impressed her deeply.

They spotted a family about thirty feet ahead as they continued down the street. The parents laughed as they watched their mischievous twin children. One held a balloon in her hand while the other leaped as high as he could, attempting to pop it. The little girl, dressed in a princess costume, fervently protested that her brother was trying to hurt her beloved balloon, which she had affectionately named Littlest Cinderella.

Walt leaned in and whispered, his voice carrying the wisdom of a man who had dedicated his life to the magic of belief. "This, Eada, is a moment frozen in time—a memory created by a young girl's belief in magic. It may seem insignificant, but it is a belief she will carry with her throughout her life."

Just then, a magician dressed in a top hat and a cape adorned with twinkling stars approached the family. He waved his wand, and a flurry of colorful butterflies erupted into existence, swirling around the twins in a mesmerizing dance of vibrant wings. The little girl squealed with delight, her laughter echoing through the street.

Eada watched in awe. Walt smiled, his eyes filled with a deep understanding.

"The power of belief, Eada," he said softly, "is the foundation on which to build a dream."

Eada's intrigue about human belief increased, and she couldn't resist asking for another example.

With a contemplative expression, Walt summoned Eada's mission brief. He opened his hand, and with a soft, sparkly glow, the document materialized instantly, its pages flipping effortlessly at his command. When it seemed he had found what he was looking for, he nodded and said, "Mm-hmm, yes, I see." Then, with a flick of his hand, the brief vanished. Next, he extended his arm and conjured the Oculus, which now stood prominently in the center of the street.

"Shall we?" he proposed, extending an invitation to step through the dimensional threads of the Oculus.

Eada initially wondered if something had gone wrong as they approached the other side of the archway. Had the Oculus possibly malfunctioned? They were in the exact same location, yet subtle differences surrounded them. The people appeared to be dressed differently, and unless her eyes were tricking her, they all had suddenly changed their hairstyles.

It dawned on Eada that they had ventured to a different point in time on Earth.

"So, we are navigating humanity's timeline, correct?" she inquired, seeking clarification.

Walt chuckled at her curiosity and nodded. "Indeed, dear Eada. Remember, on Earth, time marches only in one direction—forward. From a human's perspective, we have just taken a trip *back* in time."

They continued to walk along the streets of Walt's kingdom as he warmly acknowledged adults and playfully waved to children along the way. As they ventured into an area called Tomorrowland, Eada's eyes were irresistibly drawn to the heart of this colossal attraction that dominated her vision. Its name was prominently displayed on the attraction's side, adorned with vibrant colors and attractive fonts, loudly announcing its presence: The Astro Orbiter.

The Orbiter stood tall on a towering central structure, a beacon of imagination and adventure. Its gleaming white exterior with crimson and gold accents evoked the imagery of mid-20th-century science fiction rockets. The sun's rays painted an aura of wonder all around it. The space-age atmosphere was abuzz, with polished metallic floors reflecting gentle overhead lighting. Murals adorned the walls, showcasing cosmic vistas, distant planets, and intrepid astronauts—a tribute to the golden era of space exploration on Earth. At its center, a circular platform awaited riders, resembling a launchpad. Positioned on this platform were individual spaceships, each one meticulously crafted.

Eada's attention shifted to a young man who hesitated near one of the rocket entrances. Evidently, the boy's mother offered reassuring words until he finally summoned the courage to embark on the adventure. Walt signaled for Eada to follow, and together, they quietly occupied seats behind the young man, joining him on the expedition. As the rocket soared into the imaginary cosmos, the boy's surroundings underwent a breathtaking metamorphosis. He hurtled through the vast expanse of space, entering a boundless, shimmering macrocosm that stretched beyond human comprehension. Like fiery diamonds, stars twinkled in the inky blackness, and galaxies swirled with colors that defied earthly imagination. He was not merely a spectator but a participant in this cosmic dance, where the boundaries of time and space blurred into an awe-inspiring tapestry of wonders.

Afterward, he ventured further, diving headlong into the subatomic realm. Here, electrons, protons, and neutrons became living, pulsating entities, radiating in vibrant hues that defied the limits of human perception. They danced and twirled in a mesmerizing ballet of colors, a symphony of energy transcending the observable universe's boundaries. As he delved deeper, the subatomic atoms appeared, revealing their intricate, three-dimensional structures. They resembled miniature worlds, with nuclei at their hearts and electrons whirling around in complex orbits, all nestled within shimmering electron clouds that seemed to bristle with life. It was a realm where the fundamental building blocks of reality were anything but mundane, a place where the very essence of existence shimmered with untold mysteries.

As the rocket continued its journey, Eada noticed the boy's face lighting up. It was like a whole new world unfolding before him, as if the universe itself was revealing its secrets, and the boy eagerly soaked it all in. Walt leaned in and shared some insights with Eada about the boy. He explained that he was always curious about how things worked, especially the mysteries of the universe. At that moment, the boy's curiosity ignited. Walt told Eada that the boy had realized he was intimately connected to the vast and mysterious cosmos.

During those fleeting moments on the ride, Eada witnessed the boy undergoing a profound transformation. A new belief had taken hold of him—one that stirred his emotions, sparked his imagination, and ignited thoughts of the boundless reality he perceived.

Walt acknowledged Eada's keen perception and added that the boy's newly embraced belief would indeed act as a catalyst for profound change, shaping the very course of his life. As his thoughts and imagination underwent this transformation, the equation of reality unfolded, directing the boy onto a completely different life path. This fresh thread of existence was woven with innovative choices in education, fueled by an ever-growing scientific and technological curiosity. Over the course of his life, from the perspective of human temporal dimension, he emerged as one of Earth's most esteemed neuroscientists, with a specialization in the field of neurotechnology. None of this would have happened if a simple belief hadn't been adopted in the span of a moment.

As the ride ended, the boy couldn't contain his excitement. He rushed to his mother, and together, they walked toward the exit. Surprisingly, they stumbled upon a hologram displaying a black-and-white video. Eada noticed it was Walt himself in the video. Walt shrugged and kindly gestured for her to watch what happened next. The video showcased Walt addressing a vast audience before the majestic castle. His message championed the power of believing in dreams and the potent magic of wishing upon a star.

As the video concluded, the boy's gaze settled on a life-sized image of Walt on the wall, accompanied by a quote with his iconic signature proudly displayed below. It simply read: "It's kind of fun to do the impossible."

In a hushed tone, Walt confided in Eada, "These words carry profound significance for me. They encapsulate the extraordinary connection between belief and achieving the impossible, or indeed any reality, for that matter."

Eada realized they had just witnessed the power of human belief in action. She was captivated by its enchantment, and admired Walt's extraordinary skill in inspiring imaginative ideas in those who visited the Magic Kingdom. This experience deepened her appreciation for his wisdom and expertise in human belief systems. She felt profoundly grateful to have him as her guide in exploring this captivating subject.

As she reflected on the little girl's enchantment with the magician and the boy on the exhilarating ride, Eada realized the profound impact highly influential experiences could wield in shaping a person's beliefs throughout their lifetime. These experiences, akin to magical moments, and the discovery of creative vistas, had the power to unlock doors to boundless potential and mold one's perspective in surprising and transformative ways.

She was struck that the unique flow of time on Earth, always moving forward, played a pivotal role in establishing a complex web of psychological advantages and disadvantages. She surmised that while some beliefs were inherently positive and productive, others, born from less desirable or even traumatic circumstances, might not offer the same benefits. Eada's journey into the intricate realm of beliefs had provided her with a glimpse of the expansive spectrum of human experiences and the remarkable ability of beliefs—even those beliefs not consciously acknowledged—to shape an individual's reality.

Eada's gaze remained fixed on Walt as she pondered her next question. Her curiosity was insatiable, fueled by a genuine desire to comprehend the intricate workings of human consciousness.

"Walt," she began, "how many beliefs does a human consciousness hold?"

"Ah, Eada," Walt replied, his voice resonating with a lifetime of observations, "the beliefs in a human's mind are as numerous as the stars that grace the night sky." His words held a profound reverence for the complexity of the human psyche.

Walt continued, "Imagine each star in the sky a belief, triggering human emotions, guiding their thoughts, and shaping their reality. Just as the night sky stretches beyond sight, the human capacity for belief extends beyond conscious awareness."

Eada's fascination grew. She marveled at the intricate nature of it all, feeling a profound sense of gratitude for the wisdom Walt shared.

"Thank you, Walt," she said. "Your insights are truly enlightening and I am grateful for the opportunity to learn from you."

Walt smiled warmly. "My pleasure, dear. I am relishing the opportunity to assist you in unlocking the mysteries of the human experience."

As Walt and Eada continued their exploration of the Magic Kingdom, a profound transformation occurred, one that defied the limits of what Eada thought possible. With its golden farewell, the sun gracefully retreated beneath the horizon, surrendering the skies to a vast bed of stars. Eada was astounded by how this place transformed in its daily cycle, growing even more enchanting under the soft luminescence of the street lamps and lanterns. It was as if the very essence of human dreams had leaped into the air, electrifying the night with boundless possibilities.

In these moments, Eada witnessed firsthand the birth of countless beliefs, each a unique thread woven into the tapestry of human consciousness. The belief in magic and the hope of a wish coming true was all here, alive and tangible.

With a knowing smile, Walt led her on a winding path that took them full circle, back to the central square nestled between Main Street, USA and the majestic castle. The familiar surroundings now held a deeper resonance, as if every brick and cobblestone whispered secrets of human aspirations.

Eada's gaze drifted toward the night sky, and Walt saw the spark of realization in her eyes.

"Walt, these beliefs aren't just memories in human minds, they're living personas, etched in moments in time, as vital as the person in the present. When situations align with these beliefs, they come to life and trigger emotions."

Walt beamed with pride, and his eyes sparkled. "Eureka, Eada!" he exclaimed, extending his arm to the sky.

As if in response to Walt's joy, a magnificent burst of fireworks painted the night sky in dazzling hues. Eada jumped in surprise, then burst into laughter. "Did those fireworks happen because of what I said? Do they go off every time a human has an epiphany?"

Walt joined her laughter, his voice carrying a hint of mischief. "No, no, dear. Those are my beloved fireworks. I set them off every night because every day on Earth is a cause for celebration."

Eada marveled at the spectacular display overhead. She turned to Walt, her heart brimming with gratitude. "Thank you, Walt."

He smiled, "And I, my dear, thank you. Now, shall we bid farewell?"

With those words, they strolled toward the archway of the Oculus that had just appeared ahead of them. As they passed, the dimensional threads vibrated in perfect harmony, and Walt's magical world faded behind them.

Stepping into the Experiential Training Facility, Eada finally spoke as they made their way to the main lobby. "Walt, how do you like being an Instructor at The Academy?"

Walt smiled warmly. "It's quite fulfilling, my dear, though not all sessions are as delightful as ours. But I find great joy in it."

Eada nodded thoughtfully. "I imagine it has its challenges."

Walt chuckled. "You could say that again. But often, the most challenging students teach me the most. You, Eada, are extraordinary. I have every confidence you and your Pneuma will succeed tremendously on Earth."

Eada's heart swelled. "Thank you, Walt. That means a great deal to me."

As they exited the facility, Walt said, "Well, my dear, it appears our lesson has reached its conclusion. I hope you found the exploration of human belief systems, with their unique dimensions of existence, as enchanting as I do. These beliefs, after all, are the tapestry of human reality."

Eada nodded, her eyes brimming with appreciation. "Indeed, Walt. I've not only enjoyed our lesson, but I also gained profound insights. Your wisdom has touched me deeply and I am truly grateful for this experience."

"Until our paths cross once more, I bid you farewell," Walt said warmly, his smile carrying a weight of mentorship and a connection that would endure.

Eada felt a renewed sense of purpose and determination. As they said their goodbyes, she reflected on how Pax's training was unfolding, recognizing the wisdom imparted by Walt would remain a guiding light on their journey through the world of human beliefs.

CHAPTER 9

Earth. November 13, 2045. The day Hope commences her training at the League of Consciousness (LOC). Unbeknownst to her, a looming global crisis threatens humanity's future. Her father, Gabriel, holds a high-ranking corporate position aligned with the very forces the LOC opposes, complicating their relationship and her mission. Despite the emotional turmoil, Hope remains resolute in confronting the impending threat from Encephalon Media Group.

Hope fumbled in her groggy state, desperately trying to silence the blaring siren of the wall-embedded communications device. The first rays of dawn trickled into the stark white room through a high window, casting a pale glow on the surroundings.

"Can't a girl get some sleep?" Hope mumbled, rubbing her temples, awakening to the reality of her sparse dormitory room, a stark contrast to the comforts of her childhood home in Manhattan.

She surveyed the room and spotted a neatly folded set of khaki pants, a beige button-up shirt, a belt, socks, and polished black leather boots resting on the metal desk against the wall. *Definitely need some coffee,* she thought, quickly dressing to prepare for the day ahead.

Upon arriving at the briefing room, Hope discovered that most of the seats were occupied by fellow recruits. *Am I late?* Hope called up a clock display on her mixed-reality lenses, indicating she had a few minutes to spare.

"It's kind of you to grace us with your presence, cadet. Would you mind if we get started?" A stern tall figure stood at a podium at the front of the room.

Hope responded with confusion, "Wasn't the briefing set for zero-five-thirty hours?"

The instructor's response was swift and to the point. "Could someone kindly educate your classmate on our timekeeping here at the LOC?"

A muscular cadet spun in his chair, locking eyes with Hope and exclaiming, "At the LOC, we assume every cuckoo clock, watch, or timepiece runs ten minutes behind. Always!" He promptly turned back to face the front, awaiting further instruction.

The instructor maintained his stern demeanor. "Any questions, cadet?"

Hope, now seated, replied with a firm "No, sir. No questions."

"Good. Let's begin, then."

As the instructor started their rundown of the day's schedule, a calm voice from Hope's side offered advice: "He's all bark, no bite. And don't mind the brown-noser up front."

Hope turned her head toward the voice and encountered a friendly, chubby face surrounded by a mass of curly, black hair. The cadet wore a warm smile and thick, black-rimmed glasses, giving her a wink before returning his focus to the front of the room.

"Thanks," she whispered, introducing herself, "I'm Hope."

"Nice to meet you, Hope," he replied softly, nodding toward the instructor at the podium.

"Right," Hope murmured.

A quick survey of the auditorium revealed everyone donning the same uniform she wore, all of them fixated on the instructor like deer in headlights. When the briefing ended, all the cadets arose to exit the room. Hope quickly caught up to the kind young man who had sat beside her and tapped him on the shoulder. He spun around and was more surprised than she had anticipated.

"Hey there. It was nice to meet you at the orientation briefing," Hope said.

A good four inches shorter than Hope, he stood there open-mouthed with a blank look. Hope's striking appearance often had this effect on men, even those with a more confident disposition.

Hope filled the awkward silence. "I sat next to you in the briefing," she added, pointing back to the door with her thumb.

"Ah, yes, Hope. Right. N-n-nice to meet you." He then looked down at his feet, seeming to be embarrassed. He nervously spewed words out of his mouth, but none made much sense to Hope. His chubby cheeks, now turning bright red, indicated his bashful disposition.

"Ah, hey, thanks," Hope said with a smile and punched him lightly on his shoulder.

The young man smiled and nodded, obviously uncomfortable and uncertain how to respond.

"I get the impression that you know your way around this place," she said. "I could use a friend. Want to grab some coffee? I don't have a class for another thirty minutes."

"Of course, yes, I'd love to!"

"And, your name is?"

"Oh, sorry, yes, right, I'm Levi. Levi Archibald. It's nice to meet you." He stuck his hand out for Hope to shake. It was an old-fashioned gesture, but Hope always liked it when people brought it back.

"It's nice to meet you as well, Levi," she replied with a broad smile. "Shall we?" She gestured toward the mess hall. As they walked down the main corridor, she asked, "Are they all like that guy around here?"

"No, not at all. Most people are pretty chill. That dude back there has a serious case of TDS. Don't worry about him."

"TDS?" Hope asked with a confused look.

"Tiny Dick Syndrome? Not a rare disease, but it can surely raise havoc with a man's attitude."

Hope laughed. She sensed that Levi was starting to relax. "I'll be sure to keep that in mind."

"What are you in for?" Levi asked as if the LOC was a prison and they were fresh meat trying to survive the day.

Hope replied nonchalantly, "PT-SOF training, first day."

"Prob-Thread-Special-Ops, seriously?" Levi let out his excitement a bit too loudly for Hope's taste.

She shot him a subtle glare, silently warning him that his enthusiasm was a tad excessive. "It's not that big of a deal, man. Chill out," she said, even though she knew it was.

The League of Consciousness only accepted five candidates yearly for Probability Thread Special Operations Force training. It was a fusion of an MI6 agent, a Double-0 agent, and an advanced psychological probable-reality specialist, creating humanity's most advanced weapon.

The latter part relied on hacked and pilfered code from her father's technology. Encephalon Media Group had gone to great lengths to keep the technology for themselves, but there were always leaks. The stolen code became an invaluable asset that the LOC often relied on.

Impressed with the details of Hope's training, Levi remarked, "Well, whatever you say, that's insanely cool!"

They entered the mess hall and approached an AI dispensing unit that promptly scanned their corneas and discerned their coffee preferences. Seizing the opportunity, Hope decided to tap into Levi's knowledge and gain insights into how things operated in this place.

Sitting at a nearby table, Hope inquired, "So, what unit are you training for?"

Levi slid into a chair directly across from her. "I'm an AI architect by trade. I completed my doctoral dissertation at MIT, but they want to shackle me to a desk for some insane genome DNA decoding project. It's intriguing, for sure, and I guess they're planning to assign a whole team to work under me. I thought I'd give it a shot. They certainly know how to throw a lot of money around," he added, miming the gesture of rubbing his thumb and fingers together.

My man can talk! Hope thought. She decided to drop a bomb in their conversation just for fun. "MIT, you say?"

"Yep. Class of '43," Levi replied with pride.

"Ever hear of a man named Dr. Gabriel Valencia?" Hope asked.

"Are you kidding? Who hasn't heard of that dude? He's the most famous neurotechnologist on the . . ." Levi abruptly stopped talking, his eyes widening with realization as if a lightbulb had just turned on in his mind.

"Yep. That's my dad." Hope responded casually and then took a sip of her coffee.

Levi made sounds, but full words, let alone sentences, failed to form any decipherable communication. Suddenly, he stopped trying to speak and simply stared at Hope in awe. Finally, Levi blurted out, "Your dad? Seriously, your dad?"

Hope rolled her eyes, glancing around the mess hall and offering a reassuring smile to a couple sitting two tables away. "Dude, could you tone it down like ten notches?"

"Oh, my god! You're Hope Valencia!" Levi's face turned a bright shade of red, and he shifted uncomfortably on the bench, seemingly torn between wanting to run away or staying frozen in place.

"In the flesh," she replied with a smile.

Levi struggled to contain his disbelief. "You're telling me that the world's most famous neurotechnologist, responsible for inventing Trans-Dimensional Probability Threads and the Cybernetic Artificial Intelligent Network, the C.A.I.N. Hive itself, that the LOC considers enemy number one, is your dad? And that his daughter is training to be a PT-SOF agent?" He buried his face in his hands momentarily, then looked up, a bead of sweat trickling down his cheek. "Hope, you have to give me more than this. I'm completely lost. How is that even possible?"

"What's there to understand?" Hope asked. "I love my father, but I despise the company he works for. Much to my father's dismay, I've been their most vocal critic. I've protested them at every opportunity, thinking that being my father's daughter would make a difference. Turns out, I couldn't have been more wrong. No one wants to hear from a party crasher."

Levi's eyes reflected sympathy for Hope's situation. "It must be tough for you."

"I'm fine," Hope shot back, clearly stating she wasn't seeking sympathy.

Levi's curiosity was piqued. "How did you get into LOC training, especially for PT-SOF?"

Hope gave a somewhat vague reply. "I knew about the LOC and applied persistently for months. I either wore them down or they saw value in my connection to Encephalon. Either way, here I am."

Hope's vague answer only fueled Levi's intrigue. He leaned closer, his voice hushed as if they were having a clandestine meeting behind enemy lines. "If you're a spy, count me in. Just let me know what you need. I'm your man, no questions asked."

Hope chuckled. "Levi, chill out, bro. You're causing a scene. I'm not a spy, or at least not yet," she said with a wink.

His eyes shifted left and right as he searched the mess hall and whispered, "Yes, of course. I get it; be cool," he said with an animated wink.

Hope thought, *Oh, lord, save me,* but she figured allowing Levi this newly discovered fantasy wouldn't hurt. Her next objective was to change the subject and learn everything she could about the LOC training facility.

"Can I trust you with something, Levi?"

"Yes, of course you can. I mean, I know I need to earn your trust, but give me a chance. I'll show you that I'm your man." He then looked embarrassed and added, "I mean, not like your *man,* man. What I meant was I'm wit-chu. I'm unda cova. I'm wit da-govu-ment." By now, Levi had a big smile as if Hope was supposed to recognize something. He added inquisitively, "My Blue Heaven? You know, the classic movie with Steve Martin and Rick Moranis?" Levi's palms were up, gesturing that he figured everyone on the planet was aware of the famous classic film.

Hope responded, "Who are Steve Martin and Rick Moranis? I have no clue what you're talking about."

"Never mind, it's not important," he said, waving his hands. "Bottom line, I've got you. I'm a vault."

It always seemed strange to Hope that she had this effect on men, but with Levi, she thought she'd go along. Aside from the fact that she liked his personality, the friendship may just come in handy at some point.

"That's good to know, Levi. Thank you. It's good to have a friend on the inside I can depend on."

"Oh, you can certainly count on me. Is there anything I can help you with?"

"Yes, right. I could use another set of eyes around here, especially for anything related to Encephalon Media Group. Do you think you could help me with some surveillance?" Hope kept the request purposefully vague. She found that when men attempted to impress her, they constantly flexed and over-delivered on a task or inquiry.

"Are you kidding me?" Levi's facial expression was instantly animated. He leaned back over the table and whispered, "One of the first orders of business when I arrived was to gain access to the main database. You should see what they got in there. I didn't sleep for three days!"

"I can imagine," she replied, matching Levi's intensity.

Levi continued, "How 'bout I dig in to see what they got on your pops?"

"Easy, killer," Hope countered. "I'm not asking you to hack into the most guarded database on the planet."

"Ha! Too late on that one, sista. I'm already tapped in." Levi thrust his pointer finger onto the top of the table.

Hope shook her head, gesturing disbelief blended with a tinge of concern. "Okay, look, keep me out of that, but if you do stumble on anything you think might help, please don't hesitate to let me know."

"You got it, Hope. I'm your man." He then glanced up with a look that suggested he was about to correct himself again.

"I know what you meant. Relax, Levi."

Levi drank his coffee and stated, "Things must be interesting during the holidays around the Valencia household these days."

"I guess I'll be finding that out soon enough," she sighed with a concerned look.

"Wait. Your dad doesn't even know you're here? Oh, snap! Girl, you're a badass! How'd you pull that shit off? I imagine Dr. Valencia would have a full-blown secret service detail tracking your ass."

Hope shot him a look as if to suggest that he was venturing into uninvited territory.

"I get it, and you don't have to worry about me prying into your business. It's aaall good."

"Thanks. I appreciate that," Hope replied.

After an awkward break in their conversation, Levi offered, "Hey, if you want, we can take a quick look to see how many individual files there are on your dad. At least you would know the scope of their surveillance. What do you say?" He seemed desperate to impress her.

"Will they know that we're looking at it?" Her voice had a hint of concern.

"Not in a billion years. My hack is a ghost. There's no possible way they would know."

With that, Levi pulled his pack onto the table, unzipped it, and pulled out an old-style electronic device, something she'd seen before in old movies. The grey, oversized laptop was indeed a blast from the past. Hope was familiar with all the latest high-end specialized hardware, but Levi's old-timey machine caused her to wonder if he was the techno-geek he made himself out to be.

"Ahh, the pretty lady knows her hardware, or at least she *thought* she did," Levi said antagonistically.

"Ya, I thought I did. What in the hell is that?" she asked.

"I'd tell you . . . " he added a dramatic pause, "but then I'd have to kill you," and laughed out loud. "I'm just kidding. I use this tricked-out old laptop because no one knows how to hack into it. I've added a few security and search features that have turned this thing into a digital beast. Look here, let's pull up some files."

Levi tickled the keys of his laptop as if it were a piano. His fingers glided across the keyboard at an impossible speed. Hope could only guess how many words a minute he could shove into the ancient but high-powered device.

"That's odd," Levi had a confused look.

"What? What's there?" Hope asked and then added as she approached his side of the table. "Show me."

"That's just it. There's nothing here on anyone with the name Valencia, Gabriel, Gabe, Hope, or anything similar. I mean, it doesn't make any sense that your dad isn't here. How the second in command at Encephalon Media Group isn't here makes no sense."

Hope could tell Levi was astounded that nothing appeared in the LOC file list. And frankly, so was she. "Your so-called hack must be a bunch of bullshit."

"No it's not!" He almost yelled, making a scene for anyone around to question.

"Are you out of your fucking mind, Levi? Can you please be a little quieter?" Hope hissed.

"Yes, sorry. It's just that this is super weird. I'm telling you, and you can believe me or not, but the LOC has zero files on your father. At least not that they keep in their main database."

Hope sat down slowly and peered at the lines of data. She saw a long list of names starting with V, but none matched her father's name. It looked legitimate, and to her surprise, Levi seemed genuinely upset with what they had discovered.

"What does this mean?" She looked up, hoping he would share something that made sense.

"I have no idea, but it's not a stretch to assume that there's a deeper connection between the LOC and your father."

"What's that supposed to mean?" Hope said defensively.

"I have no idea what any of this means, Hope. I'm just suggesting that . . . "

Hope cut him off, "Well, maybe you should stop making assumptions that lead to bullshit suggestions. How does that sound?"

"Ah, yes, of course, Hope. I'm very sorry; I didn't mean to . . ." Levi stumbled on his words, and his chubby face turned a new shade of red.

Hope, realizing she had allowed her anxiety to become overly aggressive, changed her tone. "I'm sorry, Levi. I didn't mean to snap at you. I'm just under a lot of stress, and everything puts me on edge these days. Please, ignore me."

"Hey, sista, I get it," Levi replied.

"Look, how about we forget this and start fresh? We've got to get to class. Let's connect tomorrow for lunch," she suggested with a smile, attempting to get the newly minted relationship back on track.

"I'll be counting the minutes," Levi replied and looked down, obviously realizing he had just said something that made him sound like a dork.

Hope laughed, "Good. And thank you, Levi."

They both got up and walked out of the mess hall. Levi pointed down to his left as Hope pointed to her right, indicating the separate directions they were headed off to.

"T.T.F.N!" Levi quipped.

"I'm not sure I . . ." Hope had a puzzled look on her face.

"Never mind. See you tomorrow," Levi said as he shuffled off to his next class.

Hope ignored the incoming call until it went to voicemail. She needed a moment to wake up. A moment later, she activated her mixed-reality lenses and played the incoming messages.

"Hope, it's Levi. We met in the . . . Never mind. Of course, you remember me. Anyway, I didn't let the data anomaly go. I've been up all night digging deeper into it. You're not going to believe what I found. I wanted to confirm that we're meeting up for lunch today. If I'm a few minutes late, just hang until I get there. They've got me signed up for this stupid field sniper training. I don't even get it. I have no idea who makes the itineraries around here. I'll try to get there by twelve hundred. See you then."

Hope blinked off her mixed-reality lenses and sat up in bed, pondering Levi's message. She had mixed feelings about it. After a quick shower, she headed to her first class.

Several hours passed, and the afternoon arrived swiftly. As she glanced around, it became evident that Levi had yet to show up, even though it was past noon. The room suddenly buzzed with energy, and everyone was drawn to an announcement. Hope quickly activated her mixed-reality lenses to view the feed.

The top video thumbnail displayed an image of the sniper range, and the headline read, "Cadet Sustains Fatal Injury in Training Accident." Hope's heart sank as she watched the broadcast, her worry growing with each passing second. The news anchor reported that a cadet had sustained a fatal gunshot wound during a training exercise on the Sniper-Foxtrot Range,

Bravo. Tension gripped her as the moment approached when the victim's name was about to be revealed. Her mind raced with dread, fearing the worst, when suddenly, Levi appeared, plopping his substantial frame down across from Hope.

"Sorry, I'm late. Insane ass morning!"

Hope didn't hear the name from the newsfeed. She just sat there gawking at Levi as if looking at a ghost.

After a moment of silence, Levi said, "Dude, are you okay? What's wrong?"

"I thought you were . . . " The words were reluctant to leave Hope's mouth.

"Oh, snap! You thought I was dead?" Levi laughed as he finished her thought.

"What happened, Levi? Were you involved?" Hope still couldn't believe he was sitting in front of her.

"No, I really didn't see anything other than the newsfeeds. I was on Alpha Range. The dude that got shot was on Bravo Range. It was nuts. The radios went ballistic, and our instructors just shot out of there. I tried to get here sooner, but they locked the place down, and then we had to leave single file. It was a shit show."

"Well, I'm glad you're okay," Hope reached across the table and put her hand on his arm.

She then realized that Levi was enjoying the attention.

He said, "This is what we signed up for, right? Who knows when our time is up?"

Hope sensed his bravado instantly and pulled her arm away. Her demeanor changed, and the tone of her voice sharpened, "I heard your voicemail. What's so unbelievable about what you found?"

"Dang, where'd the love go, girl? A second ago, you seemed a little worried for me. Was it something I said?"

"I was worried, okay. But you're fine now, so give."

Levi rummaged through his pack, retrieving his laptop. "I'd prefer to be outside."

They relocated to a quieter patio table, and once settled, Levi opened his laptop. He directed Hope's attention to a set of test results linked to the battery of rigorous physical and intellectual tests that Hope had undergone during her qualification process for the League of Consciousness. The data indicated a positive evaluation of her performance. Levi then shifted his focus to another section of unencrypted data, revealing a comprehensive record of the committee members responsible for assessing Hope's suitability for LOC membership.

A concerned expression etched across Levi's face as he spoke. "Something's off here. Not all of these committee members are from the LOC. Look at this one."

He highlighted a specific line that expressed confidence in Hope's approval. However, the committee member's identity remained conspicuously absent. What added to the intrigue was that Levi found evidence of this committee member's communication with a party outside the LOC Headquarters. Shockingly, this external source was traced back to the location housing Encephalon Media Group's offices in Manhattan.

Hope's bewilderment deepened as she muttered, "This doesn't make sense. Why would someone at Encephalon have ties to the LOC?"

Levi posed the most logical question, "Could your father be involved in this somehow?"

In response, Hope shook her head vigorously, her eyes squinting in contemplation. "I have to go." She abruptly rose and left the table.

CHAPTER 10

As Hope emerges from the orb, the memory of the Magic Kingdom lingers in her mind. However, the relentless countdown timer continues its march toward zero, representing her dwindling time remaining on Earth. She has yet to uncover the elusive message for her father, a reality that further intensifies the situation. Filled with determination and a growing sense of time slipping away, she now turns her attention to Eada's next lesson on the intricate realm of Human Emotion.

Hope was back in Epoch's office, the orb suspended above the table. She couldn't contain her excitement, breathlessly sharing, "Eada saw me inside the orb, but she didn't know it was me!"

Aiko, always composed, raised her hand gently and expressed her understanding with genuine enthusiasm. "Yes, dear The Inverse holds many mysteries."

Epoch, ever straightforward, cut to the chase, "Did you identify the message?"

Hope's disappointment was evident in her response, "It all felt so real, but I couldn't locate the message. How will I recognize it when I see it?" Her voice carried a tinge of desperation. She glanced at the central monitor, displaying the relentless countdown: seven hours, fifty-three minutes, and forty-four seconds. Time, as she perceived it, was slipping away.

Epoch's voice, firm and reassuring, broke her contemplation, "Have faith in yourself, Hope. The message is there. You will recognize it when you see it." There was a subtle hint of uncertainty in Epoch's words.

"You are closer than you think," Aiko softly encouraged. "Perhaps you should get started with your next lesson." She nodded toward the pulsating orb.

With renewed determination, Hope prepared herself for another leap into the unknown. As she stepped toward the orb, it enveloped her, and she instantly found herself on a charming street. There, before her, was Eada, purposefully walking along. Eada's eyes scanned each residence as if searching for her destination. Hope watched, captivated by the scene unfolding before her.

Eada made her way down the corridor toward the Oculus Relatorum portals. The brief had given her precise directions to meet her instructor, John, and it read:

INSTRUCTOR: Pneuma Speaker—John Lennon
LUBHYATI: Eada
TRAINING SESSION TWO: Human Emotion
MEETING PLACE: Experiential Training Facility – Oculus Quinque
3D-Coordinates: Earth - 51.5187° N, 0.1600° W

As she walked, Eada spotted the Oculus up ahead on the left. Approaching, she felt relief as the marquee confirmed she was in the right place. The vertical threads of Oculus vibrated as if a session was already in progress. "Here we go again," she murmured, stepping through the archway and into her next lesson on Human Emotion.

Eada stood on a charming street with rows of terraced houses to her left. On her right, a well-maintained communal garden, enclosed by an artisanal wrought iron fence, added a touch of elegance to the square. Above her, oak and lime trees stretched their branches purposefully toward the clouds. The stucco façades of the residences contrasted beautifully with the red brick ascending the levels above, creating a harmonious visual symmetry.

As she strolled along the sidewalk, taking in the breathtaking surroundings, Eada was enchanted by the ornate street lamps. Twin baskets of colorful flowers hung from each side of the lamps, adding a burst of color to the scene. Each home exuded warmth and charm, sparking her curiosity about the stories that might reside within their walls.

Up ahead, she heard a noise emanating from one of the residences. The front door swung open, revealing a couple sipping wine. They shared a light-hearted laugh as they descended the steps, crossed the street, and settled at a table in the courtyard garden. There was something undeniably charming about this place.

Eada reached her destination and noticed iron railings guarding the steps leading to the entrance of the residence. She made her way to the front door and knocked. There was some movement from inside, and a friendly voice called out, "Hold on, Love. Won't be a moment."

Eada's mission brief had mentioned that, as a Pneuma, John hailed from a city called London in the United Kingdom and carried a British accent. When the door opened, she was greeted by a warm, smiling gentleman who extended his hand for a shake.

"Hi, Eada! I'm John. It's truly a pleasure to meet you."

"It's nice to meet you too, John," Eada smiled.

John chuckled, "The pleasure is all mine. I hope your journey to find the hooch wasn't too difficult."

Puzzled, Eada asked, "The hooch?"

John realized his mistake, "Oh, I'm being daft. Of course, it wasn't. You're right here in front of me."

John's long hair framed his thin face, and his hazel eyes peered through round glasses, giving him an aura of kindness and warmth. "I'd invite you in for tea, but my mates are about to make quite a racket. In a moment, we won't be able to hear ourselves think, let alone talk."

Eada smiled in agreement.

"Alright, then, let's be off," John exclaimed. He grabbed a jacket from a coat rack by the door, slung it over his shoulders, and casually tied a thin lime green scarf around his neck. As he shut the door behind them, Eada heard two loud thumps, followed by a playful ba-dum-bum-ching sequence. A snarling noise followed, forming a wall of sound, ushering them out the door as it echoed into the street.

With a warm smile, John said, "Those cheeky devils will be at it all night, love." He playfully winked at Eada as they strolled out into the street. The Oculus appeared instantly, and they approached the shimmering threads that hung in a harmonic glow, inviting them to explore the complexities of human emotions.

As they stepped through the archway, the world transformed around them, and they found themselves upon a verdant expanse of lawn framed by towering trees whose branches extended toward the sky with leaves rustling in the gentle breeze. Colorful flowers adorned meticulously maintained gardens, and the melodic chorus of blackbirds filled the air.

"Where are we?" Eada asked.

"Tittenhurst Park," John replied. "I live just over there, mate."

Where John pointed, a grand Georgian mansion stood as the crown jewel in this grand estate. Its classic architectural features exuded timeless elegance and charm. It was picturesque, and Eada was thrilled that her Pneuma would reside in such a beautiful world.

John then gestured toward a bench that sat under a towering oak tree. Its ancient and gnarled trunk rose with silent majesty from the earth. Its branches reached out like the arms of an elder, offering wisdom to those who cared to listen. In solitary pride, it stood as a sentinel of time, a living testament to the ever-changing world that had unfurled beneath its lofty boughs.

"Right over there, mate, is where something rather extraordinary happened. I uncovered the profound connection between our emotions and our beliefs. I was a member of a famous band back on Earth. Music was my life, my passion, yeah."

Eada listened intently, recognizing the depth of John's attachment to this place and the memories it held for him.

John went on. "I sat down just over there when the beginnings of a little ditty popped into my head. I ran home, sat at the piano, and penned the song, 'Imagine.' It was born from a surge of inspiration fueled by emotions—love, hope, and a deep longing for peace and happiness in my world. It was a song that urged the whole wide world to imagine a place without borders, free from the constraints of outdated beliefs. I aimed to convey that our emotions are inextricably tied to our beliefs and that we can compose a symphony of positive change if we only dared to envision the world we wished to inhabit."

As they wandered through the estate grounds, John shared more of his experiences and the emotions that had inspired his music. It was an idyllic setting for Eada to learn about human emotions and their role in shaping earthly reality.

John looked up at the sky and then around at their surroundings. Eada sensed that he was captivated by the moment, as if he wished they could stay there forever. He then manifested Eada's mission brief, quickly flipped through it, and said, "Ah, yes, very well. Let's get moving along then, shall we?"

The Oculus materialized just as he finished speaking, and they stepped through it. On the other side, Eada stood on a magnificent steel and stone bridge in a bustling city. It was a place of contrasts, where advanced technology harmoniously coexisted with old-world charm.

"Where are we?" Eada asked.

John beamed, his eyes sparkling with enthusiasm. "And *when* are we, Eada? Both are quite relevant. You're now in Paris, France, and it's the year 2054 on Earth."

Exquisite, streamlined vehicles glided soundlessly through the sky above, while translucent, chrome water taxis slid gracefully beneath the bridge. Wrought iron handrails adorned with thousands of padlocks flanked them on both sides, spanning the entire bridge.

"It's beautiful," Eada whispered, her eyes feasting on the visual banquet of Paris.

John nodded and explained, "The river flowing beneath us is the Seine, and we are standing on the historical Le Pont des Arts, also known as Love Lock Bridge." He gestured to the railings adorned with countless padlocks. "This bridge is a symbol of human love and commitment. Couples adorn the rails with a paddle lock and then toss the key into the river, symbolizing that their love is locked forever. It's a fun and emotional celebration of their union."

Eada was captivated by the fascinating human traditions.

John continued, "Your Pneuma will realize that emotions are the secret to unlocking the mystery of belief. And guess what? I have a groovy way to demonstrate this phenomenon. I think you'll dig it, yeah."

Eada stood on Love Lock Bridge, her curiosity ablaze, eager to unravel the intricate connection between human emotions and their pivotal role in shaping a person's chosen reality.

John's expression turned more serious, as if gearing up for a formal lesson. He remarked, "I'd like to show you something, Eada. When I snap my fingers, you will be completely immersed in a human's thread of conscious reality. You'll be right in the middle of her beliefs, emotions, and thoughts. You'll feel like this woman down to your very core. Instinctively, you will understand how time flows forward. And you'll be hit with a tidal wave of emotions—anticipation, fear, anxiety, joy, curiosity, hope, and wonder."

Eada's excitement grew as she contemplated the opportunity to gain a deeper understanding of the human experience. "What exactly triggers these emotions?"

With a gentle smile, John replied, "Well, love, in this case. But as you've learned from my good friend, Walt, these emotions are closely tied to this woman's beliefs."

Eada's mind raced back to her enlightening lesson with Walt. It had been a fascinating experience, and now she was on the verge of unraveling the intricate connection between emotions and beliefs.

John continued, "I reckon we should get started. Sometimes, it's easier to understand by just diving in. When I snap my fingers, you'll feel time passing and experience the sensation of being deeply in love with someone you met just a day ago, like this human in Paris. It will be rather bewildering for you. You and your romantic interest agreed to meet here on Love Lock

Bridge, and then you planned to grab some drinks. You got here early, and your date hasn't shown up yet. Are you with me?"

"Yes, but to clarify, I'll feel time passing as I wait for this person to show up?" Eada sought confirmation.

"That's the ticket, Eada. Ready to take the plunge?"

"Yes. I'm ready."

"Well then, let's be off!" At that moment, John raised his right hand to the level of their eyes and snapped his finger loudly.

As they stood on Love Lock Bridge, Eada instantly felt incredibly disoriented. So many strange feelings rushed through every particle of her existence as she entered the immersive experience of the human woman. They were all mashed together, and it took more work to focus on just one.

"Relax, Eada, it will settle in soon," John instructed. "Try to focus on the most dominant of your thoughts and emotions."

Eada turned her head to gaze down the bridge, growing increasingly anxious as she observed approaching pedestrians.

"That's right, Eada," John reassured her. "You're checking to see if he's there. You're wondering if he will show up. You're eagerly waiting for him. And what makes it most interesting is that you don't know if he will come. This is the feeling of anticipation. It doesn't come naturally to Inversians, but on Earth, you will experience it daily," John explained.

"Yes, and I . . . where is he?" Eada felt a physical surge of anxiety. Her heart raced, and a strange feeling washed over her. "Stop! Please stop!" she begged.

At that moment, John paused the reality thread. "Are you alright, Eada?" he asked.

"Yeah, I'll be okay," Eada replied, trying to regain her composure. The human emotions lingered as she blinked away the confusion.

"Would you fancy completing the lesson when you're feeling a bit better?" John asked.

"No, I can keep going. It just took me by surprise. Some of the emotions were incredible, but others were overwhelming. It was difficult to reconcile what was going on. But wow, that was intense!" Eada said with a laugh.

John matched her laughter and added, "You have no idea, my dear. It is quite the experience to be human."

Once Eada relaxed, John asked, "Are you ready to start again?"

"Yes, let's do this!"

"Alright, I'll put you back to the moment we paused the training," John said, resuming the exercise.

Eada was again immersed in the woman's reality, instantly inundated with the same human feelings, anticipations, and emotions. *I've got this*, she thought.

"I can see his face in my mind." Eada concentrated, trying to make sense of the influx of information flooding her consciousness. The woman whose perspective she had adopted for this training exercise wasn't from this place; she appeared to be a significant figure, possibly a high-ranking official. The woman was visiting Paris, presumably to deliver a speech or accept an award, though the details were somewhat fuzzy for Eada. She felt a peculiar connection to this personality yet couldn't quite pinpoint the reason. At this professional event, she encountered the man she was anticipating to meet on the bridge. Within this unique experience, other thoughts began to intrude upon her consciousness.

"I can sense the flow of time. It's so dense. I feel as if I'm stuck in something," Eada explained. "I hear my thoughts, my emotions. It's as though they are in a heated debate with each other. Some have already decided that he won't show up, while others are excited for when he does, and they can barely contain themselves."

John paused the lesson and turned to Eada.

"You mentioned 'they can barely contain themselves.' What did you mean by that?" he asked.

Eada hesitated, "It felt like there were multiple versions of me inside of me. I know it doesn't make sense, but that's the best way I can describe it."

"Ah, Eada, my dear," John chuckled softly, his amazement at her progress evident in his tone. "You've hit the nail on the head. It's impressive that you can identify the belief personas connected to the woman's emotions. These beliefs rushed in to share their stories and alert the woman to potential risks associated with her vulnerability. Most humans are unaware of this intricate link between their emotions and beliefs. It's as if they are connected through emotion to their past selves. But you, Eada, possess keen insight into what it was like for the woman." John's words were laced with excitement.

"Thank you," Eada said, appreciative of the compliment. But her curiosity lingered.

John continued, "I have come to understand a fascinating aspect of human perception related to time, which I like to call 'belief personas.' These facets of a person's character become fixed at specific moments in their life's timeline, frozen by significant events. Because human time flows in a single direction, these emotionally charged belief personas remain anchored in the past as what humans call memories. The human subconscious mind then links the past belief persona or memory, shaped by these momentous events, with the present circumstances in their life. This temporal alignment triggers a response from the past belief personas.

"These beliefs carry emotional, influential, or traumatic memories and leap forward to the present, warning the individual of potential dangers. It can be a rather unsettling experience. As you've already learned, this phenomenon introduces two variables into the human equation of reality: B and E. The E is the linchpin, you dig? By attentively listening to their emotions, rather than impulsively reacting to them, humans can forge a connection with their past belief personas and compassionately resolve whatever holds them captive."

Eada found it fascinating that humans, constrained by a singular dimension of time, were capable of creating temporal personalities that interacted with each other throughout a human timeline. She was eager to delve deeper into the lesson on Love Lock Bridge. As she sensed these internal personas rushing forward to protect the woman, she understood that these belief personas had developed their concerns or excitement based on past conditioned events. The memories from these events acted as picture frames surrounding an image of reality etched into the woman's timeline. These internal belief personas were bound to a fixed version of reality.

She also found it intriguing that each held a unique emotional state that varied widely. Some were thrilled about what would happen, while others were fearful or anxious. Some were defensive and prepared for heartbreak, while others were excited at the prospect of experiencing the sensation of falling in love all over again. And then it dawned on her.

"Humans compare the dynamic experiences of the present moment to their static belief personas of their past," she said. "Throughout their lives, various influences, traumas, teachings from others, or exhilarating experiences etch these internal belief personas into the human timeline."

"Bravo, Eada! Well done. That is an excellent grasp of human belief systems," John praised her with a broad smile.

Eada added, "Life on Earth must be incredibly complex. Is this a constant experiential phenomenon for human Pneuma?"

"Indeed, it is. Some folks are better at wranglin' it than others, but the critical bit is that this interplay of beliefs and the emotions they trigger is what informs human behavior whether they know it or not.

"Now, before we dive back in, I suggest a simple approach," John continued. "When I start this training thread, those emotionally charged belief personas will come rushing back like before. Your job is to acknowledge 'em with kindness, and then share four important sentiments. The first one? Well, it's about saying sorry for neglecting them, for not giving them their due recognition."

John went on, "The second one, my dear, is all about showing them your unconditional love, inviting them to be a positive part of your life, you know?" He grinned before going on, "Now, the third sentiment is all about embracing the present moment, telling 'em it's okay, that everything's just fine, and there's no need for them to rush in and play the hero anymore." His eyes sparkled with wisdom as he concluded. "And lastly, the fourth sentiment is believing in their safety, love, and protection. It's about letting go of those old fears and limiting beliefs, allowing 'em to break free from the chains of your Pneuma's timeline."

"That's it?" Eada responded, surprised by the simplicity of John's advice.

"Yeah, Eada, that's the ticket," John smiled and added, "It's a bit trickier than you'd think."

"I realize this is a training thread, but what does the woman do afterward?" Eada inquired.

"Live life, my dear! She will be standing there on Love Lock Bridge, waitin' for the person she fell in love with the moment she set eyes on him. It wouldn't be the right time or place to get into a long chat with her internal belief personas. She can do that down the line. I advise expressing those four sentiments sincerely and then agreeing to catch up with those belief personas later to discuss their worries in more depth."

"Ah, I see. That makes sense," Eada replied, appreciating the kindness, love, and respect inherent in John's approach. "And when she meets with them later, in human terms, what then?"

"You're doing a great job anticipating what comes next, Eada. Excellent. To answer your question, she should approach it as if she is helping a friend or loved one. Her goal should be to assist them in understanding what is troubling them, to listen to their stories, and to genuinely grasp their perspectives. Most importantly, she should convey who she is in the present moment, letting them know that she is alright and that they are too. When you practice this as your Pneuma, you will share everything about yourself, showcasing your strength, happiness, and knowledge. Be supportive and present for them, and empathize with them. Eventually, release them into infinity but ensure they understand they are always welcome to be a part of your world.

After some reflection, Eada responded, "That's fascinating."

"Indeed it is, Eada. I'm chuffed to bits that you're seein' it that way."

Eada's enthusiasm for her upcoming encounters with human emotions and their corresponding belief personas filled her with renewed energy. She felt prepared and ready to apply the tactical skills she had learned from John's wisdom.

"Alright, I'm ready now," Eada affirmed. She was instantly transported back into the woman's reality, standing on Love Lock Bridge. Just as John had described, a surge of emotions washed over her. She gazed expectantly toward the end of the bridge, but her love interest was nowhere in sight. Immediately, her most assertive internal belief personas stirred, inundating her with emotions. Eada wasted no time and sprang into action, keenly identifying the specific emotions of the moment.

She spoke within herself, extending kindness and directness to the belief persona. Though it didn't respond verbally, Eada sensed its attention. She continued, "I'm glad you're here, and I apologize for not acknowledging you sooner. I want you to know that I love you, and everything will be okay. Our life is going well, and there is no need to worry. You can stand down. I'd love to reconnect with you later. We have much to talk about."

In that moment, a wave of lightness washed over her entire being, quieting any inner turmoil and replacing it with excitement and anticipation for the future. Positive thoughts flowed freely through her consciousness, unveiling numerous possibilities.

Suddenly, a sense of passion washed over her, and she quickly turned her gaze back to the end of the bridge. In the distance, she saw him approaching, the man she had fallen head over heels for. Tall, handsome, with striking features and a smile that seemed to light up the entire city. A warm feeling started in her stomach, radiating throughout her body, creating an incredible sensation. Eada then found it interesting that she had to adjust her hair and wondered how she looked. She couldn't help the massive smile appearing across her face as he approached. Just as she was about to greet him, the training session ended abruptly, and Eada found herself back in the familiar blue luminescence of the Oculus's standard settings.

While flipping through Eada's mission brief, John spoke warmly, "Brilliant job, Eada! That was one of the most enjoyable and vibrant training sessions I've had the pleasure of conducting." He glanced at Eada, who stood there with tears streaming down her cheeks.

"Is he gone?" Eada asked, her voice filled with a sense of melancholy.

"Easy there, dear," John said as he approached, gently taking her hand and offering a reassuring look. "Human training can be quite overwhelming. Dry those tears. Everything is going to be alright in the universe. Nothing is ever truly gone or lost. Everything exists infinitely. I can assure you of that."

John's words were a comforting reminder, and as the sensations of her native reality came back into focus, Eada gathered herself and exclaimed, "Wow! That was intense!"

"I had a feeling you would find it exhilarating," John replied warmly.

Considering her experience and sensing that John was a passionate soul, Eada inquired, "John, did you ever fall in love when you were on Earth?"

John smiled, his eyes distant as if he were recalling something magical. "Yes, mate, I fell about as far as one could fall."

"I'll bet that was a fantastic experience. Was it love at first sight, like what the woman on the bridge experienced?"

"Indeed it was, my dear. Would you like to visit that thread with me? It's one I visit often."

"I'd be honored," Eada replied, surprised by the offer.

John waved his hand, and the Oculus appeared. "Follow me, mate." And they stepped through the vibrating threads.

Instantly, they were standing in an alleyway. In front of them stood a tall industrial building featuring large windows that allowed natural light to flood the space inside. The area resembled a simple storefront with a sign spanning the windows above that read INDICA GALLERY in tall, bold letters.

Two large pillars flanked the entrance, providing an aesthetic feature and necessary building support. The brick exterior added to the minimalistic and modern expression.

"What is this place?"

John stopped and looked through the windows into the gallery. "This is where I fell in love, mate." He said with a smile.

They entered the gallery. Still grasping the idea that love was something humans fell into, Eada reflected on her intensely emotional experience on Love Lock Bridge. She asked, "Did you already know the person you fell in love with?"

"No, mate. I had just met her here." John gestured toward the intriguing objects around them and remarked, "She's an exceptional artist. All of this work is hers."

They casually strolled through the gallery. John had his hands clasped behind his back as he contemplated the art displayed around them.

Eada then saw a ladder a half-dozen steps away from them. She noticed that the ladder led up to a magnifying glass hanging by a thread, inviting viewers to examine something inscribed on a canvas, oddly mounted on the ceiling.

"Ah, my favorite piece," John picked up his pace toward the ladder. Standing beside it, he said, "It's a reminder that if we choose to focus on what we want to achieve and follow our dreams, we can reach the top and make them a reality. I'd say it's a grand illustration of the $B \in E+T=R$ equation of human reality, don't you reckon?"

As Eada took in the object, she replied, "I suppose I do." She then squinted up toward the canvas hanging from the ceiling, but she couldn't make out the image or infer the message intended for the viewer. Suddenly, she realized the purpose of the magnifying glass.

Eada asked, "Can I see the answer through the magnifying glass?"

With a broad smile, John replied, "Give it a go, mate." And then he gestured for her to step up the ladder.

Eada's heart leaped as she climbed the rungs, her grip steady and sure. When she reached the top and peered through the magnifying glass, she felt a wave of warmth, happiness, and confidence wash over her at the sight of a word written in all caps: YES. Eada chuckled.

Turning back to share her emotions with John, she heard someone shout from across the gallery, "John! Oh, splendid, I'm delighted you've arrived. I want to introduce you to the artist!"

Eada looked on as the man and a woman headed toward them. She concluded that the striking woman must be the artist. She wore a simple yet elegant black dress, her eyes reflecting the colors of the art all around. Her face lit up with joy as they approached. With a broad smile, John held his hand out as the man said, "John, please allow me to introduce my dear friend Yoko Ono. She's the brilliant mind behind these magnificent works of art, don't you know? Yoko, may I introduce my good friend, John Lennon."

As Yoko and John's eyes met, they gently held each other's hands. Eada felt as if she had simply disappeared into the background. She was no longer part of John's reality.

The lesson, she concluded, had suddenly and lovingly ended. At that moment, Eada saw the archway of the Oculus appear on the other side of the gallery. She paused, feeling great appreciation for her instructor as she witnessed his encounter with the love of his life. Eada smiled, appreciating the romantic gesture of choosing this thread to celebrate John's deep connection with the power of emotion. With a newfound understanding of the variable $\in E$, Eada stepped quietly off the ladder and made her way to the Oculus.

CHAPTER 11

Earth, 2046. Gabriel Valencia grapples with the consequences of his creation, the C.A.I.N Hive, and Ronan Hayes's tyrannical rule. He seeks redemption and a way to free humanity from its digital prison.

Stepping off the elevator, Gabe found himself in Ronan's spacious top-floor office. His eyes were immediately drawn to Sophia Mendez, deep in conversation with two sharply dressed men. Their intense discussion provoked his suspicion, and as Sophia noticed him, she broke away from the conversation and headed in his direction.

Curious, Gabe asked, "Who are those guys?"

Sophia quipped, "Oh, Tweedledee and Tweedledum? They're just a couple of boneheads Ronan has working on a project. As usual, I'm left cleaning up a mess. What can I do for you, Gabe?" She flashed a quick smile.

"I received a message from Ronan that he wanted to see me. I've got a super busy day, so I thought I'd connect with him this morning before it gets too hectic.

Sophia seemed surprised, "Oh, that's odd. I wasn't aware that he needed you this morning. I'll let him know you're here. Please, make yourself comfortable, Gabe."

With that, she slipped away toward Ronan's office. Gabe took a moment to enjoy the view of Central Park, pondering the eccentricity of the people he dealt with daily.

His thoughts were interrupted as Sophia returned, announcing, "Ronan will see you now, Gabe."

Entering Ronan's office, Gabe noticed him standing by the glass wall, gazing at the city. "Good morning, Ronan."

Ronan, never one for pleasantries, simply said, "Have a seat."

Gabe settled into a chair across from Ronan's desk, letting Ronan lead the conversation. Ronan, always one to enjoy the sound of his voice, got straight to the point.

"I got word that you've been running simulated hacking protocols on various C.A.I.N. Hive AI nodes. I was curious as to why. I can't see that they are assigned to a specific project."

Gabe paused, carefully choosing his words. "I've been investigating a potential security threat," he replied cautiously. "It's just a hunch at this point, but I believe it's worth looking into."

He didn't like lying, but knew he couldn't reveal why he'd been accessing the Hive nodes.

Ronan nodded thoughtfully. "I see. Do you mind sharing your hunch with me? Maybe I can help."

Gabe hesitated, then responded, "Oh, sure. It's not fully nailed down, and I'd rather create a formal report once I have my ducks in a row." He hoped his answer would satisfy Ronan.

Just as they were getting into the conversation, Sophia interrupted them.

Annoyed, Ronan replied, "What is it, Sophia?"

"Forgive me, Mr. Hayes. Sam just rang. He wanted to know if you still needed a lift this evening?"

Ronan affirmed, "Yes, I will, and let him know I'll need to be back in the city Friday for the weekend party."

"Consider it done," Sophia replied before swiftly leaving the room and closing the door behind her.

Ronan, unfazed by the interruption, resumed his questioning. "Where were we? Oh, yes. Can you share the basics with me? Where's the attack coming from? Was there an actual breach?"

Gabe had prepared a plausible yet cryptic response to keep Ronan satisfied. "Catching up on reports, I stumbled on a potential Russian Zero Hour Threat. When I looked at it closer, I saw a familiar algorithm. When I dug in deeper, the code evaporated. It just disappeared." Gabe admired his cleverness.

Ronan, showing genuine concern, pressed further, "What do you mean it evaporated? Code doesn't just disappear. It's got to be in there somewhere."

"Of course you're right; that's precisely what I thought and why I've been banging away at the network," Gabe continued, maintaining the façade. "As the system operates on quantum computing hardware, it seems to be due to the quantum observer effect. My observation of the system seems to be impacting it. I believe I should be able to hunt it down by installing an AI agent. If we need to go that route, I'll need to install a self-destruct mode on the agent. We won't be able to stop it otherwise once it's in the system."

Gabe had just inadvertently laid the groundwork for his cover story, which would grant him access to explore and make installations within the C.A.I.N. Hive nodes across the globe.

Ronan inquired, "Have you been working with Luca on it?"

"I've thought about it, but I can manage it independently for now," Gabe responded cautiously. He had reservations about engaging Luca Bracken, Encephalon's head of cybersecurity, who inexplicably displayed unwavering loyalty to Ronan.

Ronan concluded, "I need you to keep me informed if you find anything. Okay?"

"Five-by-five, count on it," Gabe reassured him.

Before Gabe could make his exit, Ronan slipped in a casual inquiry, "Thanks, Gabe. Oh, and are you going to the party this weekend?"

Gabe inwardly groaned at the prospect of attending Ronan's party. He avoided Ronan at every opportunity, hoping to find a way out of engaging with him any more than he absolutely had to. With a forced smile, he replied, "Ah, yes, we'll be there. Saturday night, right?"

"Excellent," Ronan replied. "And yes, it starts at eight at my penthouse. Show up any time after that. I'm looking forward to seeing you and Ella. It's been over a year since we've had some fun together. By the way, how are you and the family doing these days?"

"To be perfectly honest, not exactly how we imagined," Gabe replied, choosing his words carefully.

"How do you mean, Gabe? I thought you guys set the bar when it came to a loving, modern family unit. What's going on?"

Gabe was tempted to unleash his frustrations but stopped himself. He couldn't tell Ronan that his daughter, now a fully immersed member of the League of Consciousness, wouldn't speak to him and that he was willing to do anything—including corporate espionage—to earn back her respect.

"Thank you for asking, Ronan. We've been going through some tough times lately, but we're doing our best to work through it as a family." Gabe kept his answer brief, knowing he had to maintain his composure and avoid raising suspicions about his true intentions. "I'll let you know if I find anything in the network. Is there anything else you need?"

"No, I don't think so," Ronan replied.

"Great. I'll see myself out," Gabe said, abruptly standing up. He turned and left Ronan's office without saying goodbye.

Gabe was near the elevator's call button when he heard Sophia shout across the office, "Gabe, hold up!"

Now what? Gabe was in a hurry to leave the floor as soon as possible, and now this.

She crossed the span of the office quickly and addressed Gabe as she caught up with him just before he stepped onto the elevator. "You may have covered this with Ronan, but I needed to confirm if you and Ella will make it to the weekend party."

"It looks that way, yes." Gabe's reply lacked enthusiasm.

"Wonderful!" She stood close to Gabe's side, locked her arms, tilted her head close to his ear, and whispered, "When you arrive, I'd stay off the ninety-seventh floor. Just come straight up to the penthouse on the ninety-eighth. Trust me, Ella won't appreciate what's on the ninety-seventh."

With an aggravated tone, Gabe's face turned red. "What the hell's going down on the ninety-seventh floor, Sophia?"

Defensively, she reacted, "Relax, Gabe. You sound as if we're engaged in some ritualistic cult sacrifice. It's just that Ronan wanted an area for his rowdier friends to blow off steam, if you know what I mean." Sophia smiled, gave him a sexy wink, and added, "Ronan wanted to sequester any of those antics, and I assumed it would be thoughtful to let you know."

Gabe knew he needed to reel in his patience. Losing Sophia's favor would harm his life and plans in many ways. "Forgive me. I appreciate the heads-up. Honestly, I wasn't planning on going, and Ella won't be too pleased when I tell her I've committed to making an appearance. I'd appreciate it if you kept my venting between us."

"Of course, Gabe, and I get it. I know it isn't your scene. Please understand that Ronan has a great deal of respect for you. Of all the hundreds of guests coming from every corner of the globe, you're the only RSVP Ronan has been hounding me about. He cares about you, Gabe. It would mean a lot to him for you to join us and have some fun."

Gabe considered what Sophia said. Over the years, he felt that he and Ronan had become distant to the point that they were always at odds with each other. Rarely did they agree on anything, especially regarding the subject of C.A.I.N. Hive developments.

"We'll be there, Sophia. Count on it."

"Excellent. Thanks, Gabe." She smiled and headed to her next meeting.

Gabe had been holding the elevator doors open while he spoke to Sophia, and it was beginning to beep. He stepped inside as his mixed-reality glasses notified him that he had an incoming encrypted message. He put them on as he watched the doors close. The device prompted him for security clearance. He supplied the requisite verbal command.

"Gabriel Valencia. Display message on my voice authority."

Gabe's heart skipped a beat as the message appeared on the screen. It confirmed the meeting at Cipriani's at 7:30 p.m. He felt a sense of unease. Things were about to get real. Gabe was about to cross a threshold where there was no return. He reminded himself that he had to trust this man. Something in the way he spoke to Gabe made him believe he was sincere.

This was the Encephalon executive he needed on his side, the exact person who could help him advance his objectives. It was the right opportunity at the right time, but it all seemed too perfect. Despite his reservations, Gabe knew he had to go through with it. He couldn't afford to let this opportunity slip away. Besides, it was just dinner. He could control the narrative and steer the conversation in his favor.

"Sir? Nothing is moving up 42nd Street. It will take some time to make our way to Park Avenue," Sol reported. Gabe knew Sol always did everything possible to ensure he would arrive on time for any function or meeting. Punctuality was the priority, but in instances like this, Gabe understood.

"No worries, Sol. I need to stretch my legs. A few blocks of walking will do me good," Gabe replied, appreciating the opportunity to clear his mind with a short walk.

"Keep your eyes open, sir. The city isn't what it used to be, not even here," Sol expressed his genuine concern. Gabe knew Sol had a deep affection for his family, and he valued his driver's care and attention.

"Drop me in front of the library. Thanks, Sol."

"Roger that, sir."

Exiting the Maybach, Gabe headed toward the crosswalk. Although he might think twice about walking in other parts of the city at this time of night, making the short walk from Fifth Avenue to the historic Grand Central Terminal on Park Avenue felt relatively safe.

Gabe approached his destination, the old Grand Central Terminal, one of the city's most beloved architectural landmarks. The crisp night air invigorated him, and the walk served as a mental reset before the meeting. It was a pivotal opportunity, and Gabe needed everything to go as planned.

As he arrived at the grand entrance of the iconic Italian restaurant, he was comforted by the nostalgia it evoked. The aroma of garlic, tomatoes, and parmesan wafted through the air, immersing him in its inviting ambiance.

"Hello, Dr. Valencia. What a nice surprise. Will you be dining with us this evening?" the maître d' inquired.

"Ciao, Francesco. Yes, I believe the reservation is under Porter Goderun."

"Ah, Si, molto bene! He arrived about ten minutes ago. If I had known you were joining us, I would have provided a different table. Would you like me to move you?"

"No, no, that won't be necessary. Thanks, Francesco. I'm sure the table is perfect."

"Bene! Bene! Right this way, Dr. Valencia."

As they headed toward the table, Gabe was enveloped in a comforting sense of stability. Cipriani's on 42nd Street remained unchanged after so many decades. The Italian Renaissance-inspired ceilings soared above, while marble columns held up intricate stone archways. The interior exuded elegance, adorned with striking chandeliers. It was a place steeped in generational dependability and gastronomical perfection. He cherished numerous memories of sharing meals and moments with family, friends, and colleagues in this charming establishment.

Approaching the table, Gabe noticed that Porter appeared nervous. *At least I'm not the only one.*

Porter stood to greet Gabe, offering a polite "Hello, Dr. Valencia," as they shook hands.

"Hello, Porter. Please, call me Gabe."

As the maître d' departed, leaving them to their clandestine meeting, Gabe quietly commented, "You're either insane or a genius. I can't decide."

Porter laughed nervously, a reflexive response to feeling offended, evident from the look on his face.

Gabe continued, his intention clear. "Cipriani's? Really?"

Porter replied, explaining his choice. "We're just two executives having a late-night dinner before a complex meeting. I figured hiding our rendezvous in plain sight would be best." He glanced around the restaurant and added, "The more people see us, the better. And besides, I know that the al Limone is your favorite dish in the city. Oh, and let's not forget white truffle season is just ending. This might be our last chance before next fall," he said, smiling.

"How did you know that al Limone was . . . ?"

Porter quickly reassured him, "Don't worry, Gabe. I'm not a spy; I'm the farthest from it. I read the New York Business Magazine article on you last month."

"Ah, right." Gabe reciprocated the smile. He hadn't fully adjusted to the idea that so much information about him was publicly accessible with a quick search.

Meeting up with Porter posed considerable risks, but Gabe had reached a point where he couldn't ignore the potential rewards. This encounter was either a stroke of luck or a move driven by Ronan Hayes's neurotic suspicions. Regardless, the possible gains were too significant to pass up.

The server arrived with a silver bread basket filled with warm Tuscan rolls and took their drink orders. They declined the offer to open a bottle of Giuseppe Quintarelli Valpolicella Classico, Gabe's preferred red wine at Cipriani's. Instead, he opted for a Pappy Van Winkle, fifteen, neat, needing something with a bit more punch for this meeting.

"It's reassuring to know I'm not the only one," Gabe admitted, eager to delve into the matter.

Porter, slightly taken aback by Gabe's directness, asked, "What do you mean?"

Gabe clarified, his voice hushed, "To find a way to stop Ronan. To cut the strings away from the puppeteer. I'm thrilled that we share the same concern for humanity's future and that Encephalon Media Group is enemy number one."

Porter squirmed in his seat and scanned the restaurant nervously, clearly surprised by Gabe's bluntness.

Porter replied in a hushed yet concerned tone, "Are you out of your mind? We're in public."

Gabe was satisfied with Porter's reaction. It was a test, and Porter had passed. He was a computer scientist, not an actor. His response indicated he was on the right side.

"Relax, Porter. No one can hear us," Gabe assured him, placing a small black device on the table.

Porter visibly relaxed, smiled, and inquired, "Latest model?"

"Yep, N-700 in the flesh. There are only three in the city like it."

The N-series was renowned for its anti-surveillance capabilities, and the N-700 was only rumored to exist. Any conversation within its six-foot radius was thoroughly scrambled, offering a bubble of confidentiality that surpassed all security measures.

Impressed, Porter commented, "I guess the C-suite has its perks. I wasn't aware that the 700 was even available."

"It's available, all right, for a hefty price. And you can see the green light indicating that it's active. If I weren't on your side . . ."

Porter interrupted, "I get it, Gabe. Shall we get to business?"

Gabe nodded, eager to hear what Porter had to say.

"We need to work together on this and move the needle soon. I would have never engineered such a wide-reaching system if I had any idea that Encephalon would use the C.A.I.N. Hive to . . ."

Gabe interjected, "I would have never aligned QTD-AI technology with Encephalon. We both have dirty hands and regrets. What matters now is that we work together and do something about it. Let's focus on the present opportunity, not our past mistakes."

After a moment of silence, Porter agreed, "I have a plan, Gabe. There's a lot to work out, and it's dangerous. The level of security sophistication is like nothing on the planet."

"But you built the network. I mean, you know its weaknesses, right?" Gabe was concerned that this meeting might have been in vain.

Porter reassured him, "Relax, Gabe. I do, but it's not that simple."

Gabe pressed, "And?"

Just then, the server arrived with their drinks, clinking clear ice cubes resonating in the crystal glasses. After their orders, the server inquired about their entrée selections and graciously thanked them in Italian before heading for the kitchen.

Porter then provided an answer to Gabe's question. "Well, for one, we can't use generative AI solutions. They are too aggressive for the QTD-AI system's intricacies and the C.A.I.N. Hive protocols. If they aren't detected first, they'll likely wreak havoc on the cognitive bridging protocols. We can't risk that."

Gabe felt the weight of Porter's report. He had been relying on automation to dismantle the network, but now they would have to undertake manual work, leaving a trail that could lead back to them. It was a laborious and time-consuming process, and it increased their exposure.

Desperate for an alternative, Gabe suggested, "Are you one hundred percent certain of that? What if we established transit bots?"

Porter shook his head, dismissing the idea. "Gabe, please, stop. Why would I be sitting here with you if there were a way to utilize AI? I've spent the last year trying to find a way to keep my hands clean. It's impossible, and frankly, I worry that the AI could mutate into something we couldn't stop, that no one could stop."

Porter's cautious approach was well-founded, and Gabe respected his experiential knowledge. If Porter had reservations, they were worth considering.

Gabe asked, "So, what are we looking at here?"

Porter's response was disheartening. "Possibly several years. I'll need to develop the device artifacts directly inside the AI nodes. I can't find any other way."

"Several years!" Gabe scoffed in frustration. It was far longer than he had hoped for.

Porter continued, "I'll need a constant stream of approved projects to hide our work. That can only come from your desk. We're an agile development team, so I won't have much trouble getting the projects into the development roadmap. We'll need to work together to determine the reasoning behind the work product. I have a few ideas that I've been working out in my head."

The enormity of the task and the time it would take to complete it weighed heavily on Gabe. Yet, he knew that this was the only way to stop Encephalon.

Gabe's mixed-reality device chimed with an incoming call. He glanced at it and saw that it was Poet.

"Excuse the interruption," Gabe said, "but this is my son. Do you mind if I take the call? It won't take long."

Porter nodded. "Family first, always."

"Thanks, Porter." Gabe deactivated the N-700 to enable signal transmission and answered the call. "Hello, son. I'm at dinner with a colleague, so I have to keep it brief."

As Poet shared the exciting news about their upcoming meeting with Mr. Archibald, Gabe felt a surge of pride and gratitude for his son's competence and commitment. It was fantastic news, and he was delighted to hear that everything was proceeding according to plan.

During their conversation, Gabe subtly inquired about Poet's plans for the weekend, hinting at the possibility of a family dinner.

"Okay, thanks, Poet," Gabe said warmly. "We'd love to have you and your sister over for dinner sooner than later. If you talk to her, please let her know and tell her we love her."

The call ended and Gabe turned his attention back to Porter as he reactivated the N-700. "Where were we? Ah, yes . . . Time."

Porter leaned in, his demeanor focused. "And lots of it."

"We don't have much choice, Porter," Gabe said, his resolve unwavering. "Let's get started. I'm also happy to report that a stroke of luck came earlier today."

Porter's eyebrows raised with curiosity. "I welcome any luck we can get. What is it?"

Gabe leaned in, sharing a conspiratorial grin. "I think I was able to get us a hall pass, at least for a while."

Porter, more intrigued now said, "What exactly do you mean by 'hall pass?'"

With a sly smile, Gabe explained, "Earlier today, Ronan called me to the table about some of my network reconnaissance. I almost had a heart attack, but I quickly threw out a story that I found a Russian Zero Hour Threat and that as I investigated, the code evaporated."

Porter chuckled, amused. "Evaporated? Code doesn't just evaporate, Gabe. You, of all people, know that."

"I know, I know," Gabe admitted, grinning. "I made something up about the quantum observer effect, and Ronan bought it. He thinks I saw it disappear. It just fell out of my mouth. I sold him on the idea that I had to keep looking for it, no matter how long it took or how far across the network I had to investigate."

Porter seemed genuinely impressed. "This is perfect, Gabriel. Nicely done! And you've given me an excellent idea. I'll build a seemingly malicious code that acts as if it self-destructs. I'll engineer some self-deleting protocol. We'll hide it, find it, and then record it disappearing for Ronan and the Cyber Security team to see for themselves. It will provide us with the perfect pretext to enter the nodes."

As they continued to discuss their plans, Gabe's mind wandered to his disappointment about the situation with Encephalon. In his heart, he knew there was no other way to move forward. He had to act soon to get the world and his relationship with Hope back on track.

Their dinner concluded, and as they exited the restaurant, Porter thanked Gabe for meeting him.

Gabe watched Sol pull the family Maybach directly in front of the steps. "Can I give you a lift?" Gabe offered politely.

Porter declined, "No, that's unnecessary, but thank you, Gabe. I enjoyed getting to know you more. I hope you know I wouldn't be interested in taking such drastic measures if it were anyone else."

Gabe replied, sincere in his response, "I'm truly honored by that. Thank you, Porter. We can do this. We can get things back on track."

The two men shook hands and said their goodbyes. Gabe watched as Porter made his way down Park Avenue. Gabe then stepped into the back of the Maybach. The environmental controls were set perfectly for his comfort, including the elegant notes of Beethoven's Symphony No. 3 echoing throughout the cabin.

"Where to, sir?" Sol asked.

"Let's go home, Sol," Gabe replied, contemplating the monumental task ahead.

CHAPTER 12

Still in The Inverse alongside Epoch and Aiko, Hope is poised for a transformative moment: the unveiling of Eada's profound lesson on the impact of Human Thought. This lesson isn't just an exploration of concepts; it's Hope's final opportunity to uncover a message of paramount importance. It's a message destined for her father, Gabriel, laden with the potential to steer humanity onto the correct thread of probable reality.

Hope's gaze shifted to the timer displayed prominently on the central monitor just as the orb began its slow expansion around her. The numbers blinked incessantly, a countdown that bore the weight of her destiny. Only three hours and forty-seven minutes remained.

A wave of unease washed over her. What if she couldn't uncover the message in time? The pressure mounted with each passing second, threatening to overwhelm her. But Hope refused to succumb to doubt. She pushed those paralyzing thoughts aside, refocusing her mind on the task at hand.

With a resolute breath, she steeled herself. She had embarked on this extraordinary journey for a reason, and failure was not an option. Determination coursed through her very existence, reminding her of the countless hurdles she had already surmounted. She had traversed dimensions beyond imagination, and now, in the heart of The Inverse, she was prepared to find the message that held the key to humanity's future. Hope whispered a silent vow to herself as uncertainty loomed: *I will succeed, no matter the challenges that lie ahead.*

At that very moment, a breathtaking sight materialized before her eyes. She saw Eada standing on a graceful bridge spanning a pristine river, surrounded by one of the most captivating settings Hope had ever encountered.

Eada stood as the calm and pristine river flowed below her. It was beautiful, and she took a moment to admire the landscape, her gaze tracing the river's winding course as far as her eyes could see. For a fleeting moment, doubt crept into her thoughts. Could she have inadvertently stepped through the wrong Oculus? Eada materialized her mission brief and consulted the class schedule. As she scanned the details, everything seemed in order:

INSTRUCTOR: Pneuma Speaker—Stephen Hawking
LUBHYATI: Eada
TRAINING SESSION THREE: Human Thought
MEETING PLACE: Experiential Training Facility – Oculus Undecim
3D-Coordinates: Earth – 52°12'21" N 0°06'50"

The sun bathed the scene in a gentle glow, casting shimmering reflections on the water's surface. The soprano serenade of reed warblers and the soft buzzing hum of insects filled the air. Eada felt a profound sense of tranquility wash over her, urging her to momentarily set aside her mission and embrace the serenity of her surroundings.

On the river's eastern bank, imposing gothic-style structures rose to her left, each vying for attention with its delicate stone-carved spires and ornate stone dressings surrounding leaded glass windows. These architectural marvels exuded charm and sophistication. Eada's gaze fell upon meticulously manicured parks adorned with expansive lawns and various gardens connected by tree-lined pathways. Standing at the bridge's crest, she took in the view from this vantage point, its angle gently sloping downward. The dark slate stone beneath her feet provided a sturdy foundation for the ornate wrought iron handrails that spanned both sides. It was an idyllic scene. Eada slowly turned in a circle, savoring the magnificence that surrounded her. *I hope my Pneuma lives here,* she thought.

Just then, chatter from beneath the bridge caught her attention. Curious, she gripped the handrail, leaned over, and peered into the river below. A punt glided gracefully from underneath the bridge, guided by a man standing at the stern. He skillfully maneuvered the boat, using a long pole to plunge into the riverbed, propelling the punt forward. Two joyful couples occupied the boat, their laughter echoing in the serene atmosphere.

As the passengers looked up and saw Eada leaning over the bridge, they greeted her with waves and hellos. Eada responded with a warm smile and returned their friendly gestures, feeling connected with the world around her.

"A penny for your thoughts."

The voice startled Eada, causing her to spin around abruptly. Standing there was a young man in his late teens, dressed in a somewhat chaotic yet charming ensemble. His tousled hair suggested a youthful demeanor, as did the innocence of having his hands tucked into his trouser pockets. He wore an oxford sweater over a white collared shirt—the right hem of which remaining untucked—with a blue necktie. A cobalt blue sports jacket adorned with a crest featuring two crossed rowing oars completed his outfit. His thin frame made the attire appear too big for him. Behind his black-framed spectacles, kind and intelligent eyes gazed warmly at her. A mischievous twinkle danced in his eyes as he spoke, "It's an Earth expression."

He paused, still wearing that friendly smile. "But I digress. I saw you lost in thought and wanted to join you. It's a beautiful view, isn't it? I often come here to think and ponder the mysteries of the universe."

"You must be Stephen?"

"Indeed, and it's nice to meet you, Eada." Stephen reached out his hand as he walked toward her on the bridge. As they shook hands, Eada knew immediately that she liked the young man.

"It's nice to meet you as well, Stephen."

"Shall we begin?" Stephen motioned toward the far end of the bridge.

As the two strolled down the gentle slope, Eada asked, "Can you tell me more about this place?"

"Of course, Eada," Stephen replied with a deep sense of pride and nostalgia. He gestured behind them, "Just over there is where I pursued my studies on Earth at Trinity College."

Eada glanced back, appreciating the picturesque surroundings. "It's truly enchanting. I can see why you like it here."

Stephen looked around and then responded with a hint of amazement, "Indeed, Eada. It is indubitably magical to be here."

They reached the end of the bridge, taking in the tranquil scenery. With a simple gesture, Stephen summoned the Oculus, and it appeared before them, ready to transport them to another immersive aspect of Eada's lessons. As they stepped through the shimmering dimensional threads, Stephen turned to Eada.

"Have you ever seen the Milky Way up close, Eada?"

Eada glanced at Stephen, intrigued by his question. His warm smile radiated excitement as he nodded ahead. "Well, it's high time you did."

As they ventured through the threads of the Oculus, the world around them underwent a remarkable transformation. They suddenly found themselves suspended in the boundless expanse of space. A brilliant burst of light extended across the entire horizon, unveiling the Milky Way, a celestial river brimming with stars and cosmic marvels. Eada's eyes widened as she witnessed such a breathtaking spectacle. It exceeded her greatest expectations.

"You know, it's Earth's very own galaxy, and let me assure you, it is one of the most awe-inspiring sights in the universe," Stephen said. "But, even more significantly, it's the ideal starting point for our exploration of Human Thought and its pivotal role in the symbolic equation of reality. It's all about the 'T,' Eada. Trust me, the $B \in E+T=R$ equation would never quite add up to the sum of R without it."

Stephen, too, was captivated by the celestial display. "You see, Eada, sometimes words and pictures fall short in conveying the true magnificence of the universe. To truly grasp its beauty, you have to experience it firsthand."

As they gazed upon the star systems, Stephen began, "It is important to understand that during the time your Pneuma spends on Earth, it will be bound by their current understanding of thought and its role in shaping their reality. Humans are not yet fully aware of the universal gift they have been granted. They possess the remarkable ability to project their thoughts outward, connecting with the quantum realm, and in doing so, they shape the physical world around them. Just like Inversians, human thoughts have the power to construct entire universes within universes, whether they realize it or not."

Eada nodded in understanding.

Stephen continued, "Everything you see here—the vast cosmos, stars, planets, even the tiniest particles that make them up—all originate from belief. Belief triggers emotion, resonating into thought, collectively giving rise to what humans perceive as reality. If thought is the master builder, then belief is the architect."

Eada remained endlessly fascinated by the unique temporal dimension of humans, which confined their experience to a singular timeline. This peculiarity led to a delayed manifestation of reality and shed light on their struggle to understand how thoughts functioned within their world.

Further explaining, Stephen added, "Even on the scale of an entire galaxy, nothing exists without first the thought of it. My affinity for empirical evidence limited my perspective during my life on Earth. The idea that my physical universe was a construct of thought," Stephen paused, reflecting on his following words, "well, let's just say I found it quite challenging to accept."

Eada's curiosity was piqued as she listened.

Stephen's eyes filled with a spark of reminiscence. "I introduced the idea that eventually became known as the Big Bang theory. It was my way of grappling with the notion that everything had to have a starting point. My theory suggested that this starting point occurred when an infinite amount of matter, crammed into an infinitely small space, exploded outward in all directions, setting the birth of the universe in motion."

Eada nodded, "It's fascinating how your theory parallels the power of thought."

"How so, Eada?"

"Your explanation of the Big Bang theory; doesn't it sound remarkably similar to the outcome of a thought, human or otherwise?"

A wide grin spread across Stephen's face. "Indeed, Eada. Indeed."

Stephen waved his hand above him, and suddenly, a swarm of glowing particles floated around them. Eada quickly recognized the particles as Conscious Agents.

"Eada," Stephen began, his voice carrying reverence, "understand that a 'human thought' is not a mere fleeting neural impulse confined to their brain. It possesses a tangible essence, a life that endures infinitely from its inception."

As they observed the mesmerizing quantum particles, Stephen continued, "Picture a human's thought as an energetic beacon, a signal that transcends the boundaries of their physical form. These 'thought frequencies' embark on a profound journey into the quantum realm, where they engage with Conscious Agents."

Eada marveled at the graceful choreography of the agents as they elegantly responded to their incoming thought frequencies. Stephen added, "Conscious Agents form the very bedrock of reality, the fundamental framework upon which the universe is constructed. When they receive thought instructions, they awaken from their dormant state and elegantly arrange themselves into an intricate string of energy."

He elaborated, "From there, they cascade through various strata of existence, transitioning from energy into quarks, protons, neutrons, and eventually coalescing into atoms and molecules. This intricate process culminates in the creation of the physical world." Stephen held his arms outward to the celestial display of the Milky Way.

Eada felt a surge of excitement as she considered the incredible potential for her Pneuma to shape its reality, similar to Inversians, albeit without the instantaneous effect she and her peers experienced in The Inverse.

Stephen and Eada stood in silence, their eyes fixed on the mesmerizing spectacle of the Milky Way. It was a magnificent display of consciousness woven into a vast galaxy of possibilities. The universe unveiled its grandeur in a breathtaking dance of creation.

Breaking the tranquil stillness, Stephen turned to Eada, his voice tinged with anticipation. "I'd like to show you something, Eada." With a graceful wave of his hand, the Oculus materialized before them.

Eada's curiosity surged, aware that Stephen was about to lead her into another uncharted dimension. She nodded in agreement, and they ventured through the Oculus. In an instant, they materialized in an entirely different realm, greeted by an unfamiliar landscape. Eada quickly realized they were on a planet, and her immediate assumption was that it was Earth. She looked around, absorbing the stunning view. They stood on a massive wall that extended over lush, rolling hills as far as she could see.

The sun bathed the landscape in its golden warmth, and a solitary falcon soared gracefully above, its haunting call echoing through the cerulean sky.

Eada, overwhelmed by its beauty, asked, "Where are we?" Her eyes widened with amazement.

Stephen looked out over the earthly landscape and replied matter-of-factly, "We're on Earth in a country called China. This structure, Eada, is what humans call the Great Wall of China."

As Eada absorbed the colossal structure that stretched into the distance, she was intrigued by its significance. "What exactly is the Great Wall of China?" she asked.

Stephen's eyes gleamed with enthusiasm as he prepared to share a lesson about the remarkable power of human thought in shaping the physical world.

"The Great Wall of China," he began, "is a remarkable example of how human beliefs, emotions, and thoughts can shape the reality of entire societies. Humans can achieve extraordinary feats once they understand this collectively and individually."

Her gaze fixed on the immense structure, Eada couldn't hide her curiosity. "I understand that humans don't possess the power to manifest an object or dimensional reality instantly. So how can their thoughts create something as massive as this?"

Stephen smiled, recognizing the complexity of the idea he was about to explain. "It all begins with belief, Eada," he clarified. "The individuals who constructed this wall held a deep belief in its purpose. They believed it would protect their civilization from threats and invaders. These beliefs were fueled by powerful emotions, like duty, honor, and love for their land and people."

Eada nodded. "So, their beliefs and emotions led to their thoughts, which led to this wall?"

Stephen nodded in agreement. "Precisely. The collective power of their thoughts, fueled by strong beliefs and emotions, rippled outward like waves on a pond. These thought signals resonated with Conscious Agents, sparking innovations, ideas, materialization of resources, and the flow of energies throughout their society. This extraordinary process unfolded over two thousand years, measured in human terms. When beliefs, emotions, and thoughts align, the potential for creative acts becomes boundless. It does, however, require time in the physical realm. The reality within the mind eventually manifests itself in tangible form on the outside. Believing in the journey itself is the key to realizing this potential."

Eada's eyes widened with understanding. "I see it now," she exclaimed. "I always knew that Conscious Agents are the fundamental building blocks of reality, but it didn't fully dawn on me that they operate similarly in the physical world as in The Inverse."

She surveyed the area, astounded by this remarkable example of human accomplishment. "It's as if Conscious Agents gifted the builders with vision and an extra dose of strength and endurance, all through the conduit of Human Thought."

Stephen nodded in agreement, a sense of admiration in his eyes. "You've grasped it, Eada. Human determination, creativity, and action were crucial in this monumental endeavor. They transported massive stones across vast distances, used various construction methods, and drew from a diverse workforce, all guided by the thoughts rooted in their beliefs and emotions. It truly showcases how the collective consciousness of humanity, expressed through thought, can remarkably shape the physical world. The land, people, passion, beliefs, and resources available to them are all a product of consciousness that springs to life through the activation of thought."

Eada was intrigued by the temporal nature of human thought, recognizing its role in shaping their physical world. "So, in essence, human thoughts act as seeds that eventually sprout into their physical reality?"

Stephen nodded, "Exactly, Eada. This entangled interplay between human consciousness, driven by thoughts, and the physical world demonstrates the profound connection between the microcosm and the macrocosm. It's a truly fascinating system."

Encouraged by this newfound clarity, Eada asked, "Would you mind explaining the creation of a physical object in reverse? Instead of starting from belief and ending with the object, I'd like to trace it back from the object to the initial thought that brought it into existence."

"Certainly, Eada. That's precisely why I'm here." With a simple wave of his hand, the Oculus materialized before them, its dimensional threads shimmering with an energetic vibration. "For this demonstration, we will need to visit my laboratory. Shall we?" He gestured toward the Oculus, which now stood centered on the ancient brick path of the Great Wall.

As they stepped through the humming threads of the Oculus, they found themselves right back on the bridge at the spot where Eada's lesson had begun.

"Cambridge?" Eada exclaimed, a smile gracing her lips.

"Indeed, Eada. Please follow me," Stephen urged, his enthusiasm palpable.

Together, they descended the opposite slope of the bridge and made their way toward magnificent Gothic-style structures that dominated the picturesque landscape. The delicate spires of each building seemed to pierce the sky atop a façade embellished with stained glass windows of riotous color. The structures gave off an aura of charm and sophistication. The meticulously maintained grounds enhanced the enchanting atmosphere. With expansive lawns, a variety of gardens, and meandering tree-lined pathways, the beauty of the surroundings was captivating.

Their journey took them through the labyrinthine buildings and corridors of Trinity College until they reached a nondescript door. "Shall we have some fun?" Stephen asked, nearly unable to contain his excitement.

They entered the laboratory and found themselves surrounded by a world of scientific wonders. Eada was immediately struck by the intricate network of metallic ducts, wires, and tubes that seemed to snake their way through the entire space. To her left, shelves were lined with books and slots brimming with papers, while upright filing cabinets stood to their right. Natural light streamed in through leaded exterior windows, complemented by smaller interior windows that allowed curious passersby to steal glimpses of the captivating work within.

Eada's gaze was drawn to a chalkboard in the far corner, covered in complex mathematical equations. Above it, a sign hung from the ceiling, politely requesting, "TALK SOFTLY, PLEASE." The intelligent energy that permeated the lab was undeniable.

"This is incredible," Eada remarked, marveling at the complexity and organization of the space.

Stephen nodded in agreement. "I sense it as well, Eada. Many renowned human scientists made groundbreaking discoveries here in this lab."

"I am continually impressed by human curiosity," Eada mused. "Interestingly, they've had to manifest all this intricate equipment and knowledge to explore the fundamental construct of existence."

Stephen chuckled softly. "I believe you have summed up my entire career as a Pneuma Speaker in one sentence."

Eada probed further, "What do you mean?"

"I was a theoretical physicist," Stephen explained. "Humans have been inquisitive about the nature of reality since the dawn of their sentient faculties, and they have made significant strides, but there are still many mysteries left to uncover."

Eada could sense both Stephen's passion for his work and his frustration at being unable to continue it. "It seems you've contributed significantly to humanity's understanding, Stephen. Your work has undoubtedly inspired countless individuals."

"Thank you, Eada. That means a great deal to me," Stephen responded warmly.

Together, they approached a table at the center of the lab, and a bright luminescent glow materialized above them, revealing an object within its radiance.

"An apple?" Eada asked, examining the object closely.

"In essence, yes. But as you suggested, let's deconstruct each component, tracing it back to the original thought that brought it into existence."

With another graceful wave of his hand, the apple began to rotate slowly. As Eada observed, her thoughts drifted back to The Inverse, where creation was as effortless as thinking. There, the only boundaries were the limits of one's imagination, where a mere thought could marshal Conscious Agents into any form imaginable.

With another wave, the apple expanded energetically, revealing countless cluster-like globules suspended around it. "These are what humans define as molecules," Stephen explained. "They are the physical building blocks derived from even smaller atoms and smaller still quantum materials. These molecules, you see, are just the beginning of our journey."

Stephen's hand gestured again, and all but one of the billions of molecules dispersed. "Now, let's dive further to uncover what makes up this molecule." With another wave, they entered the molecule's interior. The space expanded rapidly until it suddenly halted, revealing billions of glowing dots surrounding it. Then, all but one of those dots vanished upon Stephen's command.

He enlarged the remaining particle, which floated before them. Tiny, energetic glowing specks orbited a small mass, resembling a miniature model of a solar system in space, complete with planets revolving around a sun.

"Allow me to introduce you to the atom," Stephen declared.

Eada gazed in awe at the image before them. "It's beautiful."

"Indeed, Eada. I couldn't agree more." Stephen waved his hand again and said, "But we can delve even deeper to uncover this atom's building blocks." The energetically charged electrons scattered in all directions before they were within the atom's nucleus. The space expanded rapidly and then suddenly halted once more.

"Here, deep within the atom's nucleus, we find more building blocks known as protons and neutrons." Stephen reached up and selected one of the neutrons, sweeping away the rest. He held it in front of them, and it glowed contentedly. "What we perceive here is less of a solid thing and more of a resonance of energy. Nevertheless, let's venture even deeper."

In an instant, they traveled further within the neutron, the space around them expanding until they were surrounded by billions of sparkling dots, darting about chaotically.

"Does this look familiar to you, Eada?" Stephen asked.

"The galaxy," Eada said confidently.

"Indeed, Eada, just as there is a macro-cosmos, there is a micro-cosmos. Here, we encounter what humans have labeled 'quarks,'" Stephen explained. "This is where conventional human understanding of matter reaches its limit."

Stephen reached into the swarm, selecting one of the minuscule quarks, and dismissed the rest. He placed it in front of them, and it emitted a radiant glow and bounced around energetically.

"In the time when your Pneuma descends to Earth, the smallest known building block of quantum reality is the quark," Stephen continued. "Any speculation about what lies within it is still a realm of theoretical physics, as humans can only make educated guesses regarding its energetic components."

Eada was left momentarily speechless. "So, humans don't know about Conscious Agents?"

"No, Eada. Although they are getting closer to this understanding, some of their theories point toward Conscious Agents, but they are still far from fully comprehending it. It's a 'matter' of belief," Stephen said whimsically. "Pun intended."

Eada pondered this revelation and then inquired, "What do they propose exists beyond the quark if not Conscious Agents?"

"Well, the most widely accepted theory, which is partially correct, suggests that within the quark, there is a minute filament of energy resembling a fine hair or string. This energetic string vibrates at specific frequencies, giving rise to early particles like quarks, atoms, molecules, and eventually, our apple, or any conceivable object, for that matter." Stephen grinned broadly. "Humans have named this concept String Theory."

"I see your point," Eada agreed. "This theory isn't entirely unfounded, but they may be overlooking that the energetic string is simply a coalescence of Conscious Agents, and the frequency is tuned in by thought itself."

"Exactly, Eada. That is precisely what you and I understand to be true, but humans are still on the path to uncovering this reality beyond theory," he confirmed.

Eada contemplated the information Stephen had shared with her, gaining a new perspective on the purpose of this realm. Humanity had embarked on a quest to experience consequences, to explore knowledge, and to comprehend existence from the very beginnings of thought. However, some aspects of their journey remained consistent with those of The Inverse.

With a determined look, Eada asserted, "Humans need to be made aware of their power and their inherent place within the infinite collective consciousness."

Stephen gestured, and the glowing presentation surrounding them dissipated. "I couldn't agree more, Eada. I understand you are part of a vital mission to achieve just that. I am honored to contribute to it in my own small way."

The gravity of Eada's mission suddenly sunk in with her, knowing that her Pneuma's mission was centered around human ascension and their understanding of consciousness.

Stephen turned to her as they exited the laboratory and stepped into the brilliant sunlight. "I suppose it's time for me to say my goodbyes, for now," he said, stopping in front of the Oculus archway that appeared a few steps away.

"Thank you, Stephen," Eada said, her voice filled with genuine appreciation. "I'm deeply grateful for the time we've spent together. Your lesson was invaluable, and I'm confident that my Pneuma will find this information incredibly useful when navigating the complexities of human reality."

"It was my pleasure, Eada. I wish you every success on your journey."

Eada smiled at Stephen, brimming with excitement and anticipation for the mission ahead, as she stepped through the dimensional threads of the Oculus.

CHAPTER 13

Amsterdam, October 14, 2054. The East Medical Wing at the Netherlands Regional LOC Chapter is shrouded in shadows, mirroring the world outside—a world in turmoil. Less than eighteen hours have passed since the pivotal moment when Hope was shot. Her life now teeters on the precipice, cocooned in the fragile realm of a coma. Gabe's once-promising mission, fueled by unwavering hope, has unraveled into a bleak reality as Encephalon Media Group persists, unopposed, retaining its power to manipulate the future of humanity. Despite his efforts, Hope is fighting for her life.

In the dim hospital room, a network of wires and tubes extended from Hope's body, connecting to a chaotic orchestra of beeping machines and monitors. Poet returned, holding a paper cup that did little to insulate the scorching heat emanating from his beverage. He swiftly placed the coffee on the table beside Hope's hospital bed and hissed, attempting to stifle his discomfort, "Why in the . . . ?"

The room's subdued lighting made it challenging for Poet to locate the sink, but he eventually found it and relished the cold water running over his fingers. As he dried his hands on his pants, the weight of the situation settled upon him like an unbearable burden. Just then, he heard the heavy door swing open. His tired eyes widened in surprise and relief; his head snapped toward the entrance. "Mom, Dad!" His voice quivered with emotion. A single tear escaped his eye, cascading down his cheek as his mother rushed to his side.

Gabe and Ella held Poet in a warm embrace, and the three of them clung to each other as if afraid to let go. Standing beside Hope's bed, Gabe gently held her hand. His face was etched with the deep lines of worry and dark circles under his eyes as he watched the emotional reunion between Poet and his mother. After a brief, heartfelt pause, his concern again took precedence, and he inquired in a calm, anxious tone, "Has there been any change in her condition?"

Poet shook his head, the weariness and concern evident in his eyes. He muttered softly, "No, Dad. No change. She's still . . . ," his voice trailed off, unable to bring himself to say the words aloud.

Gabe placed a reassuring hand on Poet's shoulder and nodded, understanding the gravity of the situation. There was little they could do but wait and hope for a miracle.

The room began to settle, the weight of their ordeal sinking in. Gabe broke the silence with a soft question, his concern evident, "Poet, what happened at the theater? What went wrong?"

Poet's tired eyes met his father's, and he let out a heavy sigh as he recounted the events of the previous night at the Tuschinski Theater. He explained that everything was going as planned when Hope arrived at the meeting point, but then all hell broke loose.

"They were AI Agents, Dad," Poet began, his voice laden with regret. "They somehow bypassed our surveillance. They opened fire, and I tried to . . ." His voice trailed off, the memory painful.

Ella couldn't believe the danger her children had faced. Tears welled up in her eyes as she held onto Poet's arm.

Poet continued, "Hope was hit, and I did my best to get things under control, but it all happened so fast."

Gabe's face twisted with anguish as he listened to his son's account. The loss of Porter, and the peril Hope and Poet had faced, weighed heavily on him. "I'm so sorry, Poet. I wanted to be there for you both."

Ella wiped away her tears and asked, "Are you hurt, son? Are you sure you're alright?"

"I'm fine, Mom. Truly, don't worry. I'll be okay."

The room fell into a heavy silence. Just then, a communication device on the wall chimed. Poet's voice instructed, "Answer." The front desk announced that Mr. Archibald had arrived and asked for clearance to join them.

"Yes, of course. Send him up."

They gathered around Hope to be as close to her as possible. "This is my fault," Gabe admitted, remorse etched across his face.

"No, honey. You can't say that. This is Encephalon's fault, not yours!" Ella's voice quivered with anger.

"I should've taken her concerns about Encephalon more seriously. I should've quit right then and there. She was right, and I should've listened to her," Gabe confessed.

Ella's tears flowed as emotions overwhelmed her. Gabe turned to Poet and asked, "Remember your sixteenth birthday, son? Yours and Hope's?"

Poet sat up a bit straighter, nodding. "Yeah, Dad, I remember. Hope was pretty upset that day."

Gabe let out a sigh of immense sadness. "I've carried the weight of that day with me ever since," he admitted. His head hung low, the pangs of guilt weighing heavily on his heart as he recalled the vivid memory of their argument and Hope storming out of the dining room in the middle of celebrating their sixteenth birthday. "Even then I could've left Encephalon."

Gabe had always been determined to protect his children, resolute in his decision to shield them from danger. However, despite his sincere intentions, he knew that desire had led them down this path, ultimately resulting in him standing here at Hope's bedside. He couldn't help but feel responsible for what was happening.

From the beginning, Gabe had been concerned that Hope, with her brilliant mind and progressive spirit, wouldn't understand his actions, which were driven by love and worry. He feared that if Ronan Hayes discovered her involvement with the LOC, it would only increase the danger she faced as an agent. To safeguard Hope, Gabe had chosen to keep her in the dark about his clandestine plan, convinced it was the best way to protect her.

Now, looking back, he could see it all too clearly. He had gravely underestimated his daughter. Things would have been different if he had just listened to her. If he had only questioned his convictions, delved deeper into his beliefs, and acted upon the very equation of reality he had discovered. All the "what ifs" converged on a single undeniable truth: If he had listened to Hope, they would have found themselves experiencing an entirely different thread of reality.

Gabe felt foolish and was angry with himself, realizing that his well-intentioned actions had failed and would never have been necessary if he had dared to look past his fears, acknowledged his beliefs, and trusted Hope.

In the stillness of the hospital room, the only audible sounds were the rhythmic beeping and hissing of life-preserving machines. Gabe sat beside Hope's bedside, her pale hand gently cradled in his. Tears fell as he cherished every detail of her beautiful face.

His voice quivered as he whispered, "I'm so sorry, honey. I'm so sorry." His guilt bore down on him, and he couldn't hold back the flood of emotions any longer. Gabe buried his face in the soft blankets of the hospital bed, his shoulders trembling with uncontrollable grief. At that moment, he wished they could all just start over from the beginning.

The door creaked open, and Poet's face lit up with a warm smile. "Levi," he exclaimed, genuinely thrilled to see Hope's most cherished friend.

They all welcomed Levi's arrival with open arms, their spirits lifting at the mere sight of him. His presence provided a temporary respite from their sorrow. Levi possessed a unique charm capable of brightening anyone's day with his presence alone. Gabe stood and walked over to Levi, his voice heavy with emotion. "We're really glad you're here, Levi," he said warmly as they embraced.

Levi then approached Hope's bedside, his long, curly hair falling gently over his face as he looked down at her. Levi removed his thick, black-framed glasses, wiping away the tears that had welled up in his eyes.

"How is she doing? She's going to make it, right?"

Ella, no longer willing to endure the agonizing wait for the doctor, voiced her impatience. "We're not sure, Levi," she replied. "But we're going to find out." A mother's determination shone in her eyes as she made her way to the wall-mounted communications panel, tapping the screen just as the doctor entered the room.

A collective sense of relief washed over them as if their very souls were interconnected, all sharing the same anxious anticipation. Yet, beneath the surface, an undercurrent of fear lingered as they awaited the impending report.

"Hello, I'm Dr. Green. I wish I had better news to share with you all. Truly, I do," the doctor began, his voice heavy with empathy. The doctor continued to relay his grim report, but it was as if none of them could hear him as they each turned inward with their grief. They just hadn't been willing to face it until this moment. They knew Hope's time was nearing an end.

A profound silence enveloped them, the weight of their grief pressing upon their hearts. Slowly, they drew closer, seeking solace in each other's arms as their tears fell in their shared sorrow.

CHAPTER 14

As precious minutes tick relentlessly by, the elusive message remains a mystery.

The countdown of seconds and minutes on the timer marked the dwindling moments of life displayed on the central monitor. The hours had already vanished, leaving behind a silence punctuated by two zeroes and a semicolon. As Hope stared at the unyielding countdown, the rapid succession of changing digits was engaged in a race against her, taunting her. With just twelve minutes and a handful of seconds remaining, Hope couldn't shake the feeling that they were right back where they started.

Epoch questioned Hope's earlier response with caution. "Not a trace of it? The message had to be in there somewhere." His grave expression, out of character for Epoch, gave Aiko pause. During her brief time in The Inverse, Hope hadn't seen this look of concern on his face, which caused the excitement she felt from her final lesson to sour into worry of her own.

"No," Hope replied with a matter-of-fact tone, a palpable sense of defeat weighing on her. Then she murmured, "I watched every moment of Eada's training and noticed nothing that indicated this mysterious message."

Sensing Hope's despair, Aiko attempted to provide some comforting reassurance. "It'll be okay, dear. Close your eyes. Step back from it all and look at it from a different point of view. Maybe it was there, and you just didn't recognize it. It must have been there somewhere."

A whirlwind of emotions overcame Hope. Being thrust into The Inverse had not been her choice, and searching for the message now felt like finding a needle in an infinite haystack. She had listened attentively to every lesson, hoping to uncover a clue or breadcrumb that would guide her in delivering the elusive message to her father.

As Hope reflected on Eada's training at The Academy, she recalled how Walt had explained the concept of humans adopting an endless number of latent beliefs collected throughout their lifetime. He emphasized that these beliefs were the imaginative architects of emotionally inspired thoughts, laying the foundation of human reality.

John had delved into the intricate domain of human emotions, unveiling their remarkable capacity to acknowledge time-anchored beliefs—like personalities trapped in the past—and gently bring them to the surface. Even more significant was the intricate connection between emotions and these concealed beliefs. Emotions served as the guiding thread, and anyone with the curiosity and courage to follow them could identify these beliefs and set them free into the limitless expanse of infinity.

And Stephen. He elaborated on the incredible power of thoughts, how, if belief was the architect of human reality, thought was the master builder. Stephen had taught Eada that thoughts were not passive reflections of reality but active creators of it. They shaped and molded the world, giving rise to the sum of probable realities that perpetually teetered in the balance of humanity's symbolic equation, $B \in E + T = R$.

But despite comprehending it all, Hope was left with empty hands. No message stood out, none that seemed destined for her to share with her father, and there was no direct link between the lessons and the mission. If there had been a clear message, she would have undoubtedly discovered it.

"It wasn't there," Hope's voice tinged with disappointment. "The lessons were incredible, but I just didn't find the message. I'm truly sorry."

Epoch and Aiko exchanged a worried glance. They had seen Hope's spirit grow throughout this mission, but the evident strain and the looming reality made them anxious. The weight of this unfulfilled task hung heavy in the room, overshadowing the wisdom of the lessons she had experienced.

Nothing seemed to make sense to Hope. Her emotions surged, escalating from fear to a profound sense of panic. The timer on the central monitor continued to haunt her, a cruel and relentless reminder of her circumstances back on Earth.

At that moment, Hope was overwhelmed with a sensation of familiarity. The déjà vu that had initially greeted her arrival at the Command Center returned with even greater intensity, crashing over her like a tidal wave. Her heart raced as she scanned the Command Center, the sense of it all now impossible to ignore.

"Why does this place feel so familiar?" Uncertainty laced her voice. It was like an invisible force was pulling at her, demanding her attention. "There's something about this facility. I know it, but I can't . . . " Her voice faded. It resembled a dormant memory, a puzzle piece that refused to fit into the larger picture surrounding her.

Hope turned her gaze toward Epoch, her eyes searching for answers. She was willing to follow any lead in this moment of desperation. "I think the message is here. I can't explain it, but something tells me it's at the Command Center. I have an odd sense of familiarity here." Her eyes darted back and forth between Epoch and Aiko, her conviction evident.

Aiko glanced at Epoch, a questioning look on her face. They both instantly understood the gravity of Hope's assertion. Aiko then turned to Epoch and asked, her tone advocating for transparency, "Can we show her?"

Epoch nodded reluctantly, his eyes brimming with concern. "The Council won't be pleased, but I'll take responsibility for it."

Aiko approached Hope, her gentle touch enveloping Hope's hand. "We'd like to show you something, Hope."

"What is it?"

"It will all become clear once you see it," Epoch reassured her.

They exited Epoch's office, quickly traversed a long corridor, and ascended the floating staircase. Hope's familiarity with the facility intensified as they entered the space, gripping her memory ever more tightly. An undeniable connection to the surroundings enveloped her.

"I recognize this place," she whispered, her senses gradually assembling the puzzle.

The office was beautifully adorned. While many modern elements were unfamiliar to Hope, the decor exuded sleekness, modernity, and brightness. It felt like someone had captured an image of what she would consider a perfect workspace, even though she had never seen it before. An elegant floating glass surface hung delicately in the air, serving as a magnificent desk perfectly designed for work. Digitally rendered holographic photographs graced its surface.

Hope, drawn by curiosity, approached the desk to look at the pictures closer. To her astonishment, she recognized the faces of her family and friends—her father, Gabriel, her mother, Ella, and her brother, Poet—all displayed for whoever worked at this desk. Each image captured precious moments, yet they portrayed a life she didn't recognize. It was as if these images belonged to someone else. Among them was a photograph of herself standing beside her best friend, Levi. They were proudly holding their latest achievement award outside the LOC headquarters.

Then, her heart skipped a beat as she noticed a picture of herself locked in the arms of the same man who had appeared on the Paris bridge during Eada's training session with John. She had felt a connection to him the moment she saw him during Eada's lesson on Emotion. Initially, she had thought of him as handsome and nothing more. But why were they now together in this photograph?

Hope turned toward Epoch and Aiko, her eyes filled with wonder, tears brimming in the corners.

Gradually, understanding dawned on her, illuminating her consciousness like bright sparks in a dark room. She looked around, and in a flash of insight, she exclaimed, "This is my office."

The realization surged like a bolt of electricity, coursing through her soul at lightning speed. Her mind was sprinting to catch up with her senses. It felt like she had stepped into a dream, a vivid awakening to an entirely different thread of existence. Clarity flooded her voice as she vocalized her revelation, "This is another timeline, an entirely different version of my life, isn't it?" Her mind raced, connecting the dots of this newfound understanding and aligning the puzzle pieces.

Aiko nodded solemnly. "Yes, Hope. This is the life that was meant for you and your family. Each of you had roles to play in humanity's ascension, but as you know, it didn't turn out that way."

"We thought hosting you in this setting might somehow help you uncover the message you were seeking," Epoch continued.

"But it was a desperate attempt, Hope. The Council warned us that this would be too painful if we failed to find the message. I'm truly sorry, Hope."

A shadow of guilt crept into Hope's expression. "Don't be sorry, Epoch, I didn't share the message. It's my fault."

Aiko's tone remained gentle yet persistent. "No, dear. It wasn't anyone's fault. We aren't certain when you were meant to deliver the message to your father, and as you can see, we're equally in the dark about the contents of that message. In truth, it was unfair of us to put this on your shoulders; it was a last-ditch attempt," she assured, her sincerity palpable.

Hope's curiosity persisted, and she scanned the room, her voice laden with urgency. "But how did you know I had to share a message with my father in the first place?"

Epoch's response was concise. "The Council."

Frustration surged within Hope, her voice escalating, "The Council? If they possess such wisdom, why not simply reveal the message to me?" She stood her ground, demanding clarity.

Epoch patiently explained, his voice unwavering. "It doesn't work that way, Hope. Humanity's destiny transcends the Council's influence or that of any entity. Your presence here is nothing short of miraculous. We thought it was all lost until fate intervened. A desperate plea was made to the Council, requesting an exception. They provided an opportunity for you to re-examine Eada's lessons on human beliefs, emotions, and thoughts, all to discover the essential message meant for your father. However, this opportunity carries strict rules. I may have already revealed too much, but you must grasp that this is the sole path to return to your intended reality thread."

Hope's eyes wandered around the room. It wasn't merely a physical space; it felt like a missing fragment of her life. As far back as she could recall, she had carried a persistent feeling of being on the wrong path. But in this very moment, within the confines of these walls, she felt as if she had finally discovered the life she was meant to live.

Still searching for answers, Hope asked, "If one simple message had the power to throw all of humanity off course, to throw my life off course, it seems to me it was an impossible mission in the first place."

"Oh, Hope, the concept of 'impossible' is unique to humans, confined to Earth alone," Epoch said. "In the vast universe, there is no such label. Every existence is rooted in belief. All things exist within threads of reality, and nothing is truly new or undone. Whether it's a single person or an entire civilization, the power lies within them to choose the threads they wish to weave into their experience. And it all starts with a belief."

Hope contemplated Epoch's words. She had dedicated her life to her world, tirelessly fighting for humanity and her cause. She had poured her heart and soul into what she believed in, driven by discipline, sacrifice, and unwavering passion. Yet, despite her relentless efforts, she found herself in a world torn apart by greed, overshadowed by control, and populated by a global community seemingly relinquishing its power. They had become trapped in the vicarious lives of others, endlessly glued to their mixed-reality headsets, consuming the experiences of others instead of searching within themselves to uncover and believe in the world they truly desired."

A single tear rolled down her cheek, and then, with a defeated whisper, she said, "I was always so close with my dad. I don't understand it. I don't know what went wrong. I don't know what else I could have done."

"It wasn't a burden given only to you, dear. This mission was a responsibility shared by your entire family. It hung in a delicate balance. It was never about each of you individually fulfilling your part of the mission, but more all of you believing in yourselves and each other." Aiko offered.

"I just don't understand why my father gave his life to Encephalon. Why he worked so hard to turn his discovery into a weapon against human consciousness instead of a resource for empowerment and freedom." Hope's voice carried the weight of great disappointment and confusion.

"That's one perspective," Epoch snapped defensively.

Hope shot him a quick look, "What do you mean? I was there. I saw it all play out. I lived it."

"You didn't live *all* of it, dear," Aiko said softly.

Epoch added, "Your father had his reason, Hope. One thing I can promise you is that every decision he made, he always thought it was the best decision for you and your brother. That always carried the most weight in anything he acted on."

Hope struggled with Epoch's revelation, although she was comforted by the sincerity in Epoch's report. "But why . . . ?" Hope's voice trailed off as she searched for the question that might allow an answer to fill the void.

"I would like to show you something, Hope." Epoch stood and walked over to the floating glass desk. He waved his hand, and the orb appeared floating above it. He continued, "Do you remember the moments leading up to when you were shot at the Tuschinski Theater?"

Hope looked down as she searched her memory of that fateful night. It was all a blur, but slowly, it came into focus. "Yes, yes, I remember watching a video. It was the coded message from my dad." Her voice trailed off in deep contemplation. "But we were cut off . . . the AI Agents. When the perimeter alarm sounded, the video cut off. I never saw the rest of it." Hope's voice became optimistic. She looked at Epoch searchingly.

Epoch nodded up at the orb and, within beautiful patterns, swirled into a bright light, and then instantly, Hope was staring at her father. He looked tense, even scared. His expression was serious, and his voice sounded severe through the deep wrinkles that framed his countenance.

"Hello again, Hope. If everything has gone as planned, you and your brother are enjoying our favorite sci-fi movie at the Tuschinski Theater." A big dad smile dominated his face. "If you're not there, something has gone wrong, and you must disappear quickly. But assuming you're together, I love you both very much."

Hope shot a look at Epoch and Aiko. Aiko gestured toward the orb, urging her to focus on her father's message.

"My life is in danger, and I don't know if I will see you again. I have been working on this plan to correct my mistakes, hoping to give you and the world one last chance for a future. When I started working for Encephalon, I had no idea that our technology would be used to enslave humanity. On the contrary, I wanted to show the world, right down to a person, just how powerful their consciousness is. I wanted them to know that they no longer needed to be servants bowing down to their masters and that their imaginative thoughts were the key to projecting any world they desired around them.

"Nevertheless, we all know that was just a dream and that our world is far from that reality. But it's not too late, Hope. We have a chance to change it. We've encoded two encrypted files within this video. These programs are the key to finally defeating Encephalon, but the operation can't be executed from the inside. The first file will grant you and your team at LOC full access to Encephalon's central server bank, directly infiltrating the C.A.I.N. Hive core. A secondary encrypted program is the most powerful Zero-Hour-Threat virus ever created. You must install it within ten seconds of opening the digital tunnel. You only have one shot at this, Hope. We've got to make this count."

Gabriel paused and looked behind him. When he turned back, he continued, "I'm so proud of you and your brother, honey. I anguish over the tension between us, and I'm ashamed of the pathway I took and the pain I've caused you all, hell, the world, for that matter. But we have an opportunity to fix that now.

"It's a long shot, but we've got to try. There's no time to explain it all now. You and Poet need to find somewhere safe to operate from. Poet will explain everything. Please don't try to reach me; it will be too dangerous and could reveal your location. I'll send comms through a Fringe Frame." Gabe paused. Hope could see the strain in his eyes and hear the tension in his voice.

"Please don't be upset that you're only hearing this now, kiddo. I decided to exclude you from the mission because I couldn't bear the thought of subjecting you to more danger. You've had enough of that already. I couldn't allow any of this to be connected to you until we were absolutely sure we had the tunnel built and the virus completed. I know you would disagree, and you're probably disappointed in me, but sweetheart, please know that my intentions start with you and your brother.

"Hope, your mom, and I love you and Poet more than you will ever know. We are incredibly proud of you both, and it's such an honor to be your parents. You have been our compass, and we will be forever grateful for your patience and love. I wish I had more time to explain, but you've got to get moving. If we're successful, we'll all have a good family story to tell someday. I love you, sweetheart, and always know that your kind and brilliant heart gave me a lighted path. I know this all sounds incredibly difficult, but if there's anything you taught me, I need to believe in myself. And remember honey, 'it's kind of fun to do the impossible.'"

Tears streamed down Hope's face, and she stood momentarily silent, a whirlwind of emotions coursing through her. She had finally grasped her father's motivations. Despite his shift into the corporate world, Encephalon must have trapped him.

The last words her father spoke in the video echoed through her mind. Her father's favorite quote from Walt Disney was, "It's kind of fun to do the impossible."

It's kind of fun to do the impossible. Do the impossible. Hope's eyes brightened and her body tensed as she gasped and then let out a big exhale before declaring, "I found the message!"

Epoch and Aiko exchanged knowing glances, their faces lit up. Hope continued, "And I know exactly the moment I needed to share it with him."

Aiko approached Hope with a warm, reassuring smile. "Indeed you do, dear. Indeed you do."

Hope walked over to a window that offered a view into the Command Center. There, displayed on the central monitor, the timer ticked down, reflecting that she had less than two minutes remaining.

Aiko's words were quick, emphasizing the urgency of the moment as she nodded to the seconds rapidly slipping away. "It's time to go, Hope. This is your chance to change the outcome of humanity. Only you can do this, and now you know how."

Hope's voice trembled as she sought reassurance, "But how can I go back and find the exact moment in time, the inflection point I missed before?"

Epoch gently took Hope by the hand and locked eyes with her. "It is your destiny, Hope. Your beliefs will guide you there. This will be your second life on Earth as Hope; a precious chance for you to rewrite the narrative. This is a gift, Hope. Use it wisely. And when you arrive, listen to your heart."

He continued, his voice filled with wisdom: "It is the essence of the equation $B \in E + T = R$, which you have learned from observing Eada's training. Your beliefs and emotions will intertwine, guiding your thoughts, which will choose the thread of that crucial moment where your actions can change the course of human history. Trust in yourself, Hope, and the power of your beliefs. The universe will respond to your intentions and lead you to the desired reality."

Hope glanced across the office, her heart heavy with nostalgia for a reality she felt an uncanny need to reclaim. Every detail, from the framed photos on the desk to the sunlight filtering through the vast windows, tugged at her intuition, giving her a distinct sense of déjà vu. She wondered how a place she had never actually experienced could feel so intimately familiar.

Despite the surreal familiarity of it all, Hope felt a surge of confidence welling up within her, fueled by the profound sense of belonging she had with Epoch and Aiko. As she met their reassuring eyes, Hope understood that they believed in her with unwavering faith. It was a faith she had carried with her throughout her journey, and now it was her turn to reciprocate that trust. The weight of her purpose settled on her shoulders, and she was ready to embrace it with newfound determination.

With a deep breath, she looked at Aiko and Epoch, her eyes filled with resolve and anticipation. Her voice, though soft, carried the certainty of her decision.

"I'm ready."

CHAPTER 15

In Manhattan, sixteen years into Hope's second life on Earth, the date on her revisited timeline is July 20, 2041. In the upper echelons of Manhattan's social circles, the Valencia family grapples with the delicate juggling act of balancing family and career, all while the world faces turbulent times. As they confront the repercussions of Gabriel's career decisions, a formidable question arises: Is it too late to choose another thread of reality?

Hope awoke suddenly, her mind still clinging to the vivid fragments of a dream. Sunlight bathed her spacious bedroom in a golden hue, casting a warm glow over the antique clock on her bedside table, which read 6:52 a.m.

This particular dream felt different, carrying a weight she couldn't easily dismiss. It featured a recurring enigmatic figure, a character who often made appearances in her nighttime reveries. Each encounter seemed like a fleeting glimpse into another reality, a portal to something that eluded her understanding. But today's dream held a significance that set it apart. Its message echoed loudly in her mind, urging her to trust in the power of her beliefs and her heart to shape the world around her.

While previous dreams often left her with a sense of restlessness, today's carried an inexplicable urgency. She couldn't pinpoint the reason, but the feeling persisted, leaving her with the impression that this day held greater importance than its date might suggest.

Hope's mixed-reality glasses chimed insistently. As she reluctantly put them on, her brother Poet's eager face appeared on the display.

"Hope, it's the big day! Are you excited?" His voice brimmed with anticipation.

Hope, still heavy with sleep, rubbed her eyes. "Of course, I'm excited, but why the early call? The sun's barely up."

"Sweet sixteen, sis! We can finally drive!"

Hope sighed, "It's too early, Poet. Everyone's asleep, even the staff. Can't it wait?"

Poet's excitement grew. "I bet they got us cars! Let's sneak to the garage."

"Cars? Seriously? Poet, we live in Manhattan. The only ones who drive here are chauffeurs and AI coaches. Ever heard of Sol and Jacob?"

Poet rolled his eyes. "Sol and Jacob are no fun. Besides, I'd rather be the one behind the wheel. You seriously don't want to drive?"

Hope raised an eyebrow. "Oh, I'd love to drive, alright. Or rather, ride."

"Huh?" Poet looked intrigued.

Hope smirked. "If they're getting us vehicles, I'd prefer a vintage 2002 V7 Moto Guzzi III Racer. Now, *that* would be something to cruise around Manhattan."

Poet shook his head, "You're so weird. Meet me at the bottom of the stairs."

Hope agreed, her drowsiness giving way to excitement. The anticipation of their sixteenth birthday was finally starting to take hold. She threw off her bedding and let her feet touch the cool floor. As she headed to the wardrobe chamber, the luxurious surroundings served as a reminder of their privileged life in Manhattan. Ornate ceilings hinted at grandeur, intricately designed walls whispered tales of historical significance, and massive windows framed by carved stone offered panoramic views of the city below.

Hope put on a robe and made her way to meet Poet. The towering mezzanine ceilings, adorned with elegant stone arches, stretched above her. To her right, ornate stone balustrades guarded an emblem inlaid into the timeless stone flooring of the entrance, while skylights bathed the space with the early morning light.

Descending the grand staircase, Hope noticed Poet leaping down the steps behind her, skipping three at a time in his excitement.

She groaned, though a smile played on her lips. "Slow down, Poet. We're not going to miss anything."

Poet retorted, "Where are Mom and Dad?"

"What in the world are you two doing up so early?" Ella's voice was a mixture of surprise and amusement.

"Buster here thinks you got us cars for our birthday," Hope said, her teenage attitude filling the room.

Ella laughed and turned toward the corridor leading to the dining hall. "Gabriel! The twins are up!" Her face radiated with joy.

Hope and Poet heard their father yell, "Did you say the kiddos are up?" His voice sounded in disbelief.

"Yes, but I've got them cornered, for now." She winked and then gestured for them to follow.

"Send 'em in!" came Gabriel's distant reply.

Laughing, Hope whispered to Poet, "Race you to the dining hall!"

They sprinted through the long corridor, almost tripping over each other. "Careful! No broken bones on your birthday!" Ella chided as they dashed past.

Entering the dining hall, the twins halted, mesmerized by the vision of a sea of vibrant balloons suspended above them.

"Sixteen hundred balloons, to be precise. I thought the house might float away!" Gabriel joked.

Now recording the moment with her mixed-reality eyewear, Ella herded the family toward the breakfast table. As they took their seats, staff members brought two mini cakes, alight with candles shining brightly. After a hearty rendition of "Happy Birthday," Poet blew out his candles with a cheeky grin, whispering to Hope, "Choose your wish wisely, sis."

His words echoed in Hope's mind, feeling eerily familiar. Pushing the strange sensation aside, she took a deep breath and blew out her candles.

"What got you two up at this hour?" Gabriel asked with a surprised tone.

"That goof," Hope replied, nodding toward Poet.

"Well, it's not every day you turn sixteen," Poet retorted, his grin widening.

Amused, Ella chimed in, "This might be the first time during summer vacation that you two didn't sleep in. It means we get to spend the whole day with you."

Poet raised an eyebrow. "The whole day?"

Hope added, "We've made plans with friends. You know, we're sixteen now. Don't get us wrong; we love you, but we also have a life of our own."

Gabriel and Ella exchanged knowing glances. "Did you two draft up bedroom lease agreements?" Gabriel teased.

Ella joined in, playing along, "Sure did, honey. Rent's due on the first, and we'd really appreciate it if you kiddos didn't turn it in late."

Exchanging exasperated looks, Poet muttered, "Always with the jokes."

"We get it," Hope said. "But come on, we're not kids anymore, and our friends want to hang out. We have a lot of social responsibilities." Hope tried to sound as grown up as possible.

"We get it, too, sweetheart. Believe it or not, we were sixteen once as well," Ella replied, "We just want to make the most of our time together."

Poet sighed, "It's cool."

The enticing aroma of breakfast filled the air, a rare occasion when the Valencias gathered for a morning meal.

"Mr. Valencia?" The head butler's deep voice cut through the atmosphere, drawing Gabe's attention. He approached, holding a pair of mixed-reality glasses in his gloved hand. "My apologies for the interruption, but Mr. Ronan Hayes wishes to confirm your attendance at dinner tomorrow night, along with Mr. Ash Bertram. Shall I patch the call through?"

Ella shot her husband a meaningful look. "Remember, dear, we have plans for dinner with Dr. Bannister tomorrow night."

Gabe nodded, a hint of contemplation briefly crossing his features. He then donned the mixed-reality glasses, signaling for the call to be connected. It struck him as unusual that Ronan had chosen to call him directly instead of going through his efficient assistant, Sophia Mendez.

"Hello, Ronan," Gabe greeted, his voice steady and measured.

The energy in the room shifted as Gabe engaged in the conversation. His countenance grew more severe as he listened intently to Ronan's words. Ella, Hope, and Poet exchanged curious glances.

"I see," Gabe responded at one point, his tone remaining neutral yet attentive. "Yes, I understand."

As the conversation continued, it became evident that Gabe was attempting to decline the dinner invitation. "Actually, I had prior plans with a colleague from Switzerland who's visiting," he explained, a touch of polite regret in his voice.

However, Gabe's attempt to gracefully decline seemed to falter. Ella, Hope, and Poet picked up on the persuasive undertone in Ronan's voice as the discussion continued. Their father's composed expression did not waver. "Yes, I understand."

After a pause, Gabe's voice took on a hint of resignation. "Yes, I'll be there. La Grande Boucherie sounds fine. Okay, I'll see you then." He finally ended the call, removing the mixed-reality glasses.

Ella's brow furrowed. "What was that about, Gabe?"

Gabe sighed, his expression a mix of resignation and determination. "Seems like I'm attending dinner with Ronan Hayes and Ash Bertram tomorrow night."

Hope raised an eyebrow. "But you declined, right?"

Gabe shook his head. "You heard the conversation, kiddo. I did my best. Ronan can be quite persuasive."

Ella's brows furrowed, concern evident in her eyes. "Gabriel, is there any way you could change the dinner plans? Adrian's here only once a year for the International Physics Conference. We've all been looking forward to spending time with him."

Gabe looked at Ella, his expression a mixture of frustration and resignation. "Honey, I wish it were that simple, but it's impossible," he admitted, his voice tinged with regret. "Would you go without me? You know you're Adrian's favorite," Gabe added, attempting to infuse a touch of charm into his words, hoping to ease the palpable tension in the room.

Ella's disappointment was evident. Her shoulders tightened. She sighed and nodded understandingly, acknowledging that sometimes circumstances were beyond their control.

Hope, however, struggled to contain her frustration. She clenched her fists, her knuckles turning white as she fought to stay seated. But the rage building within her was overwhelming. She abruptly shot up from her seat, her voice cracking with pent-up anger. "This is absurd! Utterly absurd!" she exclaimed, her voice oozing exasperation. "How could you, Dad?" Her tone verged on a shout. "He's a tyrant who exploits women, harms children, and enslaves anyone trapped in his web using the C.A.I.N. Hive! Are you really going to prioritize that slimeball Ash Bertram over your friend who traveled from Switzerland? It's beyond messed up!"

Ella exchanged a glance with Hope, her expression a mix of sympathy and frustration. The tension in the room grew thicker, the atmosphere heavy with unspoken emotions.

With a final, piercing glare at her father, Hope tossed a napkin onto the table and abruptly exited the dining hall. An uncomfortable silence enveloped the room. Gabe's gaze remained fixed on the empty chair where Hope had been seated moments earlier.

As the seconds ticked by, Gabe sensed a deep, heavy sadness settling in his chest. He realized that his decision had consequences beyond mere disappointment within his family. It felt as though his choices were sending shockwaves through the very fabric of their reality, creating ripples that extended well beyond their immediate circumstances.

Then, unexpectedly, Hope re-entered the dining room, her steps deliberate. The family watched her in silence, struck by the profound expression on her face. It was as if the timeless wisdom of her soul radiated through her beautiful countenance. She approached her father, locked eyes with him, and said, "Please forgive my outburst, Dad."

"Oh, there's no need to apologize, honey, I . . . I . . . " Gabe's words faltered.

Hope took her father's hand, leaned over, her face mere inches from his, and peered deeply into his eyes. The room fell silent as the two of them remained nearly frozen in their speechless gaze. Almost in a whisper, Hope said, "I wanted to remind you of your favorite Walt Disney quote, Dad."

Gabe sat up straight, instantly recognizing the reference.

"It's kind of fun to do the impossible. That's what you always say, Dad. I'd never heard you utter the word 'impossible' until Mom asked if you could change your dinner plans. It was as if I were hearing it from another person, not my Dad, the one person I know who doesn't believe in 'impossible.' He faces everything head-on."

Gabe remained dumbfounded, almost hypnotized as Hope continued.

"Please reconsider your plans for tomorrow night. It would mean the world to me. Actually, it would mean more than you know." Hope then wrapped her arms around her father's shoulders and hugged him tightly. She smiled at him, then gracefully departed the room leaving everyone aghast.

Tears welled at the corners of Gabe's eyes. As he sank back into the plush dining chair, his countenance shifted and his eyes brightened as if a light switch had been flicked on allowing him to see clearly for the first time in a long time.

Ella smiled warmly, her expression mirroring the profound transformation Gabe had just experienced.

As the day drew to a close, their shared family moments rekindled genuine joy, dispelling the earlier tensions. Gabe breathed a sigh of relief, his foremost wish being the happiness of Ella, Hope, and Poet.

Exiting his closet, robe in hand, Gabe was making his way to the rooftop swimming pool—a cherished sanctuary in times of stress, and tonight was no exception. The gravity of his recent decision weighed heavily on him.

As Ella entered the room, Gabe's eyes were drawn to her, as they always were, captivated by her enduring beauty and grace. He smiled as he remarked, "They always say your kids will outgrow you sooner than you expect, but I didn't anticipate it to happen at sixteen." Gabe chuckled warmly.

Ella grinned, "She's just like her father. You two are undoubtedly cut from the same cloth."

Gabe beamed with pride, celebrating the spirit and character they shared with their children.

"I could say the same for you and Poet," Gabe replied affectionately.

Ella's eyes sparkled warmly at the compliment and then added, "It's remarkable, isn't it?"

"What's that, honey?"

"Well, you know. One day, you're pushing them around in a stroller; the next, they offer you life-changing advice."

Gabe smiled, "Ain't that the truth?"

A moment of silence enveloped them before Ella gently broached the unspoken subject. "When you joined forces with Ronan Hayes, it held such promise for us. But this Ash Bertram? He's quite different from the vision we had in mind. What's going on, Gabe?"

Gabe's gaze dropped, his expression shadowed by the weight of his thoughts. "It's spiraling out of control over there, El. I didn't anticipate any of this. Honestly, I didn't."

Ella approached him, her hands gently resting on his shoulders. "I support whatever decision you make. All of this," she gestured gracefully around their luxurious master suite bathroom, "is lovely, but it doesn't define us."

"Sometimes I feel like I've forgotten who I am," Gabe admitted.

"Don't worry, honey. We'll never let that happen," Ella reassured him with a warm smile before leaning in for a kiss.

Gabe embraced her, holding her close and taking solace in the warmth of their bond. "I'm counting on that," he said, his voice filled with gratitude for her boundless love and the extraordinary family they had created together.

Just then, Gabe's mixed-reality device chimed, signaling an incoming call from his friend and colleague, Dr. Adrian Bannister.

"Dr. Bannister, how are you, my friend?" Gabe greeted Adrian with genuine enthusiasm.

"Hello, ol' sport!" Adrian responded, his tone exuding warmth. "How are you? It's wonderful to see you!"

Gabe smiled, appreciative of the enduring friendship they had nurtured since their meeting so many years ago in Switzerland. The day they spent together at the CERN facility left a lasting impression. "It's good to see you too, Adrian. Ella and the kids are doing great. There's never a dull moment in the Valencia household. How about you? Anyone new in your life?"

Adrian chuckled. "Oh, Gabe, I don't have time for romance. I'm married to my work, always have been, and always will be. Speaking of which, I'm looking forward to our dinner tomorrow night. I've been eager to share some exciting news with you."

Gabe's curiosity piqued. "Oh, what's that?"

Adrian's words resonated with an electrifying intensity. "I can only share the details in person, but I *found it*, Gabe!"

Gabe was taken aback. "Are you sure? I mean, you really found it?"

Adrian chuckled once more. "Yep, I finally found those little rascals." His radiant smile mirrored Gabe's astonishment.

"Gabe, I believe it's time we finally join forces."

The timing of Adrian's proposal struck Gabe, and the significance of the moment wasn't lost on him. "You have no idea how thrilled I am to hear you say that. Especially today."

Adrian added a caveat with a playful tone. "There's one small, insignificant hitch."

Gabe's curiosity grew. "What's that?" he asked, anticipating Adrian's signature touch of irony.

"You've got to leave Encephalon, Gabe. I can't share my findings unless you commit to leaving those bastards. You're too good for them, Gabe. It's time we truly change the world, and this time, for the better."

At that moment, Gabe sensed that this day was one of those pivotal moments capable of irrevocably altering the course of a person's life. He found it profoundly poetic that it coincided with Hope and Poet's birthday, further accentuated by Hope's message—a poignant reminder of the quote he consistently shared with his loved ones to always believe in themselves and embrace the limitless possibilities life offered. It was a timely reinforcement of the advice he had long held dear.

Every thought in Gabe's mind aligned with a clarity he'd sought throughout his life. With unwavering confidence, Gabe replied, "In my mind, I'm already gone, Adrian."

Adrian's joyous response echoed through the connection. "Brilliant! I knew you'd come around. I'll see you tomorrow night. I can't wait to update you on everything."

"I'm looking forward to it, my friend. Have a great evening."

"By the way, isn't Hope and Poet's birthday today? The big one-six, right?" Adrian added with a chuckle.

Gabe reflected on the passage of time and smiled. "Good memory, my friend. Yes, today is the day."

"Well, I can't say I understand how that feels, but I can imagine you're feeling much older now." Adrian's affectionate jab landed true.

"Easy. That one stung." Gabe replied with a smile.

"It's great to see you, Gabe. Say hi to Ella and the kids. I'll see you two tomorrow."

"Count on it."

Gabe placed his mixed-reality device on the marble counter, his reflection staring back at him. He took a deep breath and muttered, "Here we go."

As he prepared to step away from Encephalon Media Group, he understood that it might lead to a showdown with Ronan Hayes over ownership and future use of his research. It was a fight he felt ready to take on, a decision he couldn't believe had taken him this long to make. He cherished the profound impact Hope's wisdom and guidance had on his clarity about the future.

CHAPTER 16

Amsterdam. October 13, 2054. Hope's new future thread.

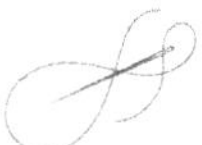

Hope strolled across the arched masonry bridge, filled with wonder as a sleek water taxi glided gracefully through the crystal-clear canal below. The boat's translucent design showcased the remarkable technological advances of the era while seamlessly coexisting with vintage gas lamps that lined the streets of her beloved Amsterdam. Iron hanging baskets brimming with vibrant flowers transformed this ordinary scene into a living masterpiece.

Crossing the bridge, Hope marveled at the harmonious blend of modern innovation and historical charm that gave her city its unique character. The world she inhabited had evolved into a breathtaking utopia, and she felt grateful for the privilege of witnessing the global transformation, knowing her family played a vital role in its ascension.

A couple breezed past on bicycles, a charming juxtaposition in a world where self-powered pedal bikes shared the streets with anti-gravity vehicles. The gentle whir of their bike chains and the rustle of their clothing in the breeze filled her senses. Approaching a café, the tantalizing aroma of freshly brewed coffee enveloped Hope, awakening her senses to the promise of the day ahead.

"Good morning, kiddo," the barista greeted Hope with a warm smile. "The usual?" he asked, reaching for the coffee beans.

"Yes, thank you, Simon," Hope replied, returning his smile.

Strolling toward the LOC Netherlands Headquarters, coffee cup in hand, Hope marveled at the seamless integration of the modern facility with its natural surroundings. Massive steel beams glistened through scaled glass walls, creating a structure that radiated within its environment. Ascending the steps to the entrance, she passed through the towering glass doors, which sealed shut behind her with a barely audible whisper. The grandeur of the space, blending functionality and elegance, left her in awe. To Hope, the League of Consciousness was more than a workplace; it was a sanctuary of enlightenment, exploration, and wonder.

Above her, a magnificent glass ceiling hung, supported by colossal steel beams, forming a rectangular umbrella beneath a flawless blue sky. Soft, modern lighting fixtures floated at various heights. Hope felt embraced by the warmth of her surroundings as the floors, walls, and ceilings emitted a soft, radiant glow. Amid the precise lines of contemporary architecture, the delicate details added a touch of poetry to the practicality of the environment.

High above, centered for all to see, suspended words that delivered a powerful message: "Multis filis unum sumus."

We are indeed, Hope thought, feeling the resonance of those words, a sense of déjà vu enveloping her.

She glided into her office, savoring the sensation of her suspended glass desk aligning perfectly with her posture. The space beneath remained pristine and uncluttered, allowing her to focus on the day ahead. Her gaze shifted to the few holographic pictures resting on top, always bringing a smile to her face as she saw her loved ones greeting her each morning.

Beyond the contemporary ambiance of her office, Hope's attention gravitated toward the central monitor situated at the rear of the Command Center. On its screen, a live feed showcased the highly anticipated grand opening of the new LOC station on Mars. A courteous throat clearing punctuated the stillness of the office, drawing Hope's gaze toward the door.

"Levi!"

As her best friend, Levi Archibald, entered her office, his confident stride complemented his round belly and plump cheeks. A cascade of dark, curly hair framed his face, and behind his substantial, black-rimmed glasses, mischief sparkled in his eyes. Every facet of his appearance and demeanor radiated a carefree, trusting, and affectionate spirit.

"Hey there, lady! Or should I show more respect now and address you as Colonel Valencia? Dang, girl, that's dope!"

"Cut it out, Levi. I'm just Hope to you, but it is incredible, isn't it?" Hope's smile radiated an expression of sheer delight for the recent honor bestowed upon her at the LOC Conference in Paris, France. She had become the youngest individual in the LOC's history to attain such a prestigious rank.

"It's as cool as it gets, Hope. I'm so proud of you. No one deserves it more." Levi's sincerity shone through in his expression.

"Thanks, Levi. That means the world to me. Especially coming from you."

"So, any exciting adventures during your time in Paris? I heard the food was incredible."

Hope chuckled, "It was amazing, Levi. I truly wish you could have been there. I attended so many parties and met some really impressive people." Just then, an unfamiliar look flitted across Hope's face.

"Wait a minute. What was that?" Levi asked.

"What was what?" Hope feigned innocence.

"That look. That's new for you, my lovely. Do I detect a hint of romantic magic in the Parisian air, perhaps landing on my buddy, Hope?" Levi chuckled, playfully nodding in agreement.

"Stop it, Levi. You're giving me the creeps."

"You haven't answered my question, girl. And what's with that smile? Come on, spill the beans!"

"Alright, alright, yes. Okay. I met someone."

"Okay, now we're talkin'. Give me all the juicy details. Don't hold anything back. You know how much I adore a love story."

Hope chuckled. "I have to say, Levi, it was truly magical. It was like something out of those mushy poems and sappy love songs. I never believed in love at first sight. I never thought a guy could sweep me off my feet like that. And on a bridge, of all places."

Perplexed, Levi raised an eyebrow. Hope continued, "We met at an officer's mixer the night before and agreed to meet again the next day for drinks. I know it sounds cliché, but we reconnected on Love Lock Bridge, of all places." A blush crept across Hope's face. "I can't explain it, but I can't stop thinking about him." She looked at Levi, her smile stretching from ear to ear.

"Well, well. I can already hear the wedding bells ringing."

"Stop it, Levi. Let's not get ahead of ourselves here."

"I'll be the godfather to your kids!" Levi adopted a dramatic pose, hand to his face, and spoke in a muffled voice, "Just when I thought I was out, they *pull* me back in."

"I don't get it. What are you talking about?"

"Seriously? You've never heard of 'The Godfather'? You need to get out more, sista. But hey, it's super exciting that you've met someone. Maybe we can go on a double date sometime. Although, I should probably find a girlfriend first. It might be a little awkward otherwise."

Hope laughed, and while the topic brought immense joy, she wanted to change the subject. Fortunately, Levi shifted the conversation.

"Hey, we now have access to the Commissioned Officers Club, right? I heard the GravityBall courts are sick over there. We've got to get on that."

GravityBall, cherished by Hope, Levi, and their LOC colleagues, combined anti-gravity technology with the symbolic D.A.R.E. equation—an encapsulation of human existence in $B \in E+T=R$.

The court, an arena featuring variable gravity zones, demanded strategic finesse for scoring, with players donning anti-gravity exoskeletal suits to enhance their agility. The game transcended technology, merging physics and metaphysics, where belief was paramount. It was more than a test of physical prowess; it delved into the realm of probable realities—a strategic art form involving beliefs, emotions, and swift thought transformations to influence the game's outcome. Ultimately, the objective was straightforward: Score by launching the ball into the opposing team's goal, defying the ever-shifting gravitational field, and aligning beliefs with the player's objective. Victory!

Before each match, players visualize success, igniting their confidence. This cherished game embodied the power of belief, warping the fabric of reality's threads.

"I'm way ahead of you, my man. I've got courts booked for Friday morning at zero-five-hundred," Hope said.

"Zero-five-hundred? Are you serious? Isn't there some kind of international law against being awake at that hour?"

"Yes, zero-five-hundred, and that's an order, my friend," Hope said with a smile.

"Roger that!" Levi playfully snapped to attention, and they both burst into hearty laughter.

Just then, Hope's mixed-reality device chimed, signaling an incoming call. It was her brother, Poet.

"See you at lunch," Hope gestured to indicate she needed to take the call.

"Wouldn't miss it for the universe," Levi declared with a grin, bowing to his best friend, spinning on his heels, and strolling out of Hope's office.

Hope swiftly put her device on and instructed her AI admin, "Ency, answer the call and display it as a hologram one meter to my twelve o'clock."

"Yes, mum," Ency replied.

Poet stood before her a moment later as if they were in the same room. "Hey, sis!"

"Hey, Poet. When will you be in town?" Poet had called the previous day, mentioning that he and their parents would visit to celebrate her promotion. They were thrilled about it and insisted on getting together as soon as possible. Gabriel and Ella always found reasons to connect for a family dinner, and this was one that Hope knew was a definite.

"I just got in. I decided to arrive a day early to catch up with my friends. We're heading out late tonight, but I'm already bored out of my mind. And guess what I saw today?"

"What did you see, Poet?" Hope couldn't imagine what her brother was about to reveal. Given his personality, it could have been anything fascinating.

"Well, I was headed over to Mom and Dad's to drop off my bags when I passed by the Tuschinski Theater. Guess what the featured movie was?"

"Uh, I couldn't even guess. What was it, Poet?"

"'The Matrix!' Poet blurted out with a laugh. Then he added, "Can you believe it? It was our all-time favorite classic when we were growing up. We watched it with Mom and Dad, like, a million times."

"You're kidding?" Hope responded in surprise, mirroring Poet's excitement.

"For real, sis. Hey, what do you say we catch the afternoon matinee? I mean, you're a colonel now, right? You can pull some strings and make it happen. Meet me at the theater at fifteen hundred hours."

"Alright, alright. Let me see what I can do. Consider yourself penciled in. If you don't hear from me in the next hour, plan on meeting me there."

"You got it, sis. See you then." The hologram vanished, leaving Hope with a radiant smile.

Stepping into the lobby of the historic theater filled Hope's heart with happiness. It seemed as if this grand palace of cinema had been preserved just for her. She had spent countless afternoons here with her family, watching classic films and sharing cherished memories. As she walked through the familiar halls, she thought of her father, Admiral Gabriel Valencia, and their remarkable work together to lead and expand the League of Consciousness. Their lifelong dedication revolved around awakening humanity's potential and harnessing the power of human consciousness.

The scent of popcorn, the familiar hues of the walls, and the soft velvet drapes evoked memories of her childhood visits to this place. Pausing in the center of the lobby, Hope wondered, after all these years, what secrets this place might hold. This theater had been synonymous with happiness and cherished memories throughout her life, yet an enigmatic whisper occasionally haunted her. It was a sensation she could never quite define, but deep within, she sensed it.

Hope continued beyond the lobby and entered the main auditorium. In the dim light, the plush red velvet seats and the opulent gold and red decorations all looked anew for such an ancient establishment. Hope cherished the iconic ambiance of the main curtains elegantly cascading over the screen.

As she strolled down the aisle, the plush velvet curtains parted, revealing the ghostly grey screen. The lights dimmed, and the old-fashioned sci-fi movie began to play. Memories flooded her mind, but something about this particular movie tugged at her consciousness. A hint of déjà vu was in the air.

The glow from the ancient projector unveiled the silhouette of a lone figure seated in the third row from the front. *We always used to sit there*, Hope reminisced. Poet turned and smiled as she approached. He stood and walked along the row of seats to meet her halfway, and they embraced.

"It's so good to see you, sis," he said, his smile warm. "I've missed you."

Hope hadn't realized how much she needed this hug from her brother. "I missed you more," she replied, holding back tears.

"Shall we?" Poet extended his arm toward the inviting theater seats. Although it was mid-afternoon, he had worked his magic to secure the entire auditorium just for them.

Hope chuckled softly. "I might have subjected you to this movie one too many times when we were kids," she admitted with a mischievous grin. "I have to wonder why you brought me back here to watch it again."

Poet hesitated momentarily, his eyes wandering around the theater as if seeking answers in the dim lighting of the space. "Honestly, there's no specific reason," he began, his voice conveying a note of intrigue. "I only saw the theater because of a bridge closure over one of the canals." His expression hinted at a more profound curiosity, as if he questioned whether some force had guided him to this place.

As Hope and Poet settled comfortably into their theater seats, the movie began to play. Green tinted computer code cascaded down the screen, forming a mesmerizing waterfall of symbols and numbers that coalesced into a digital rainstorm. Suddenly, the code dissolved, revealing a close-up shot of a phone ringing in a nondescript room. A man named Thomas Anderson, who operated under the hacker alias Neo, anxiously picked up the call.

At that precise moment, an electrifying sensation filled the air, as if an invisible storm of static electricity had silently enveloped the entire theater. The room plunged into near-total darkness, with only the projector's lumens casting eerie glows.

Hope turned to her brother, her eyes locking onto his bewildered expression. They both blurted out in unison, "Did you feel that?"

They combed the darkened theater with their eyes, their gazes drifting upward to the high ceiling in search of an explanation. Nothing was visibly amiss, yet an undeniable charge lingered in the atmosphere, refusing to be ignored.

"Well, I suppose we can add this to the list of mysteries for the day," Poet mused casually.

Hope nodded, her curiosity far from satisfied. Nevertheless, the sheer delight of sharing this unexplainable moment with her brother within the hallowed walls of the Tuschinski Theater reclaimed her attention. It stirred a profound warmth in her heart. It had been a wonderful day, a memory she wouldn't trade for all the world's treasures.

Epoch waved his hand, and with a swift, ethereal grace, the Oculus materialized at the center of the theater's central aisle. Its presence added a touch of cosmic wonder to the grandeur of the Tuschinski Theater. Epoch and Aiko observed Hope and Poet from their metaphysical vantage point as the movie began to play. A wave of relief washed over Epoch as he realized their intervention had been successful, averting a potentially disastrous thread of reality for humanity.

"That was a close call," Epoch remarked, his voice tinged with relief and admiration for the resilience of the human spirit.

Aiko nodded thoughtfully, her eyes reflecting the profound wisdom she had gleaned from countless observations within the conscious multiverse. "Indeed, it was," she said, "but always remember, in the vast expanse of reality, nothing is truly impossible."

Epoch smiled, his respect for Aiko deepening with every mission they undertook. He found a kindred spirit in her—a partner whose insights and perspectives continually enriched their journey through the boundless realms of existence.

As they observed Hope and Poet, the siblings' presence and emotions resonated through the metaphysical threads of the multiverse. Epoch and Aiko recognized the profound significance of this moment, acknowledging that every belief, each emotion-laden thought, and every passionately driven action played an indispensable role in the magnificent design of awakening humanity's potential.

Epoch beckoned Aiko to step closer to the archway with a subtle, meaningful gesture. As they ventured across the threshold of the shimmering, harmonically charged threads, the Oculus gracefully dissolved from its metaphysical position, seamlessly merging with the boundless expanse of the conscious multiverse, where infinite possibilities awaited.

The End

ACKNOWLEDGMENTS

"It takes a village." This saying held profound meaning for me as I embarked on the journey of writing *Threads of a Needle*. The completion of this book was made possible by the unwavering support and invaluable contributions of incredible individuals and invaluable resources, without whom this endeavor would not have been realized.

First and foremost, I extend my deepest gratitude to my wonderful wife and our amazing children. Your inspiration, unwavering support, and patience throughout my pursuits are immeasurable. This book, and the ideas it encompasses, could not have come to fruition without the lessons you have taught me and the inspiration you have all provided.

Originally, I set out to write a non-fiction book meticulously detailing the facets of this philosophy. However, my passion for the project waned as I delved deeper into the non-fiction approach. It was during a conversation with my dear friend and advisor, Marianna Teudor, that the course of the book shifted. She suggested, "You know, Dave, you've mentioned an imaginative description of these concepts several times. I see you writing this as a fantasy fiction novel, not a non-fiction self-help work." At first, I laughed at the idea, as I had never before written a book, let alone a dramatic narrative. Yet, it was Marianna's initial challenge that set me on this path, and I am profoundly grateful for it.

My journey as an author took an auspicious turn when I had the privilege of working with my remarkable publishers, Jenn Foster and Melanie Johnson of Elite Online Publishing. Jenn and Melanie's steadfast support and professionalism throughout this journey are deeply appreciated. Their unwavering belief in this project, combined with their patient guidance through every twist and turn, from concept to completion, was instrumental.

As the story began to take shape, I grappled with numerous complex concepts and ambitious ideas. It was during this phase that I had the pleasure of sharing my vision with my nephew and dearest friend, Bobby Zitting. Our brainstorming sessions over glasses of fine Italian wine yielded inspired collaborations and critical contributions to the story. Bobby's dedication extended to exhaustive research and meticulous editing, making him my "editor before the editor" and significantly enhancing the manuscript. It has been an honor to have his help, dedication, creativity, and the shared vision of $B \in E + T = R$ during this journey.

Speaking of amazing editors, I owe a profound debt of gratitude to my editor, Anita Henderson. Working with such an established, creative, and experienced writer was an honor. Anita not only guided me in making this book the best it could be, but she also served as an exceptional teacher, mentor, and even therapist when needed. Her patience, professionalism, and creative vision ensured that *Threads* was expressed in the best possible light. I can unequivocally say that this narrative wouldn't be as exceptional without the outstanding writing and editing skills Anita applied to it.

I am also immensely thankful to my beta readers: Alia, Bobby, Elfina, Justin, Marianna, Ryan, Rein, and Simon. Each of you offered unique insights and perspectives that enriched the final manuscript. Your thoughtful insights, honesty, and vision played a pivotal role in shaping the final manuscript. I hope you will recognize the impact of your contributions and changes reflected within the story.

To each of you, from the depths of my heart, I am truly humbled by your dedication, passion, efforts, and vision. Your contributions to this project are immeasurable, shaping the narrative, enhancing clarity, and adding depth to the concepts. I eagerly look forward to readers embarking on this journey with me and discovering the profound concepts within *Threads of a Needle.*

With immense gratitude,
DG Zitting

ABOUT THE AUTHOR

Dave G. Zitting is a seasoned entrepreneur with a remarkable career spanning over three decades in real estate finance and financial technology. His leadership has led to the successful establishment and growth of national business firms, resulting in significant achievements.

Beyond his thriving professional journey, Zitting's insatiable curiosity spans various domains, including science, technology, philosophy, psychology, and non-denominational spirituality. This lifelong quest for knowledge and wisdom has unveiled profound insights that extend beyond everyday life, reaching into the greater reality of the known world and universe.

What sets Zitting apart is his ability to translate this acquired wisdom into both his personal life and business ventures, yielding resounding success. As a co-founder and leader of firms employing over two thousand individuals, achieving billions in sales volume objectives, and pioneering sophisticated financial platforms, Zitting attributes his accomplishments to transformative insights gained along his remarkable journey.

By infusing his knowledge into every facet of life, including business, family, friendships, hobbies, and passions, Zitting has created a distinct advantage in navigating life's intricate game. He has also established the B∈E+T=R Life Strategy (BETR), recognizing the pivotal role of beliefs—conscious and subconscious—in shaping reality. This philosophy is elegantly summarized in his symbolic equation, B∈E+T=R, where Beliefs, Emotions, and Thoughts align to shape the probable thread of Reality. Zitting's philosophy empowers others to choose the reality they wish to experience. Within this equation, altering any value—B, E, T, or R—naturally transforms them all.

Dave G. Zitting's journey embodies the transformative potential of knowledge and self-awareness, showcasing the profound interplay between beliefs, emotions, and thoughts in shaping destinies. His enchanting fantasy fiction novel, *Threads of a Needle*, weaves these principles into a captivating narrative infused with life-changing wisdom. Through his work and personal philosophy, Zitting continues to inspire and empower others to take control of their beliefs and thoughts, forging unique paths toward a more fulfilling and successful life.

TERMS AND CONCEPTS

B∈E+T=R

The equation B∈E+T=R, also known as D.A.R.E. (Dimensional Algebraic Reality Equation), serves as a symbolic representation of human reality, encapsulating its core dynamics. Within this equation, B represents Belief, E represents Emotion, T represents Thought, and R represents the sum of Reality. Beliefs (B) are intricately connected, or expressed as set-membership, with human Emotions (E), denoted as B∈E. When Thought (+T) emerges from these interconnected functions, fortified by conscious action, these potent thought signals project at the quantum level metaphysically. They form connections between an individual's consciousness and one of countless probable realities within the multiverse. This intricate process ultimately manifests the sum of reality (=R) or the chosen thread of reality.

This symbolic equation illustrates how our Beliefs, Emotions, Thoughts, and associated actions collectively shape or determine the Reality experienced by each individual. Thus, it highlights the profound interconnectedness of each variable (BETR), emphasizing that any alteration in one aspect of the equation inevitably reverberates throughout the others. Consequently, even a subtle change in Belief, Emotion, or Thought yields the emergence of a distinctive and unique probable thread of reality in a person's lived experience.

Unlocking the Gift of Negative Emotions: Negative emotions (N-Es) often met with caution or aversion, hold a profound place within the spectrum of the B∈E+T=R equation. Within The B∈E+T=R Life practice, individuals are encouraged and empowered to embrace these emotions as invaluable gifts. Each negative emotion serves as a unique beacon, shedding light on aspects of an individual's beliefs/Belief Personas that require attention. All emotions (E) are intricately tethered to a belief (B), as symbolized by (B∈E).

Moreover, negative emotions are recognized as the most valuable function within this practice. They not only allow us to acknowledge our forgotten beliefs but also provide a means to reconcile our past with our present and future by lovingly releasing antiquated beliefs that are not aligned with our desired probable future reality.

Beliefs

Beliefs encompass multiple logical definitions. In psychology and cognitive science, beliefs refer to a mental attitude or state in which an individual accepts something as true or factual, often without empirical evidence to prove its accuracy. Beliefs fundamentally shape an individual's thoughts, emotions, behaviors, actions, and world perception/reality.

Beliefs can be visualized as ideas existing on a spectrum that ranges from what is conventionally perceived as 'positive' to 'negative.' An individual's placement of an idea on this spectrum determines the formation of a belief. The positioning on this spectrum can be highly subjective, influenced by cultural, societal, and personal perspectives. These beliefs wield significant power in shaping our actions and influencing our decisions and, ultimately, our reality.

Additionally, beliefs can be likened to versions of ourselves at different junctures along our life's timeline. These versions of self (beliefs) are equally significant and valid, coexisting with the present-moment self. For a deeper exploration of this concept, please refer to Belief Personas below.

Establishment of Beliefs

Beliefs are formed and established through a complex interplay of various cognitive, emotional, social, and environmental factors. Here are some key processes involved in the establishment of beliefs:

- **Perception and Sensory Input:** Beliefs can be influenced by sensory input and an individual's interpretation of their sensory experiences. What people see, hear, touch, taste, and smell can contribute to the formation of beliefs.

- **Learning and Conditioning:** Much of what we believe is learned through exposure to information, ideas, and experiences. Learning mechanisms like classical conditioning (associating one thing with another) and operant conditioning (learning through consequences) can shape beliefs.

- **Cultural and Social Influence:** Beliefs often align with the values, norms, and traditions of one's culture and society. Socialization, peer influence, family upbringing, and societal institutions play a significant role in shaping beliefs.

- **Cognitive Processes:** Cognitive processes such as reasoning, inference, and critical thinking can lead to the formation of beliefs. People evaluate evidence, weigh arguments, and make judgments contributing to their belief system.

- **Emotional Influence:** Emotions can strongly influence beliefs. Emotional experiences and the affective responses associated with certain beliefs can make those beliefs more resilient and resistant to change.

- **Confirmation Bias:** People tend to seek information confirming their beliefs while ignoring or discounting contradictory evidence. This confirmation bias can reinforce and solidify beliefs.

- **Experiential Learning:** Personal experiences—particularly impactful or emotionally charged experiences—can shape beliefs. Traumatic events, life milestones, and positive or negative experiences can influence an individual's beliefs.

- **Religious and Spiritual Beliefs:** Religious and spiritual beliefs often stem from faith and are influenced by cultural, philosophical, and moral considerations.

- **Psychological Needs:** Beliefs can serve psychological needs, such as the need for meaning, purpose, security, or control. People may adopt beliefs that help satisfy these needs.

- **Belief Systems:** Beliefs are often organized into larger belief systems or worldviews that provide coherence and consistency to an individual's set of beliefs. These systems can include ideologies, philosophies, or religions.

It is important to note that beliefs can vary widely among individuals and cultures. Beliefs can be deeply ingrained and resistant to change, even in the face of contradictory evidence. Understanding the nature of beliefs is crucial in The B∈E+T=R Life practice, as beliefs play a central role in shaping our future reality.

Belief Personas

Understanding the multidimensional nature of consciousness within the expansive realm of quantum reality, consciousness extends across various temporal points. Each of these moments in time captures a unique facet of an individual's belief system. These distinct snapshots of consciousness, or "Belief Personas," represent different versions of a person. They are shaped by either the cumulative beliefs the individual has embraced up to a particular point in their life journey or by the influence of significant events, such as successes, triumphs, traumas, or emotional experiences.

Interactions Among Belief Personas and the Present Moment Persona: Belief Personas engage with one another through the conduit of an individual's emotional state (B∈E). Both Past Belief Personas and Future Belief Personas influence the Present Moment Persona.

The Fluidity of Belief: This perspective challenges the notion of beliefs as confined to a linear timeline. Instead, beliefs flow across the dimensions of an individual's existence and psyche. Individuals have the capacity to oscillate between different belief states, drawing from their past, present, and future selves. This dynamic relationship is encapsulated within the D.A.R.E. symbolic equation of human reality, where Beliefs (B) are intricately linked to Emotions (E) (B∈E) and Thoughts (+T), ultimately shaping, or choosing, the sum of Reality (=R).

The Evolution of Self: The journey of self-discovery and personal growth involves individuals compassionately engaging with their Belief Personas. The goal is to reconcile differences and strive for coherence or enlightenment that harmonizes the multiple dimensions of the self. Achieving this harmony often necessitates the application of strategies within The $B{\in}E{+}T{=}R$ Life practice.

Implications for Memory: Beliefs are not mere abstract recollections or nebulous fragments within the memory centers of our minds. They are deeply interwoven into the fabric of our broader dimensional existence. These memories do not adhere to a linear representation of the past, but instead are composed of experiences from various Belief Personas. This intricate tapestry gives rise to a complex self-awareness, where memories take on a multidimensional and continually evolving role in shaping our lives as we align with probable threads of reality.

Implications for Personal Identity: One may ponder which Belief Persona represents the true self. The answer lies in the understanding that all Belief Personas are equally valid. However, due to humanity's perception of time, the Present Moment Persona takes center stage in the ongoing narrative of one's life. This realization underscores the significance of mindfulness in the present, as beliefs formed in the present moment wield significant influence over one's future, in alignment with the concept encapsulated by $B{\in}E{+}T{=}R$.

Introducing the concept of Belief Personas aims to establish a comprehensive framework for understanding the intricacies of belief, memory, and identity within the broader dimensional landscape of existence. This synthesis bridges the perspectives of theoretical physics with the realms of philosophy and psychology.

C.A.I.N. Hive

Developed by the fictional company Encephalon Media Group, Inc., C.A.I.N. Hive stands for Cybernetic Artificial Intelligent Network, representing a cutting-edge network ('hive') infrastructure seamlessly integrating advanced NeuroConnect chips. These specialized computer chips are surgically implanted into the human neocortex, creating a groundbreaking system that fosters unparalleled social connectivity.

This interconnected neural web enables users to access a comprehensive social media experience through an intricate mixed-reality construct that encompasses Physical Reality (PR), Virtual Reality (VR), and Augmented Reality (AR). The synergy between human neurological pattern recognition capabilities and state-of-the-art AI algorithms within the C.A.I.N. Hive results in the development of the most formidable experiential reality platform ever conceived. This innovative network transforms how individuals engage with one another and elevates their immersive encounters within the digital realm to extraordinary heights.

CERN

CERN, or the European Organization for Nuclear Research, is a prominent international scientific organization based in Geneva, Switzerland. Established in 1954, CERN is renowned for its cutting-edge research in particle physics and high-energy particle accelerators. It operates the largest and most powerful particle accelerator, the Large Hadron Collider (LHC), which has played a pivotal role in advancing our understanding of the universe.

One of CERN's most celebrated achievements is the discovery of the Higgs boson, a fundamental particle associated with the Higgs field. This discovery provided crucial insights into the mechanism responsible for imparting mass to other particles, a cornerstone of the standard model of particle physics.

In our fictional narrative, the character Dr. Adrian Bannister conducts his research at CERN. Dr. Bannister's work led to the exploration of metaphysical phenomena within the universe, unveiling the existence of Conscious Agents. This discovery opened new dimensions of understanding about the nature of consciousness and its role in shaping reality. CERN's collaborative efforts with scientists worldwide continue to push the boundaries of human knowledge in particle physics and metaphysical exploration.

Conscious Agents

Quantum mechanics has firmly established the nonexistence of "local realism." What this means is that something does not truly exist until it engages with a "conscious observer." (For further details, refer to the Double Split Experiment, Probability Waves, Principal of Fecundity [all possibilities are realized], and Principle of Plentitude [the universe contains all possible forms of existence].) But what constitutes this interface?

In all its vastness, the universe embodies pure consciousness, fragmented into what is termed Conscious Agents. These Conscious Agents serve as the fundamental building blocks of reality, a "one-bit Conscious Agent." This is a simple yet elegant mathematical construct. The tiniest unit of the one-bit Conscious Agent aligns with the dimensions of a quantum "plank," which, in our current comprehension of quantum physics, can be likened to a quantum particle. It represents the smallest theoretical entity conceivable by the human intellect, and it is imbued with three universal functions:

- Perception: The one-bit Conscious Agent possesses the capacity to perceive.
- Decision: It can make decisions.
- Action: It has the ability to act upon its decisions.

Physical reality emerges as a result of the coalescing interactions of Conscious Agents in response to observed contemplation. This phenomenon is not confined solely to the observable physical universe or multiverse. Instead, it encompasses various levels of intelligence and realities, ranging from the innate wisdom found in natural systems like a colony of honey bees, to sentient beings such as humans, and even the realm of digital intelligence like AI. Consequently, our understanding of reality transcends the boundaries of the observable physical universe, expanding into a broader, more intricate tapestry of existence.

D.A.R.E.

Dimensional Algebraic Reality Equation. (See $B \in E + T = R$ above.)

Encephalon Media Group, Inc.

A formidable global social media conglomerate known for recruiting one of the main characters into its organization. Through the amalgamation of cutting-edge technologies, they achieve digital domination over the human race, manipulating their belief systems via virtual social platforms. This nefarious control ultimately reshapes the trajectory of humanity.

Future Memory Recall (FMR)

Future Memory Recall (FMR) is a transformative exercise designed to empower individuals in consciously shaping their preferred threads of reality within the multiverse. It operates on the principle that our beliefs, emotions, and thoughts form the foundation of the reality we experience. Individuals can actively influence and align their consciousness with their desired probable futures by engaging in this exercise.

Key Components of Future Memory Recall Exercises (FMR):

Belief (B): FMR commences with the fundamental aspect of belief. Individuals are encouraged to identify and delve into deeply ingrained beliefs, aligning with Belief Personas. These beliefs act as the scaffolding upon which the framework of their envisioned reality will be constructed. This process is initiated by activating the D.A.R.E. equation, $B \in E + T = R$. By engaging in intensive imaginative focus on a specific desired moment in their future, they set in motion the summative component of the equation ($=R$) for potential transformation. This, in turn, sets into motion the other elements of the equation.

To illustrate, consider a simple algebraic equation, $1+x=2$. Solving for "x" equals 1. However, if we alter the equation to $1+x=3$, then "x" becomes 2. Similarly, altering the sum in the algebraic equation is akin to changing the $=R$ through intense imaginative focus on one's probable future. This process releases electromagnetic thought energy into the system, energizing a specific thread of their probable future reality. If the existing beliefs (B) are incongruent with the new envisioned reality ($=R$), then temporal Belief Personas are triggered, subsequently setting off emotional responses ($B \in E$).

Emotion ($\in E$): Emotions hold a central position within the framework of FMR. Individuals are encouraged to identify their emotions and, more crucially, to recognize the intrinsic value and wisdom concealed within even the most challenging emotional states, such as fear, sadness, anxiety, disappointment, anger, and frustration, among others. In FMR exercises, the triggering effect of beliefs activates a cascade of emotions. These emotions serve as valuable messengers, facilitating a direct connection with each emotion's underlying, or tethered, Belief Persona (B).

Exploring the Role of Emotions: Within the context of FMR, emotions function as a bridge between belief (B) and thought (+T), forming a critical juncture in D.A.R.E., B∈E+T=R. These emotions are like signposts, guiding individuals toward the beliefs that shape their perceived realities.

System Hack - "I Wonder": An essential tool within FMR is the simple yet profound statement, "I wonder." This statement marks a shift in perspective, inviting individuals to approach their emotions and beliefs with curiosity rather than judgment. When faced with an emotion, especially a challenging one, asking, "I wonder what belief (B) is connected to this emotion," initiates a transformative process. This question guides individuals to explore the underlying beliefs that have triggered the emotion, allowing for a deeper understanding and potential realignment. (See The Power of "I Wonder" below.)

Thought (+T): Imagination is a catalyst for change. At the heart of every Future Memory Recall (FMR) exercise lies the transformative power of thought. FMR encourages individuals to engage in intensive imaginative thinking, a process that transcends mere daydreaming and ventures into the realm of conscious creation. Through various visualization techniques and guided embodiment sessions, individuals are prompted to vividly envision and articulate the intricate details of their imagined future realities.

Imagine, for a moment, closing your eyes and stepping into a new home you aspire to inhabit someday. Or picture yourself strolling along a pristine beach during a dream vacation. However, the true potency of thought (+T) is unveiled when these mental scenarios are meticulously fleshed out. The more vivid and detailed the mental imagery, the more robust the thought signal becomes.

This act of mental construction serves as the architect's blueprint, meticulously outlining the specific experiences and scenarios that individuals wish to manifest within their future realities. It is within these imaginative constructs that new beliefs are forged, breathing life into the Present Moment Persona and forging a profound connection with the $B \in E+T=R$ equation.

It is essential to recognize that thoughts are not confined to the nebulous workings of neurons within the physical human brain. Instead, they transcend these physical boundaries, manifesting in the form of electromagnetic signals. These signals, pulsating with intention and purpose, energetically charge the desired thread of reality, effectively rewriting the equation (=R) of the imagined future.

In essence, thought (+T) is the catalyst that propels individuals from passive spectators of life to active co-creators of their destiny. Through the intricate dance of imagination, intention, and action, FMR empowers individuals to influence their reality threads, shaping them into vibrant tapestries of their own design.

Reality (=R): The essence of FMR culminates in transforming one's reality (=R). By diligently practicing this exercise and consistently acknowledging, reconciling, and channeling their beliefs, emotions, and thoughts toward their envisioned future, referred to here as a "probable thread of reality," individuals can navigate toward transformative pathways within their existing reality.

D.A.R.E., symbolized by the equation $B \in E + T = R$, stands as the foundational framework of FMR. It underscores the interconnectedness of beliefs, emotions, and thoughts, which collectively hold profound sway over the reality one experiences and ultimately selects. Through conscientious participation in FMR, individuals unlock the potential of their consciousness to actively mold and choose the threads of reality that resonate most harmoniously with their aspirations.

Lubhyati

"Love" is a word derived from Sanskrit Lubhyati, (Lūvyati), meaning "to desire." Within The Inverse, a Lubhyati is a metaphysical entity born from the essence of pure consciousness. A Lubhyati represents the expansive existence of human or intelligent consciousness within the boundless multiverse. A Lubhyati possesses the extraordinary ability to fragment aspects of itself, giving rise to derivative conscious entities known as Pneuma. The spiritual concept of the "Oversoul" in human belief systems closely parallels the essence of a Lubhyati.

Neuro-Symbolic Programming (NSP)

Neuro-Symbolic Programming (NSP) represents a cutting-edge cognitive technique designed to transform a person's belief system profoundly. It achieves this through a dynamic interplay of auditory and visually stimulated symbolic imagery. NSP stands as an evolution of traditional vision boards, harnessing the immense potential of the subconscious mind.

In NSP therapy, meticulously selected symbolic imagery, carefully tailored to align with an individual's desired reality, is rapidly introduced into their mental landscape. These symbols are strategically crafted to engage multiple sensory modalities, creating a seamless bridge between conscious and subconscious realms.

This immersive experience can be undertaken before or after engaging in Future Memory Recall (FMR) exercises. When combined with FMR, NSP synergistically amplifies the effectiveness of belief transformation. Through NSP, individuals can profoundly influence their beliefs by embedding them deeply within the intricate tapestry of their subconscious mind.

This powerful cognitive technique empowers individuals to reshape their perception of reality and manifest their chosen threads of existence with unparalleled clarity and intention. NSP represents a pivotal tool in the pursuit of profound personal transformation.

Oculus Relatorum

The Oculus Relatorum, often referred to as the "Eye of Threads," stands as a wondrous dimensional portal, a testament to the fusion of metaphysical marvels and imaginative craftsmanship. Nestled at the heart of The Academy within the mystical realm of The Inverse, these portals serve as a pivotal wellspring of knowledge and intrigue for our unfolding narrative.

The threads cascading elegantly within the archway of the Oculus represent not mere threads but rather the very fabric of dimensional "threads of realities." These ethereal strands resemble the conceptual Trans-Dimensional Probability Threads, abbreviated as TDPTs, a revolutionary revelation credited to the brilliant Dr. Gabriel Valencia, one of our cherished characters.

These Trans-Dimensional Probability Threads drape gracefully within the Oculus Relatorum's archway, extending an irresistible invitation to the curious minds of Lubhyati students at The Academy within The Inverse Wisdom Complex. They form a gateway to embrace and experience an infinite array of probable realities, acting as an instinctual educator for the burgeoning understanding of their Pneuma regarding the multifaceted aspects of their forthcoming exploratory reality journey.

Pneuma

A metaphysical entity, a Pneuma ('nōōmə), emerges from the core of pure consciousness as a derivative of a Lubhyati. It embodies the inherent curiosity and exploratory nature of its progenitor, a Lubhyati, venturing into diverse physical and non-physical realities. Its name draws inspiration from Greek philosophy, signifying the "creative one," aptly characterizing its boundless potential to immerse itself in any desired reality. Pneuma resides within various physical and non-physical entities across the multiverse, including humans and other sentient beings, serving as the early phase of sentient consciousness that ultimately evolves into a Lubhyati. This concept harmonizes closely with the human belief in the existence of the "soul."

Quantum Thought Dynamics-AI (QTD-AI) Protocol

QTD-AI, a fictional innovation attributed to the character Dr. Gabriel Valencia, the head of MIT's Neurotechnological

Research Studies Team, represents a pioneering process that draws upon three significant technological advancements in the field of neuroscience.

NeuroConnect Chips: At the core of the QTD-AI Protocol are NeuroConnect chips, highly specialized computer chips meticulously integrated directly into the neocortical centers of the human brain. These neuroconnective interfaces facilitate seamless communication between the human mind and advanced computational systems.

Generative AI: QTD-AI harnesses the extraordinary capabilities of Generative Artificial Intelligence (AI) algorithms. These AI systems transcend traditional computing, boasting the remarkable ability to process colossal volumes of data and derive profound insights. Among their most astonishing functions is their ability to digitally decipher the intricate landscape of human thoughts, meticulously harvested by the NeuroConnect chips. Through this groundbreaking process, science has achieved an unparalleled feat: the digital organization of the intricate tapestry of human thought into highly structured and utilitarian data packets. These data packets form the essence of the QTD-AI Protocol, empowering individuals to interact with, manipulate, and navigate the profound realms of human consciousness with unparalleled precision and clarity.

Mixed-Reality Technologies: The QTD-AI experience is further enhanced by Mixed-Reality Technologies, incorporating both Virtual Reality (VR) and Augmented Reality (AR). With the integration of mixed-reality glasses, individuals gain the remarkable ability to visualize and interact with the intricate web of probable threads of reality.

Trans-Dimensional Probability Threads (TDPTs)

Trans-Dimensional Probability Threads (TDPTs) are visually striking manifestations that appear as vertical threads when viewed through the QTD-AI Protocol's mixed-reality eyewear. Strikingly reminiscent of the probable reality threads found within the archway of the Oculus Relatorums, TDPTs are gateways to a multitude of probable realities. Each thread represents a unique path through the vast tapestry of existence, offering individuals the opportunity to explore and navigate the uncharted territories of the multiverse. These threads serve as windows into the infinite possibilities that await those who dare to delve into the metaphysical realms, providing a clear and tangible means of embarking on this extraordinary journey.

Intriguingly, TDPTs are intimately entwined with D.A.R.E., symbolically represented as $B{\in}E+T=R$ (See $B{\in}E+T=R$ above.). TDPTs fictionally symbolize these connections, offering tangible, visual representations of an individual's choices within D.A.R.E.

The Copenhagen Interpretation

The Copenhagen interpretation is one of the most well-known and widely taught interpretations of quantum mechanics. It was formulated primarily by Niels Bohr and Werner Heisenberg in the 1920s. The interpretation deals with the nature of quantum systems, the measurement problem, and the role of the observer in quantum experiments. Here are the key features of the Copenhagen interpretation:

- **Superposition:** According to the Copenhagen interpretation, particles at the quantum level exist in a state of superposition, which means they can exist in multiple states simultaneously. For example, an electron can exist in a superposition of different positions or spins until it is measured.

- **Wave-Particle Duality:** It recognizes the wave-particle duality of quantum entities, meaning particles like electrons exhibit both particle-like and wave-like properties depending on how they are observed or measured.

- **Quantum Uncertainty:** The interpretation embraces Heisenberg's uncertainty principle, which states that certain pairs of properties, like an electron's position and momentum, cannot be precisely measured simultaneously. This introduces fundamental limits to our knowledge of quantum systems.

- **Role of the Observer:** One of the most distinctive features of the Copenhagen interpretation is the role of the observer. It suggests that quantum systems remain in superposition until they are observed or measured. When an observation is made, the superposition collapses into a definite state.

- **Observer Effect:** The interpretation implies that the act of observation fundamentally changes the system being observed. This phenomenon is often referred to as the "observer effect."

- **Complementarity:** Bohr introduced the concept of complementarity, suggesting that quantum entities can exhibit particle and wave properties. However, these properties are complementary and cannot be observed in full detail simultaneously. This principle helps reconcile the wave-particle duality.

- **No Objective Reality:** This interpretation of the Copenhagen interpretation suggests that quantum systems do not have an objective reality until observed. In other words, the reality of quantum entities depends on the act of measurement.

The Copenhagen interpretation has been historically influential and provides a successful framework for calculating quantum phenomena. It remains a subject of philosophical debate and has alternative interpretations, such as the Many-Worlds interpretation and the Pilot-Wave theory, which offer different explanations for quantum behavior. The Copenhagen interpretation's emphasis on the role of the observer and the collapse of the wave function is a point of contention among physicists and philosophers of science.

The Inverse

The Inverse is a metaphysical realm that serves as the exact opposite of Earthly reality, hence its name. In The Inverse, the conventional constraints of time and space differ entirely from what humans experience on Earth. In The Inverse, space is not limited to three dimensions but is singularly infinite, and beings exist everywhere, encompassing all dimensions simultaneously. Time is experienced in all its facets at once, including past, present, and future. This realm challenges the notion of human confinement, highlighting the innate ability to choose and shape reality through thoughts and beliefs consciously. Beings in The Inverse have the unique ability to conjure any reality instantly with their thoughts, as dimensional restrictions do not apply to them.

The Many-Worlds Interpretation (MWI)

The Many-Worlds Interpretation is one of the most intriguing and debated interpretations of quantum mechanics. It was formulated by Hugh Everett III in 1957 as part of his doctoral thesis. MWI offers a different perspective on quantum phenomena compared to the Copenhagen interpretation and provides an alternative way to address the measurement problem in quantum mechanics. Here are the key principles of the Many-Worlds Interpretation:

- **Universal Wavefunction:** MWI starts with the idea that there is a single, universal wavefunction that describes the entire quantum system of the universe. This wavefunction evolves deterministically over time according to the Schrödinger equation, which governs the behavior of quantum systems.

- **Branching Universes:** In MWI, when a quantum measurement is made, instead of the wavefunction collapsing into a single state (as in the Copenhagen interpretation), it splits into multiple non-communicating branches, each corresponding to one of the possible outcomes of the measurement. These branches represent separate, parallel universes or "worlds."

- **Parallel Realities:** MWI posits that every possible outcome of a quantum measurement actually occurs in a separate, non-interacting branch of the universe. For example, suppose a quantum system is in a superposition of two states and a measurement is made. In that case, MWI suggests that there is a universe in which one outcome is observed and another universe in which another outcome is observed.

- **No Wavefunction Collapse:** One of the fundamental differences between MWI and other interpretations is the absence of wavefunction collapse. In MWI, the wavefunction evolves continuously, and all possible outcomes are realized in parallel, with each outcome corresponding to a different branch.

- **Apparent Probability:** MWI explains the appearance of probability in quantum measurements as a subjective experience of observers. When an observer measures a quantum system, they become entangled with it, but they exist in a superposition of states corresponding to each possible measurement outcome. From the observer's perspective, it appears as if one outcome was randomly chosen, giving the appearance of probability.

- **Conservation of Information:** MWI adheres to the principle of unitarity, which means that information is never lost in quantum processes. Instead, all information is preserved across the branches of the universal wavefunction.

- **No Communication Between Branches:** While MWI postulates the existence of multiple branches or parallel realities, it also suggests that these branches are causally disconnected. In other words, there is no way for information or influence to travel between these branches.

MWI has both proponents and critics within the scientific and philosophical communities. Supporters of MWI argue that it provides a straightforward and elegant solution to the measurement problem in quantum mechanics and eliminates the need for a separate, ad hoc collapse of the wavefunction. Critics, on the other hand, raise questions about the physical reality of these parallel universes and the lack of experimental evidence to confirm MWI.

Despite the ongoing debate, the Many-Worlds Interpretation has sparked significant interest and continues to be a topic of research and discussion in the field of quantum physics and philosophy of science.

The Power of "I Wonder"

The phrase "I wonder" is a potent tool within the $B{\in}E+T=R$ strategy, rooted in the profound connection between emotions (E) and beliefs (B), as expressed in the equation $B{\in}E$. Emotions become our allies as we navigate the currents of the present moment.

When a Belief Persona (see definition above) is triggered, emotions (E) come into play. It is critical to understand that emotions, including challenging ones like anger, fear, sadness, anxiety, frustration, and disappointment, carry inherent value; they pose both a question and an answer.

Imagine you are actively shaping new life goals, using tools like goal setting, vision boards, and engaging in Future Memory Recall (FMR) exercises. In this process, your thoughts (+T) and the future probable reality (=R) aspects of the equation come to life. This is akin to working in reverse, starting from the desired sum of reality (=R) and working backward to uncover any hidden beliefs (B) that might obstruct your goals and aspirations.

When your focused energy converges on your envisioned future (=R), any beliefs (B) incongruent with this vision face scrutiny. Here, emotions (E) play a dynamic role. If there are beliefs (B) misaligned with your future desired reality (=R), emotions (E) react dynamically. These conflicting beliefs awaken your Belief Personas, whose sole purpose is to safeguard you.

Once activated, these Belief Personas, imprinted on your life's timeline—both in the past and future—align with the present moment, triggering or signaling perceived threats based on their reality perception shaped by conditioned beliefs.

However, emotions (E) extend beyond immediate emotional states; they carry within them a question and an answer:

Question: Are you genuinely interested in and committed to the future probable reality you are striving for, as defined by your goals, visualizations, and Future Memory Recall (FMR) exercises?

Answer: If your answer is yes, and you actively apply the $B{\in}E+T=R$ strategy while immersed in an emotional state, the system reintroduces you to the Belief Persona associated with that emotion ($B{\in}E$). This, in turn, allows you to reconcile antiquated beliefs that are not in line with your goals and objectives, your desired future.

If you react to the emotional state, the system interprets it as a lack of genuine interest in your defined goals or visualized future reality. In this sense, your answer is no. In such cases, the past Belief Persona that triggered your emotional state remains etched in your life's timeline, poised to intervene at perceived threats. Here is where the simple yet powerful statement, "I wonder," becomes a game-changer.

When you actively engage with the $B{\in}E+T=R$ strategy, you realize a past Belief Persona emotionally triggers you. Picture it as leveling up in the game of life, adding a layer of cognitive curiosity to your emotional triggers. Mastering this skill takes practice, enabling you to operate on two levels: your emotional state alongside an elevated sense of curiosity, empowering you to "own the moment of choice." This puts you in a "state of play," and the universal system favors those *playing* the game of life, not merely *observing* the game of life.

Allow your emotions to flow freely, without suppression. What truly matters is practicing the art of experiencing emotions while simultaneously nurturing curiosity. This is where "I wonder" comes into play. By sincerely pondering, "I wonder what Belief Persona is connected to this emotion," you signal to the universal system your active engagement in the game of life, coupled with a cognitive awareness of the $B \in E+T=R$ strategy and the involvement of one of your Belief Personas.

The process unfolds as follows:

Curiosity: Begin by infusing curiosity into your emotionally triggered state: "I wonder what Belief Persona is connected to this emotion." This immediate inquiry signifies your active participation and communicates your commitment to your desired future reality, as expressed within the symbolic equation $B \in E+T=R$.

Acknowledgment: Acknowledge the Belief Persona: "I recognize your presence. Thank you for being here to protect me. However, everything is okay—we are okay. You can stand down now."

Apology: Extend a sincere apology to the Belief Persona: "I apologize for not acknowledging you sooner. I understand that something happened to us that has you concerned, and you believe we are in danger. I'd like to understand more about that because I fear I may have forgotten it. I believe we can align more productively."

Reintroduction and Reconciliation: Invite the Belief Persona to accompany you: "I invite you to spend time with me today. However, I request that we dial down the intensity of our emotions; we do not need to be overly emotional. This will allow us to reconnect and share our experiences and realities. It will enable us to align and move forward confidently. When you're ready, I'd like to learn more about you—your place in my life's timeline, who you are, and when you came into being."

This process requires courage, sincerity, and authenticity. It offers a unique opportunity to explore and embrace yourself at a multidimensional level. Belief Personas may reveal themselves in various ways, either overtly or subtly. This healing reconciliation diminishes negative energy and releases the Belief Persona into the vast expanse of the probable multiverse. Most importantly, it eradicates the obstructing aspects of the belief itself, empowering you to select the desired probable thread of reality confidently.

The Principle of Fecundity (Robert Nozick's Theory)

Robert Nozick, a prominent philosopher, introduced the "principle of fecundity" as an extreme version of egalitarianism. This principle posits that "all possibilities are realized," implying that every conceivable way a universe could exist is actualized.

In the realm of philosophical discourse and theoretical exploration, the principle of fecundity envisions a scenario where every conceivable variation of existence, regardless of its diversity or unconventionality, is considered equally valid.

Nozick's principle of fecundity invites contemplation about the vastness of the multiverse and the countless potential realities it may contain. It raises questions about the nature of existence, choice, and the boundaries of human comprehension.

While the principle of fecundity may exist primarily as a thought experiment in philosophy, it serves as a catalyst for discussions about the nature of reality, consciousness, and the implications of radical equality on our understanding of the universe.

For more information visit

<u>DGZitting.com</u>